"We should give the ... their parents...we would have named them."

Willow set her bowl aside and bent to touch the cheek of the littlest child. "This one is a girl." She stroked the dark tuft of hair on the other baby.

"And this one is a boy."

Charles reached out a finger and the little girl reacted instinctively, clutching it in her fist. He made a sound that was half laugh, half gasp of astonishment. "Our own Adam and—"

"Eva," Willow interrupted. "Her name should be Eva."

Charles grinned.

Willow had grown so accustomed to seeing Charles looking serious and reserved. She could scarcely credit the way his expression made him seem young and boyish.

Charles touched each of the children on the top of the head. Willow's eyes pricked with tears. Other than her father, she'd never witnessed a man who was so tender and gentle. Yet strong.

Willow couldn't account for the stab of disappointment she suddenly felt in her chest. This was a temporary situation. Once they'd found the danger to the children and eliminated it, this entire charade would be over...

Lisa Bingham is the bestselling author of more than thirty historical and contemporary romantic fiction novels. She's been a teacher for more than thirty years, and has served as a costume designer for theatrical and historical reenactment enthusiasts. Currently she lives in rural northern Utah near her husband's fourth-generation family farm with her sweetheart and three beautiful children. She loves to hear from her fans at lisabinghamauthor.com or Facebook.com/lisabinghamauthor.

Books by Lisa Bingham

Love Inspired Historical

The Bachelors of Aspen Valley

Accidental Courtship
Accidental Family

LISA BINGHAM

Accidental Family

⬧ HARLEQUIN®LOVE INSPIRED® HISTORICAL

Recycling programs
for this product may
not exist in your area.

LOVE INSPIRED BOOKS

ISBN-13: 978-1-335-36960-4

Accidental Family

www.Harlequin.com

Live joyfully with the wife whom thou lovest all the days of the life of thy vanity, which he hath given thee under the sun, all the days of thy vanity: for that is thy portion in this life, and in thy labour which thou takest under the sun.

—*Ecclesiastes* 9:9

To my grandparents, whose "storybooks" were tales from their vast genealogical records. The histories of all those family members still provide a font of inspiration to tickle my imagination.

Chapter One

January 13, 1874
Utah Territory

Charles Wanlass waited until the sound of feminine laughter had dissipated into the darkness before stepping into the cold. He paused to ensure that the side door to the Meeting House had snapped into place. Then he hurried toward the miners' row houses and his own quarters, the very last building on the left.

From somewhere deep in the woods, he heard a woman's voice call out.

"Willow? Willow, where are you?"

The cry was soon followed by a burst of laughter. Snatches of singing.

Charles couldn't help smiling. Normally, he and the other men in the Batchwell Bottoms mining community hated January. The merrymaking of Christmas was over, the wind had grown especially bitter and the nights were long and dark. With nothing to break the monotony but work, the days seem endless.

This year, however, the occupants of the little community nicknamed "Bachelor Bottoms" were more than

happy to put off spring for as long as possible. Less than a month ago, a freak avalanche had closed off the pass, marooning a trainload of women in the valley.

And none of the miners looked forward to that moment when they would go.

"Willow?"

The cry was fainter this time, the giggling more disjointed.

Charles wondered what could have happened to separate Willow Granger from the rest of the group. She was a shy little thing, so tiny she could fit under his chin. Sober and wide-eyed. He couldn't imagine what could have caused her to escape the Pinkerton guards who had been tasked with keeping the women away from the miners.

As he stepped inside and threw his hat onto a nearby table, he became aware of several things at once: footsteps running through the snow, a commotion of male voices, shouts from the center of town and cooing.

Or the soft mewling of a cat. Or...

A baby?

In that instant, he became aware of a basket on the floor in front of him. It was heaped with blankets. A note pinned to the top read: "Please, please protect my little ones and keep them as your own. They are in more danger than I can express."

Crouching, Charles moved the blankets aside, revealing not one, but two cherubic faces.

Tiny. So tiny.

A surge of protectiveness rushed through him like a tidal wave, washing all other thoughts and emotions aside.

Almost simultaneously, he heard footsteps charging into his home. He placed himself between the int and the basket. To his surprise, it wasn't a burly assailant, but one of the mail-order brides.

Willow Granger.

From the moment of their arrival, Willow had been a source of curiosity for Charles. Where the other girls were carefree and chatty—even giggly or silly—Willow stood out. The woman was reserved, seldom speaking in Charles's presence. She had a mane of curly auburn hair the same bright red-gold as a sunset. Most days, she barely managed to contain it in a thick braid. Unlike the other ladies, her wardrobe seemed limited, a pair of shapeless dresses that obscured her figure—one for every day and one for Sunday best. And she was watchful. He wouldn't doubt that those pale cornflower-blue eyes saw everything, even the contents of a person's heart.

She seemed to sense that something was amiss because she peered around him. In an instant, she took in the basket, the babies and then the note. Before he could stop her, she snatched the paper from its mooring and read the words.

"Oh."

It was a mere puff of sound, but it held a wealth of emotion—shock, concern, dismay.

Unfortunately, neither of them had time to ask each other questions, because a swarm of men were heading toward them—the Pinkertons, and close on their heels a group of miners, including Jonah Ramsey, the superintendent of mines, and Ezra Batchwell, one of the owners. To add to the confusion, the alarm bell near the mine offices began to toll.

To Charles's utter horror, the babies at his feet chose that moment to rouse from their slumber. They began to cry, softly at first, then louder, until the noise cut through the din and the crowd on his doorstep seemed to freeze in the cold winter night.

But that moment of calm was short-lived, because a deep, booming voice bellowed, "Charles Wanlass, explain yourself!"

"They're mine!"
"They're mine!"

Willow trembled when she realized that she had blurted the words at the same moment that Charles Wanlass had uttered his. In an instant, the lie had been cast, not once, but twice, heightening the veracity of the declarations, but doubling the consequences—because this was Bachelor Bottoms where, in order to get a job, a man had to sign an oath that he would abstain from drinking, smoking, cussing...

And women.

Their claims seemed to shudder through the men assembled outside the door. Willow wouldn't have been surprised if they'd been spoken loud enough for the whole valley to hear. Then a dozen pairs of eyes turned their way, and she withered beneath the stares.

She'd never been good in crowds. Becoming the brunt of anyone's attention caused her to wilt. Yet here she stood, forced to endure the focus of everyone's attention.

"What did you two say?"

The growl came from Ezra Batchwell. The owner of the Batchwell Bottoms Mine was a fierce bear of a man, his body stocky and barrel-chested. The fur coat he wore and the beaver hat pulled low over his balding pate helped give him the appearance of some great beast. In her short time at Bachelor Bottoms, Willow had steered clear of him. He had a temper. Especially where women were concerned.

She felt a hand touch the small of her back. When she looked up, she found Charles regarding her with quiet gray eyes. There was something about that look, the steadiness of his gaze, that offered her comfort and strength.

"See to the children," he murmured. His command was softened by the lilt of his Scottish burr and uttered so lowly that only she could have heard the words.

When she reached out to pull the blankets aside, she realized that she still clutched the note in her hand. Her gaze scanned the words: "Please, please protect my little ones and keep them as your own. They are in more danger than I can express."

She instantly recognized the loopy script.

No, Jenny, no.

Willow's stomach twisted. She hadn't been able to find Jenny for days now. Somehow, the other woman had slipped away from their Pinkerton guards and gone... who knew where?

Why would she leave the safety of the other women and the Dovecote, the dormitory-like building where they stayed? Why would she venture out on her own? If her labor had begun, Jenny would have had everything she needed: warmth, support, even medical help from their very own female doctor, Sumner Havisham Ramsey. The woman had only recently married the mine superintendent. If Jenny had needed an advocate to help smooth things over in the Batchwell Bottoms community, she could have appealed to Sumner.

But she'd been so frightened the last few weeks. So sure that someone meant to hurt her and the baby she carried.

No. Not baby.

Babies.

Willow crumpled the note into a small ball, surreptitiously jamming it into the pocket of her gown. Then she returned her attention to the infants.

Curiously, one of them had fallen back asleep, despite the fact that its sibling piteously squalled. Wrapping the top layer of blankets around the angry child, she lifted it to her chest and then rose again, automatically rocking back and forth as she tried to calm the poor thing.

As soon as she turned, she met the wide-eyed stares, and Willow's knees began to tremble. Thankfully, before she could sag, Charles's hand wrapped around her waist and he drew her close to his side, offering her warmth and support. Then, miraculously, the baby grew quiet.

The silence hung thick and dark and ominous, and the longer it continued, the more Willow became aware of the alarm bells in the distance. The last time she'd heard such sustained tolling, there had been a mine accident and dozens of men had been injured.

"Has another tunnel collapsed?" she breathed, looking up at Charles, needing the strength of his gaze. She became inordinately aware of the man's height, the rawboned planes of his face, the wheat-colored hair that he kept close-cropped at the sides and longer on top.

She felt his fingers tighten at her waist. The sensation was brief, but oh, so welcome.

"What's happened?" Charles asked, already reaching for his hat and settling it over his brow.

"The tunnels are fine." This time, the deep voice belonged to Jonah Ramsey, mine superintendent, and even more importantly in Willow's opinion, Dr. Havisham— no, Dr. *Ramsey's*—husband. "We were told there's been a death. We hoped you'd come with us to check things out. Just in case someone needs some spiritual support."

The words shivered into the night, seeming to trace a

cold finger down Willow's spine. The men on the steps all began talking at once. Her pulse roared in her ears and her arms tightened around the baby so fiercely that the little one squeaked in protest, then rooted into the blankets again, its eyes closing.

Dread seemed to bloom up from the tips of her toes, rumbling through her extremities, leaving her quaking.

Jenny.

No. Please, Lord. No.

Not Jenny.

She must have spoken her prayer aloud because the commotion stopped again and all eyes turned in her direction—especially those of Ezra Batchwell.

"You know something," he said accusingly.

"No, I…" Her throat became impossibly tight. "Is it Jenny?"

When Batchwell would have demanded answers, Jonah Ramsey stopped him with a hand on his arm. "What makes you think that one of the women is involved?"

"J-Jenny's been gone for a few days."

"Gone!" Batchwell barked, but Jonah moved to stand in front of him.

"What do you mean, Willow?"

"She h-hasn't been at the Dovecote." Willow fiercely blinked back the tears that swam into her eyes.

"Why didn't you let anyone know?"

"I… I—"

Willow shut her lips before she could utter anything more. She and Charles had impetuously laid claim to Jenny's children. If Willow were to reveal any more of the woman's confidences that she'd pieced together over the past few weeks…

"Has Jenny been hurt?" Willow tried to control herself, but the last words emerged in a pitch that conveyed her panic.

She saw the way the men exchanged glances. There was a furtive guiltiness to their expressions.

Because they knew.

They knew she was right.

"What happened?" she cried, and then more desperately, "What happened!"

Charles pulled her to him, tucking her head beneath his chin. "Shh." She felt his hand pass down the length of her braid. And felt safe tucked in his arms. "I'll go and find out. You stay here."

She pushed against him, ready to argue. But when his gaze dropped to the baby she cradled next to her chest, he said pointedly, "You stay here and take care of our wee children."

Willow felt torn, needing to know the truth, *now.* But she heeded Charles's unspoken message. Someone had to stay with the twins. Someone who knew that they were in dire need of protection.

"There's food in the larder, wood in a pile by the fireplace. I'll be back as soon as I can."

Then, to her infinite surprise, he bent to place a soft kiss on her brow, marking her as his own.

"Lock the door behind me," he whispered to her.

Then he was gone, the latch snapping into place behind him.

Have you lost your mind?

Charles did his best to push aside the little inner voice that nagged at him for his impulsiveness.

He'd claimed a pair of newborn bairns as his own, and then had kissed Willow Granger to boot. If he weren't tossed out of the mining camp on his ear within the hour, it would be a miracle.

Even as he inwardly castigated himself for his foolishness, Charles discovered that he didn't regret his actions.

Which was odd.

He owed a debt to Ezra Batchwell and his business partner, Phineas Boggs. He'd been a teenager when they'd snatched him from utter ruin, and since then, Charles had dedicated his life to repaying them for the faith they'd had in his potential.

Yet he'd lied.

Something he'd promised he would never do again, least of all to them.

"What's going on, Charles?"

The murmured question came from Jonah Ramsey, who seemed determined to keep pace with him.

Not knowing how to respond, Charles shook his head. His jaw tightened as he worked hard to tamp his emotions deep, deep into his soul. He would sort things out later, after he'd had some time to think, confer with Willow and appeal to God for the strength to appear calm. Maybe then he'd have an answer.

Jonah probably would have pressed him further, but they'd reached the steps of the mining office. Several men stood in the middle of the road, and as Charles wove his way through them, he caught a glimpse of the woman lying on the ground.

Even in the darkness, the prone figure of Jenny Reichmann was easy to recognize.

Willow's fears had proved to be true.

Charles sank to his knees in the snow, reaching to touch the woman's cheek. She was cold. Her eyes were partially open, staring sightlessly into the night.

"She's been murdered," someone grumbled.

Jonah held up a hand. "None of that, you hear? We don't know what happened. This could have been a horrible accident. Maybe she was injured and tried to walk to the office to find help. She might not have realized that we were all at evening Devotional."

Although Jonah's voice brooked no argument, Charles knew that the rumors would continue until someone discovered the truth. There was nothing else to do during a cold night than think and talk and spin tales.

"What about her baby?" someone murmured.

Charles knew the answer before he shook his head. The mound of her stomach had already begun to gather a skiff of snow. "She's been gone too long. There's no saving it." Even as he said the words, his scalp began to tighten and he remembered the babes in the basket.

Could they have belonged to Jenny?

He racked his brain, trying to remember the last time he'd seen her. As lay pastor, Charles had been allowed to spend time at the Dovecote in order to tend to the spiritual needs of the ladies marooned in Bachelor Bottoms. He briefly remembered that Jenny Reichmann had been different from the other girls. She'd been on her way to meet up with her husband in California before the avalanche. Although she hadn't been the only pregnant woman on the doomed passenger train, her condition had been the most pronounced. Charles had supposed that was why she'd kept out of sight, secluding herself from almost everyone, preferring to remain in her room. Charles could probably count on one hand the number of times he'd seen her.

"Move, please."

The voice came from Jonah's wife, Sumner. As soon as she'd managed to thread her way through the crowd, she came to an abrupt halt. Although Charles knew she'd been trained to keep a poker face while tending the wounded, he didn't miss the shock that flickered in her eyes. Her gaze lifted, bouncing from Jonah to Charles, then back to her husband.

"We need to take her to the infirmary and away from prying eyes," she offered in a low voice. Then more loudly, she added, "And will someone please stop ringing that bell?"

Abruptly, the noise halted—but the silence that ensued was worse. The quiet was so thick that Charles was sure he could hear the snowflakes landing on the dead woman's skin.

Sumner laid a hand on Charles's sleeve, but he barely felt it until she squeezed more forcefully. "Charles, do you think you could carry her to the infirmary for me? Maybe there, you can say a few words over her."

He nodded, his throat feeling thick and tight.

"The rest of you go home!" Sumner called out. "And keep your gossiping to yourselves for now. There's no sense riling up the whole mining camp until we know exactly what happened."

One by one, the miners began to fade into the darkness, until only Jonah, Charles and Ezra Batchwell remained.

"Jonah, give him some room. It's been less than a month since we removed the shrapnel near your spine. I don't want you hurting your back now that it's on the mend. Charles, if you're ready."

Charles slid his hands beneath the still form.

Then he carried his burden into the night.

Willow glanced up at the ticking clock on the mantel and sighed when the spindly hands marked the passing of another quarter hour.

Since Charles had left, she'd tried to make herself useful. She'd stoked the coals in the fireplace and in his range, and put enough wood on both to chase the chill from the combined kitchen and sitting area. Then, deciding that he would be cold and tired when he came home, she'd made coffee.

Soon, the babies had begun to rouse. Fearing they were hungry, Willow had fretted over how she would feed them. But thankfully, once she'd changed their diapers from a pile of flannel squares she'd found tucked into the corner of the basket, they'd fallen back to sleep.

For now.

How on earth was she going to give credence to the claim of being their mother if she couldn't feed them herself?

Sitting in the only comfortable chair in the room— a tufted easy chair drawn close to the fireplace—she'd taken turns holding the children.

A boy. And a girl.

The instant she'd cuddled them in her arms, a fierce wave of protectiveness had rushed through her. She'd felt her heart melt at the sight of their tiny fingers.

As the snow spattered against the window, she wondered how long it would be before she was punished for that untruth. Even now, her skin seemed to prickle in foreboding. It had taken only a few fibs at the Good Shepherd Charity School for Young Girls for Willow to learn that the adults in her life would brook no disobedience or dishonor.

God would punish her for the lie.

But she couldn't find it within her to confess her deceit to Batchwell and Bottoms.

A pounding sound suddenly broke the quiet, and Willow jumped. Immediately, her heart collided against her ribs in time with the banging. Panicked, she set the baby in the basket, covered both wee faces with a blanket and then searched for a place to hide them.

She should have prepared for the worst as soon as she'd locked the door.

"Willow? It's me."

It took a moment for her to absorb the words and the low timbre of the voice, but the Scottish lilt slowed the frantic thud of her pulse.

Charles.

She rushed to open the door. After he dodged inside amid a swirl of snow and ice and wind, she slammed the door shut again.

In the firelight, his features looked pinched and pale. Not for the first time, she was struck by the angular lines of his face, the sharp cheekbones, his piercing gray eyes.

"You didn't light the lamps?"

"I—I didn't know if you wanted me to use the kerosene."

He regarded her with open puzzlement, then murmured, "Daft girl. I wouldna leave you here in the dark. Take care of them now while I get out of my coat."

She hurried to light one of the waxy faggots he kept in a cup on the mantel. Holding her hand over the flame to protect it from the draft, she lit the lamp in the center of the table on what she supposed was the "eating" side of the keeping room. Then, after adjusting the wick, she blew out the taper.

Once again, Charles eyed her curiously. "Do the rest of them. We'll need to be seeing one another. Given all that's happened, you and I need to talk."

At those words, her gaze tangled with his, and she saw in the depth of those kind gray eyes a wealth of sadness.

Without being told, she knew he brought bad news.

Chapter Two

After lighting the faggot again, she stumbled through her task of lighting the lamps. When she'd finished, she couldn't deny that by chasing the shadows from the corners of the room, the buttery glow had banished some of her fear, as well.

Charles shrugged off his heavy shearling coat. He hung it and his hat on two of the pegs by the door. Then he shook his head, causing droplets of melted snow to fly from his close-cropped hair.

For the first time, Willow allowed herself to study the man intently. He wasn't what the other girls would consider handsome. His features were too sharp and angular for that. But without his coat, she could see that he was broad-shouldered, and lean—although in Willow's opinion, he could use a few good meals. Nevertheless, he radiated an aura of strength and dignity.

"How are they?" He gestured to the basket.

"Fine."

"No problems?"

"No, but…they'll be needing food soon and…"

Her cheeks flushed with sudden heat. How on earth

could she broach with a man the subject of feeding newborns?

Charles didn't seem to notice her discomfort. As he bent over the basket, his features lost their sharp angles and his expression glowed with wonder.

"I thought about that already. There are some goats in the barn by the livery. As soon as things calm down, I'll see if I can milk one or bring the animal here. I've got a lean-to in the back where it could stay for now."

He looked up at her then. In the past, she'd always thought his gray eyes were calm and peaceful. In that moment, they pierced her with their intensity.

"The twins aren't really yours, are they?"

She couldn't bring herself to lie. Not to him.

Willow shook her head.

"So, they belonged to Jenny?"

She licked her lips, her mouth suddenly dry. She trusted this man for no other reason than Jenny had trusted him.

"I think so."

"When did she give birth?"

"I don't know. She disappeared a few days ago, just like I told Mr. Batchwell. I—I wasn't sure whom to tell." She shifted uneasily. "After the Devotional, I finally decided to come to you. That's how I came to be at your house." Willow gripped her hands together. "Jenny, is she…"

It was his turn to look uncomfortable. He seemed to be searching for the right words. At long last, he said, "I'm so sorry."

Willow wasn't sure how it happened. There was a keening cry, the sound of sobbing. Then, as Charles drew her to him, she realized that she had been the one to make the noise.

Unconsciously, she gripped him, her fingers digging into the strength of his shoulders, her cheek pressing into his chest. His arms wrapped around her as she wept for a friend she'd known for only a few short months. She and Jenny had met at the docks in Liverpool and made the journey to America together. By combining their courage, they'd formed a bond that had helped them both complete the voyage.

"What happened, Willow? Do you know where she went?"

Her tears soaked into the homespun linen of his shirt. "No! She'd been upset the past week or so. I tried to get her to talk, to see if I could help, but then…she disappeared. She didn't tell me she was leaving. Only that—"

The door suddenly burst open. The lamps fluttered and sputtered as Ezra Batchwell stood in the doorway, his features overcome with fury.

"Explain yourself, madam!"

Charles was glad that he held Willow in his arms because he felt her knees give way. As he tightened his grip on her slender frame, he demanded, "What's the meaning of this? This is my home. The least you could have done is knocked."

Willow began to tremble so violently he feared that she might fall to the floor. For the first time, Charles realized how slight she was beneath her all-encompassing gown. She was a tiny thing, yet soft and feminine and smelling inexplicably of violets.

Ezra stepped into the room, allowing Jonah and one of the Pinkertons—Gideon Gault—to follow.

"No. This is my row house, my property, my silver mine! You, of all people, know the rules of this community— and you need to explain yourself this instant. As it is, if the canyon weren't completely impassable, I'd ride you both out on a rail!"

Charles had worked at the Batchwell Bottoms silver mine long enough to know that Ezra Batchwell was more bluster than substance. He had a short temper and tended to blurt out his frustrations without thinking. His partner, Phineas Bottoms, was calm and methodical, tending to examine a situation from every possible angle before weighing in. Unfortunately, since the mail-order brides had been marooned in the community, Batchwell seemed to regard the women as an open threat—to the point where even Bottoms couldn't calm him down.

Thankfully, Phineas Bottoms must have been summoned into town, because he wove through the men congregated on the stoop and stepped inside.

"Now, Ezra—"

"Don't you 'now, Ezra' me, Phineas! This man has been carrying on with one of the brides right beneath our very noses! Worse, he's had a couple of babes by her! And all the while, he's been claiming to be a man of God and preaching to us each night during evening Devotional. It's nothing but a tawdry—"

"She's my wife!"

The words blurted from Charles's lips before they'd even formed in his head. A shuddering silence descended around the room—one broken only by the whistle of the wind whirling snow into the house.

Willow trembled even more in his arms, but she didn't speak. Luckily, she'd turned her face toward him. Otherwise, she wouldn't have been able to hide her shock at his pronouncement.

He squeezed her, imperceptibly, meeting her gaze for a fleeting instant in a way that he hoped reassured her, and then offered, "Willow and I met when you sent me to England to oversee the shipment of the new machinery last spring. We fell in love and married."

Ezra made a huffing sound that was at once disbelieving and outraged.

How could he make the lie sound more convincing?

"We hadn't planned on her being marooned here in Bachelor Bottoms."

Batchwell's hands clutched his walking stick so that his knuckles gleamed white.

"So, we kept things…secret…"

"And do you have a marriage license to back up your claims?"

Charles was unable to think of a quick enough response.

"As I recall, we were never able to find all of Miss Granger's baggage," Jonah Ramsey offered. "If the document was in one of her trunks, we may not find it until spring."

Charles met his friend's gaze in surprise, wondering if Jonah knew the truth or if he was merely trying to smooth things over in the most logical means possible.

"And you've all got another think coming if you believe I'm going to take their word on the matter."

"Sir, I—"

Ezra turned to Gideon Gault, stabbing a finger in the air. "Go get that man who married Ramsey. If these two have already been legally wed, it won't make no nevermind to do it again."

Charles felt Willow stiffen, so he offered a quick objection. "Now, see here, I don't think—"

Ezra's finger pointed in his direction. "Not a word out of you, you hear me? You're a man of the cloth — or the nearest thing we have hereabouts—and I won't tolerate a big hullabaloo interfering with the men or the jobs they're supposed to be doing. More importantly, I refuse to have a scandal on my hands—or even whispers of scandal. Therefore, you'll be remarried. Within the hour. Until then, *you* will remain in the Miner's Hall." The finger stabbed in Charles's direction once more. "Ramsey, send for a few women to sit with Miss Granger. And post some guards at the door! I don't want anybody going in or out until we've seen to this matter."

Batchwell motioned for his retinue to follow him, then stormed toward the door, grumbling, "As if we don't have enough on our hands."

Charles resisted, knowing that he had to speak to Willow. He couldn't let this charade continue. Not if it meant the poor woman would be forced into marriage— to *him*.

But before he could offer a single word, Gideon Gault was at his side, looking tall and broad and imposing in his dark blue Pinkerton tunic.

"Sorry, Charles. You heard the boss. He's being high-handed, but it shouldn't hurt either of you to repeat your vows in his presence."

Vows they'd never spoken. Vows that would bind them together as man and wife.

He tried to convey a portion of his thoughts to Willow, wanting to reassure her that she could bring this whole thing to a halt, and he'd take the consequences, but her eyes were curiously shuttered. Too late, he realized that the crowd of men had remained and both he and Willow were still the center of attention.

Gideon's grip on his arm was strong and steady, pulling them apart. But Charles managed to snag Willow's hand and whisper, "I'll be back as soon as I can. Promise." Then the men pulled him resolutely into the darkness without even a coat to shield him from the cold.

* * *

Willow shivered in the quiet.

How had this happened?

Her mind worked in endless looping circles—*Charles, babies, marriage*—until the door burst open and several women dodged inside.

Leading the charge was Lydia Tomlinson, self-proclaimed suffragist. Unlike most of the mail-order brides in their group, she had no plans to marry. Instead, the avalanche had forestalled her plans to host a series of speaking engagements in California.

"Willow, why didn't you tell us that you were already married?" Lydia asked, as she draped her cape over one of the kitchen chairs.

"I—"

"Now, Lydia, let the girl breathe." Iona Skye reached to squeeze one of Willow's hands. "If Charles and Willow saw fit to keep their relationship a secret in order to preserve the man's job, it's no business of ours."

Thankfully, the other women heeded Iona's words. As the eldest member of the group of stranded females, Iona had been on her way to live with her sister's family. Because she was a widow woman, the mail-order brides tended to let her take the lead, since Sumner had moved to live with her husband off company property.

"Whatever the circumstances, we have a wedding to prepare—and not much time to do it." Iona pointed to a pair of women with identical dark eyes and dark curls. "Myra and Miriam, you keep your eyes on the babes while Lydia and I take Willow upstairs to change. Emmarissa and Marie, you take care of decorating the mantel. They can restate their vows in front of the fire, so see what you can do to gussie it up with the extra candles we brought. The rest of you can make up some coffee and find some plates for the cookies left over from the cook shack. You can't have a wedding without some refreshments."

Before Willow could insist that there would be no guests—and no real wedding—Lydia and Iona took her hands and drew her up the staircase to the rooms above.

"This will do," Lydia said, after opening the first door. Inside was one of the mine-issued cots, with a mattress rolled up tightly near the footboard. On the opposite wall was a simple dresser with a mirror and a chair.

"I brought your comb and brush, Willow, and your Sunday-best dress, but..." Lydia pulled the chair into the center of the room. "I wondered if you would like to be married in something...different."

Willow found herself staring bemusedly at Lydia. "What?"

"Would you like to wear something other than your Sunday-best dress? Since the men haven't found your second trunk yet, I thought you might like to wear something...brighter."

Willow's cheeks flamed. There was no second trunk— there never had been. She'd arrived in America with only two gowns to her name. Her Sunday-best dress was a staid, serviceable black faille, as shapeless and dreary as the dress she wore now. But when she'd announced that she would be leaving the Good Shepherd Charity School for Young Girls, the headmaster had forbidden her to take anything with her that the school had provided. She'd been reduced to supplying her meagre wardrobe from the charity barrels bound for a mission in New Guinea. Unfortunately, the recent donations had been heavily laden with maternity wear.

"I...yes, I..."

Lydia didn't seem to need any more of an answer

than that, because she left the room, closing the door behind her.

Iona gently pushed Willow into the chair and began unwinding her braid.

"You have such beautiful hair," the older woman murmured, making Willow's skin prickle with self-consciousness.

Willow shifted uneasily. The headmaster at the Good Shepherd had proclaimed her red tresses a sign of evil and had insisted that she keep them covered at all times with a scarf or bonnet.

Before she quite knew what had happened, Iona had divided the tresses into smaller plaits, which she wound in an intricate design around the crown of her head and in a swirling knot at the nape of her neck. By that time, Lydia had returned with a carpetbag, from which she removed a yellow day dress sprigged with tiny pink roses.

Willow couldn't prevent the soft gasp of pleasure that escaped her lips as the women stripped off the shapeless garment she'd been doomed to wear for months and replaced it with the fitted cotton gown.

The waist proved too large for Willow and the hem too long. However, Lydia had come prepared. Taking a needle and thread, she artfully tucked up the skirt, drawing the fullness toward the rear in a mock bustle. Then she took a length of pink ribbon from the carpetbag and tied it around Willow's waist.

"There."

Both Lydia and Iona stood back to eye their efforts.

"Beautiful," Iona murmured. "She looks every inch a bride."

Lydia's brow furrowed. "Not quite." She opened the door and called out, "Greta!"

Greta Heigle had traveled to the Territories all the way

from Bavaria. A plump, blond-haired woman with pink cheeks and snapping blue eyes, she'd boarded the train without knowing a word of English. After a month marooned with the other mail-order brides, she was beginning to learn how to communicate with hand gestures and a sparse English vocabulary.

Willow heard soft footfalls running up the staircase, then Greta burst inside and gasped, *"Die Männer sind hier."*

When the women looked at her blankly, she offered, "Men. *Men.*" Then she pointed to the floor.

"The men are here?"

"Ja!"

Greta then held out a length of lace, and before Willow could fathom what they meant to do, Lydia and Iona began pinning it to the crown of braids.

"*Now* she looks like a bride," Lydia breathed with satisfaction.

Iona took Willow gently by the shoulders and turned her to face the mirror.

For a moment, the air whooshed out of Willow's lungs. She'd spent so much time in staid black school uniforms or charity day gowns that she couldn't remember when she'd ever worn color. The soft yellow dress made her skin milky, her hair bright as a flame. And the veil... the veil softened the effect even more. She did indeed look like...

Like a bride.

Even more...she looked...

Pretty.

"*Schön.* Lovely," Greta murmured. The stout woman drew her close for a bone-crushing hug.

When she drew back, Willow fingered the delicate

veil. The lace was soft, fashioned from gossamer silk floss. "I'll return this as soon as possible."

Greta's brow knitted in puzzlement, so Willow mimed the action of unpinning the veil and handing it to her. Greta shook her head. "*Nien. Geschenk.* Gift." Then the woman beamed.

Willow's eyes welled with tears. The piece of hairpin lace must have taken hundreds of hours to complete. The fact that it would now adorn a sham marriage made her inwardly cringe. Nevertheless, she couldn't dim the joy shining from Greta's eyes.

"Thank you, Greta. I'll treasure it always."

"Miss Granger!"

There was no mistaking the booming voice that reached them from the main room. Ezra Batchwell and his retinue had returned, and he was eager to see that the formalities were finished.

Lydia hugged her as well, then Iona.

"Best wishes," Lydia said, before backing out of the room.

Iona took a handkerchief from where it had been tucked in her sleeve. Sniffling, she dabbed her eyes. "May this be the first of many happy days," she whispered, her voice husky with emotion. "I always cry at weddings." Then she hurried from the room, leaving Willow alone.

From below, Willow could hear the deep murmur of male voices combined with a few higher pitched ones. She knew she wouldn't be given much time to think.

But even as she considered running downstairs, calling the whole thing off and confessing her deceit…

She couldn't do it.

Not just because the thought of that many eyes turning her way in censure made her quake, but because Jenny had been her friend. Her first real friend. Those babies downstairs were Jenny's and they were motherless and defenseless.

No. Not defenseless.

They had her.

And they had Charles.

Pinning that thought in her mind, she smoothed a hand over the ribbon at her waist, adjusted the veil around her shoulders, then headed for the door.

Charles shifted nervously from foot to foot, feeling as if a herd of ants were crawling beneath his skin. At Ramsey's insistence, he'd taken time at the Hall to wash his face and hands, slick back his hair and don the clean shirt, vest and tie that Gideon had loaned him.

He swallowed against the dryness of his throat, easing a finger beneath the tie, which seemed to be cutting off his ability to breathe. He was sure that Gideon had tied it too tight—probably on purpose, since he'd joked that Charles would soon feel the noose of matrimony closing around his neck for the second time.

From the corner of his eye, he could see the two wee bairns being rocked in the arms of the Claussen twins.

Charles knew better than most what would happen to the babes if they weren't claimed. If Ezra Batchwell had exploded at the idea of having women on the premises, there would be no containing his ire at the thought of a pair of children running about. As soon as the pass cleared, they would be taken to the nearest foundling home. Once there, they could be separated, or worse, live their childhoods in an institution—a fate that Charles had himself endured and wouldn't wish on his worst enemy.

No. If Willow was agreeable, he'd see this charade to

the end, then sort things out when they'd both had time to plan what was best for the youngsters.

As if she'd heard him, Willow suddenly appeared at the top of the steps.

For a moment, the air left Charles's lungs. For a month now, he'd caught glimpses of the girl—at the Devotionals, behind the counter of the cook shack, or peeking between the curtains of the Dovecote. He was ashamed to admit that he hadn't paid her much mind.

He regretted that now, because the woman who stepped toward him was beautiful. The soft cotton dress she wore seemed to highlight the fairness of her skin, the dusting of freckles across her brow and cheeks. And that hair…it shone in the lamplight like a blazing sunset.

She moved to stand beside the fireplace, and then turned to face him.

Ignoring Batchwell's scowl, Charles caught her hand and leaned to whisper next to her ear. "You don't have to do this."

Nevertheless, when he met her gaze, those cornflower-blue eyes blazed with determination.

"They need us," she whispered.

"Enough!" Batchwell barked. "Let's get this over with."

Even then, Charles kept hold of Willow's hand. Despite her bravado, he could feel the chill of her fingertips and the trembling of her extremities. When he repeated his vows, she clung to him even tighter. As she offered her own promises, he thought he heard a quaver in her voice. Then, before Charles could credit how quickly his life had altered course, there was a cheer and someone was pounding him on the back.

"Kiss the girl!" a deep voice shouted, and Charles could have sworn it was Gideon Gault. Knowing that all eyes were upon them, Charles brushed a light kiss over Willow's lips.

When he drew back, her cheeks were pink with color, and he automatically drew her into the lee of his arm as the women rushed to offer their congratulations.

Soon, his home became noisy with chatter and laughter. For too long, his house had been a sterile, quiet place. He'd learned to endure the silence, but he'd never grown used to it.

However, when Ezra Batchwell pounded his walking stick on the floor, reality came rushing back as the row house became quiet again.

"It's late and some of you need to be at your shift within a few hours. I think it's time we all went home."

There were murmurs of disappointment, but the women rushed to shake Charles's hand and kiss Willow on the cheek. Then they gathered their wraps and reluctantly headed into the cold. The men followed more slowly, until only Batchwell, Bottoms, Jonah Ramsey and Gideon Gault remained.

Rather than offer his congratulations, Batchwell stomped toward the couple, his dark eyes blazing. "You broke the rules," he growled. "You knowingly brought a woman to our valley and then lied to us all."

Charles stiffened. He might not have invited Willow to join him in Bachelor Bottoms, but he *had* lied to his employers. Since there was no response he could offer at the moment to clarify the situation, he remained silent.

"Get out," the man rasped through clenched teeth. "You, of all people, are aware of the directives of this mining community and the requirements for employment. I don't care if there's a blizzard or a blocked pass, you and your...*wife*...will get out of this house, out of this valley, out of this town. Immediately!"

Chapter Three

"I resign. From my job, my position as lay preacher, and member of this community!"

Charles couldn't prevent the words that burst from his lips. It was as if they came from another person—another source.

"And as an outlier to the community, I claim the same ability to shelter in one of the row houses like the other families who were marooned here by the avalanche."

Ezra Batchwell grew so red-faced that Charles wouldn't have been surprised if the man's head exploded.

"How dare you?" Batchwell whispered accusingly. "How *dare* you treat our rules so frivolously?"

Charles stiffened his shoulders. Batchwell was right. Charles owed the owners everything.

And yet...

He glanced at Willow, who hovered uncertainly near the twins' basket. Unconsciously, she'd provided a barrier between the babes and Batchwell. Charles took in her wide, startled eyes, and that glorious hair limned by firelight. Behind her skirts, he could see the blankets moving.

Please, please protect my little ones and keep them as your own. They are in more danger than I can express.

Those defenseless babes needed him. Even if it was only temporary.

"As you can see, Mr. Batchwell, I've got a family to take care of, and their welfare takes precedence. If that means giving up my job, so be it."

Batchwell opened his mouth—probably to offer another tirade. Jonah stepped slightly in front of the man, putting a hand to his chest. "You can't fault a man for focusing on his family."

Then Phineas added his own two cents. "If you ask me, the boy hasn't done anything wrong, Ezra. It's not against the rules to be married here at the Batchwell Bottoms Mine. Half our workforce is married—" he pointed to Jonah "—including our mine superintendent. It's only against the rules for them to live together on company property. And seeing as how Charles has resigned…well, I don't see as how you've got any right to be carrying on this way."

A low rumble began in Batchwell's chest, making it clear that he was ready for a rebuttal. Before he could speak, Phineas limped toward the basket a few feet away and drew aside the blanket so that the two sweet faces were exposed.

"There comes a time in every man's life when his family has to come first, Ezra. What with the death of that young girl and the storm…seems to me there would be something amiss in Charles if he didn't decide that he should protect the ones he loves."

Phineas glanced up then, his shrewd gaze piercing straight into Charles's soul. Charles prayed the older man hadn't uncovered the deceit that lay there.

"Far as I'm concerned, you're welcome to use the row house. It's not like there's anyone else waiting for it. Once the pass clears, we'll see what needs to be done."

Phineas lifted his arms and made a shooing motion. "Now, get out of here. Get! You, too, Ezra. You're letting in cold air that these babes can ill afford. Even worse, it's late and dark. Any of those conditions can make a man say things he oughtn't." He offered a bitter chortle. "And let's just say that there's nothing more that needs to be said until morning. Get!"

The men reluctantly turned and filed from the room. Phineas was the last to leave, poking his wizened head around the edge of the door.

"A good evening to you both. Charles. Mrs. Wanlass. You take good care of those little ones, you hear?"

Charles couldn't be sure, but for a moment, Phineas's eyes seemed to twinkle. Then the door snapped shut, and they were left in silence.

Alone.

Together.

There was a calm that fell over the empty row house. Then Willow shifted to adjust the blankets on the babies. Unsure of what to do, he walked to the door and bolted it, locking them in.

Unaccountably, his palms were sweating and he unobtrusively wiped them down the sides of his trousers. Truth be told, he'd never been in any woman's presence for more than a few minutes, let alone locked in a room with one. He wasn't sure what he was expected to do. Since he'd never lived in a family setting, he had no history to draw from.

Willow shivered, spurring him into action.

"I'll throw more wood on the fire and warm things back up."

She regarded him with wide eyes. "But…shouldn't you ration your supplies?"

Ration his supplies?

There were plenty of logs next to the hearth and another pile stacked along the wall of the lean-to outside. Even if they managed to burn through the entire collection, thick stands of pine and aspen surrounded Bachelor Bottoms. It would be easy to gather more.

Willow stood wringing her hands, obviously as uncomfortable as he was with their situation, so he offered gently, "There's plenty out back. I doubt we could burn through it in a month."

"Oh. Oh, I see."

Despite his reassurances, she seemed to regard the extra fuel as an extravagance, and Charles wondered if he'd somehow given her the impression that he couldn't provide her and the children with basic needs.

But then, they didn't know anything about one another, did they?

"We don't want the children to catch a chill."

"No. No, of course not."

The fact that he'd put the needs of the babies first seemed to dismiss her fears of wastefulness. Not wanting her to change her mind, Charles hurried to throw two big logs onto the fire, then fussed with them until he had no other option than to face Willow again.

She stood in the same spot, her hands clasped at her waist, her eyes wide and unblinking. A bit stunned. But not horrified. He'd been so afraid that he would have offended her with the pack of lies he'd been spinning—or worse, that she would be dismayed at being rushed into a marriage she'd never wanted.

"I, uh… I hope I didn't upset you with everything… with what I said about…us already meeting and…"

She shook her head. "No."

"Good. Because I didn't want them—didn't want anyone—thinking…"

Why was he so tongue-tied with her?

Her brow suddenly knit in consternation. "You shouldn't have quit your job. Why did you quit your job?"

He strode toward her, then his arms around her. Willow was such a wee thing, fitting perfectly beneath his chin. She shivered and he pulled her closer to the fire.

"I haven't done anything that can't be undone eventually."

She drew back to eye him askance. "Except marrying me."

There was that.

Thoughts skittered through his brain like water on a hot skillet, but he was finally able to grasp on to one coherent thread.

"We can always get an annulment. Later. When the pass has melted and we've figured out how best to protect the children." He drew back, bending so that she could meet his gaze. "I promise, Willow. I would never force you to do anything you don't want to do. If you want, I'll go out there right now and explain the whole thing. No one will ever blame you. All this was my doing from the very beginning."

He took a step back, reaching for his hat. Before he could grasp anything but air, she stopped him.

"No, Charles! I'm as much to blame. And…" Her eyes grew huge, so blue and beseeching that he was rooted to the spot. "What happened to Jenny?" she whispered.

He wasn't sure how much he should tell her. The two women had been friends. If anyone had been privy to Jenny's fears and emotions, it would have been Willow.

"Sit here," he said, gesturing to the chair by the fire.

When she would have demurred, he said, "I'll tell you everything you want to know, but… I could use a cuppa, and I'm sure you could, too. And if I don't get out of this tie…"

He tugged at the string, but the knot only seemed to tighten.

Willow pushed his hands aside. "Here, let me."

"I think Gideon Gault did this on purpose," Charles said. "He's promised never to marry, himself. Something about being raised with a houseful of older sisters."

The tie suddenly gave way. Charles felt some of the tension in his body rush out as he was finally able to take his first real breath. He quickly released the top button of his shirt and yanked the boiled collar free, instantly feeling more like himself.

Willow's smile was shy and quick, and he was relieved to see that she didn't seem to mind that he found the trappings of polite society confining.

When she reached for the pins holding her veil in place, he quickly offered, "Let me help. You don't want to snag the lace."

In reality, he was sure that she could perform the task quite well on her own, but he wanted to offer her the same little kindness that she'd given him. It was important to him that she knew he had no intention of lording over her. Granted, he didn't have much experience with marriage—or even married folk, for that matter. But he'd seen the way that Jonah and Sumner treated one another, as partners and friends, as well as sweethearts. In Charles's opinion, that seemed the best way for him to handle things.

One by one, he gently removed the metal hairpins. As he did, his fingers brushed against her hair. The tresses were softer than he'd imagined. He'd thought that such curly hair would have a wiry texture, but the strands were silky. He couldn't help wondering what it would feel like if her hair was unbound. Free from their braids, would the curls be wavy and thick, or would they spring into riotous ringlets?

Before he could even finish the thought, the task was finished, and Willow stepped away.

For a moment, the air shimmered between them—like the stillness right before a spring lightning storm. Then Willow stepped toward the chair, and the energy shifted back to awkwardness.

"I'll just…" He pointed in the direction of the teapot on the kitchen table. It was surrounded with the remnants of the impromptu wedding—used cups and saucers, half-eaten cookies, a platter with only a few remaining sweets.

Draping the veil over one of the chairs, Charles quickly found two clean mugs on his shelves. He rued the fact that Willow would have to drink her tea from the no-frills cups. She should have something fancy. Refined. But the pretty things that the women had brought with them from the Dovecote had all been used.

"I don't see any milk. Do you take sugar?"

"Please."

Again, he had nothing fancy. Merely the shavings from a sugar loaf. But he gave her what he hoped was the right amount. Then, after hooking his finger through the handle of both mugs, he grabbed one of the chairs from the table and positioned it near the fire, then handed Willow her tea.

She sipped the brew, and he took comfort from the fact that she didn't grimace. For several moments she stared into the flames—long enough that Charles could take a quick gulp from his own mug.

Then she turned to him, her eyes direct, resolved, and a brilliant crystal blue.

"Tell me about Jenny."

Willow feared that Charles would try to shield her from what he'd discovered. She'd seen the behavior of enough of the miners from Batchwell Bottoms. Since the men were denied the presence of females in their community, they invented reasons to interact with the women. In doing so, they tended to put them on a pedestal, insisting that they be pampered and sheltered from the slightest discomfort. The men worried that the women found the wind too cold, the nights too dark, the food too limiting.

Willow had lived in the real world far too long to indulge in such fantasies. She'd known cold and darkness and hunger far worse than any she'd encountered here at Bachelor Bottoms, and she had no desire to abandon those lessons for the false security of half-truths.

So when Charles's gray eyes met hers, she didn't look away. Instead, she willed him to give her the information she craved.

Because she wouldn't rest until she knew the truth.

He exhaled slowly. Then bent forward, resting his elbows on his knees, his mug held loosely in his hands. For a moment, he stared into his tea.

"She was found in the street near the mining offices. It's not clear if she stumbled there, looking for help, if she fell, or if she…was left there."

"Left there?" The whisper pushed from Willow's lips involuntarily.

Charles looked up.

"She could have had an accident." His words sounded too forced, as if he wanted to convince himself of their veracity.

"But you don't think so."

He reluctantly shook his head.

"It looked to me like she'd been struck." He lifted a hand to the back of his head. "Here…" his palm shifted to his temple "…and here." He met Willow's gaze again before saying, "Her skull was crushed."

"You're sure someone did this to her? That it wasn't an accident?"

Charles's lips narrowed as he thought things through, and she appreciated the way he appeared to be so deliberate. Clearly, he wasn't a man prone to jumping to conclusions.

"Maybe I could have given that possibility some credence." His gaze became intense. "If it weren't for the note we found on the basket."

"Who could have done this?" Willow whispered.

"Was there anyone who was bothering her?"

Willow shook her head. "Not that I can recall. The first few weeks we were here, she seemed really…happy. I thought it was a little strange, since the avalanche kept her from reuniting with her husband in California. She didn't complain about being marooned, like the other ladies."

"Did she have any trouble with one of the other women?"

"No!" Willow vehemently shook her head. "You can't possibly think that one of the mail-order brides did this."

"I'm just trying to gather as many facts as I can."

"Jenny kept to herself. I think she was self-conscious about her pregnancy. She believed herself to be ungainly and…unattractive. She seemed incredibly preoccupied about the loss of her figure. She remained in her room for the most part. It was only after we all moved to the Dovecote that she perked up. She began taking walks in the mornings and afternoons. But with the guards keeping us near the dormitory, she couldn't go far. She just circled the meadow around the Dovecote. She was always alone…" Willow's words petered off. "But I can't remember her having any disagreements with the other women. If anything, they tried their best to draw her out and help her."

"Did she have any contact with anyone else?"

Willow scoured her brain, trying to remember the smallest details. "Those first days, when there were so many injured…she was in the same room with a few of those who'd suffered broken bones. That would have been one of the porters from the train, Mr. Beamon, and the conductor, Mr. Niederhauser. The rest of them would have been mail-order brides. I don't think she ever took a shift in the cook shack, so she wouldn't have met anyone there. The Pinkertons were in and out of the Hall on a regular basis—Jonah's assistant, Mr. Creakle, and that nice Mr. Smalls. Once we moved to the Dovecote, the guards tried to keep the miners at arm's length, but that didn't prevent someone with a good excuse—a load of firewood, a box of supplies from the storehouse, the offer of a book to read—from getting a word with one of the girls. Even so, I don't remember anyone seeking out Jenny in particular."

"You said she was happy at first."

Willow's brow creased. "Yes. The fact that she would have to stay here for months didn't seem to even dawn on her. She was eager for her baby to be born, so I thought that maybe she was hoping she could reunite with her husband looking like the same girl he'd left behind in England, rather than being…in the family way."

Willow felt a tinge of heat seep into her cheeks at being so frank with someone of the opposite sex, but she forced herself to continue. "But after Christmas, her mood changed. She became weepy and emotional. When I tried to find out what was wrong, she said she was tired—tired of being awkward and unattractive. She wanted her baby to come. Then, just before she disappeared, she seemed uneasy and jumpy—almost fearful. What could have happened?" Willow asked aloud.

"Who would have done this to her?" Her gaze fell to the basket. "And why was she so sure that the babies were in danger, as well?"

Charles shook his head. "I don't know. But judging by everything that's happened, I don't think we can brush her warning aside." His gaze dropped to the basket. "Right now, we've got to put our heads together and see to the bairns. Then we'll focus on other matters."

Such as what happened to Jenny.

A soft sneeze from the direction of the basket caused Charles's steeliness to disappear from his gaze.

"You said the babies will need milk. Anything else?"

"I, uh…warm water to bathe them, more blankets, perhaps more flannels. Eventually, I'll need fabric to make layette gowns. They don't seem to have a change of clothing."

"Then let's focus on what we can do for them tonight." Charles stood and reached for a pail near the stove, then his coat and hat. "I'll head to the barn for milk. Why don't you rustle through the larder and see if you can scrape up something for us to eat besides leftover cookies? Tomorrow, I'll go to the company store and get whatever else we need."

"But…your job. You won't have pay coming in…"

He paused in buttoning his coat, then came back to her. Touching her shoulder, he said, "It's all right, Willow. I have a great deal of credit with the store that I've put aside as part of my wages. It's about time I used some of it."

"If you're sure."

"I'm sure."

He traced her cheek—and she couldn't resist the urge to lean into that caress, ever so slightly. "Right now, we're in this together. These children need us. And Jenny, God rest her soul, has put them in our care. For now, that's where we'll put our focus."

The words roused her fighting spirit, and Willow was instantly flooded with a fierce determination. "Yes. You're right. I'll have something for us to eat by the time you return."

"Thank you, Willow."

Tugging his hat securely over his brow, he unlatched the door and stepped outside.

If possible, the night had grown even colder in the last few hours. Charles hunched deeper into his coat, stamping down the stoop and into the darkness. As he was about to turn the corner, he couldn't help glancing back at the row house. There in the inky blackness and whirling snow, his windows blazed with a warm, welcoming light. Charles could just make out the flickering shadows caused by the fire and the shape of a woman passing into the kitchen.

A woman.

In his home.

A wife.

No. Not truly a wife—even though they'd exchanged vows.

Turning, he trudged through the ever-deepening snow in the direction of the barn. In the space of an hour or two, he'd crashed through quite a few of the commandments—envy, dishonesty, and now he was about to add stealing to his list since, as a *former* member of the mining community, he had no real claim to any of the animals or their milk.

But the need to ensure the well-being of the babes— who couldn't be more than a few days old—seemed to have brushed all his principles aside.

Tomorrow, he could talk to Jonah about paying for the use of a goat—or he could make arrangements with the company store or the cook shack. Then again, the fewer folk who knew about the bairns needing milk, the better. He had no doubts that the Bachelor Bottoms gossip mill would be chewing furiously on the news that Charles Wanlass had married in secret, fathered two children, *re*-married his sweetheart and resigned from his position. He didn't need anyone puzzling over why the mother couldn't feed them herself.

He glanced behind him again. By now, he was out of sight of the row house, but he could see the golden radiance easing into the dark night like a beacon.

And in that instant, quite inexplicably, Charles didn't feel so alone.

"What's going on, Charles?"

He started, his hands automatically coming up into fists—a reaction he hadn't had since he was a boy. When he found Jonah Ramsey watching him from the entrance to the infirmary, Charles quickly dropped his hands.

Ramsey closed the door firmly behind him, twisted a key in the lock, then jammed his hands into his coat pockets.

"Where you headed?"

"The livery."

Ramsey's brows rose, but he merely said, "I'm headed that way myself. I'll keep you company."

They walked in silence, their boots crunching in the snow, and Charles scrambled for something to say to ease the uneasiness that hung between them. Granted, Charles had never been much of a talker—and he hadn't spent as much time in his off hours with Jonah Ramsey as Gideon had been prone to do. But the two of them shared a comfortable friendship.

"Are you meeting Sumner at the livery?" Charles asked, for wont of anything else to say.

"Nah. As soon as she looked over Jenny's body, I sent her home with the sleigh. I knew this storm would only get worse and I wanted her heading to safety as soon as possible. That's why she wasn't at the wedding."

Charles felt the man shoot a glance his way, but he refused to look up.

"I'm sure Sumner will be right disappointed to have missed it. She and Willow are pretty close."

Charles hadn't thought about that. It would seem strange that Willow had never confided an affection for him all this time.

"In fact, I'm pretty sure that Sumner told me on more than one occasion that Willow was part of the group of mail-order brides destined for California. As I recall, my wife said something about Willow agreeing to marry a bedridden man with a houseful children."

Charles had forgotten about that, too. He knew that Jonah was waiting for him to comment, but for the life of him, Charles didn't know what to say.

This time he couldn't help meeting Ramsey's gaze, and by thunder there was a glint in his friend's eyes, even in the darkness.

"I'm sure Sumner will be relieved to hear that she was mistaken," Jonah continued when Charles failed to speak. "She was worried that Willow's arrangement might be less of a marriage and more a lifelong term of servitude."

They'd both eased to a stop in front of the livery, where a lantern hung by the door offered a small puddle of light. Charles studied his friend hard, wondering if there were hidden meanings to the words being offered. Once again, he wondered if Ramsey somehow suspected the true parentage of the twins. If so, he would know that Charles's claims of an earlier marriage ceremony in England were false. But if that were the case, he would have called a halt to the vows that had just been exchanged.

Wouldn't he?

"What brings you out on a night like this, Charles?"

What on earth could he say to that?

"I… I needed to have a word with Smalls."

Willoughby Smalls oversaw the livery, the mules used in the mine and the other various animals that kept the mining community in milk, meat and even wool. Since Charles often helped him with the blacksmithing, he had a logical reason to talk to the man.

"I thought he should hear about my resignation from me."

Jonah nodded. "That's good of you. But I think I saw him head up to Miner's Hall. He and Creakle were probably thinking of getting their fiddles out and providing a little music. I'm sure they'll be easy to find."

The man opened one of the side doors to the stables, then turned at the last moment. "Oh, and Charles…"

Again, Charles could have sworn that Jonah's dark eyes flashed with amusement.

"While you're at it, tell Smalls that I've given you permission to take one of those goats off his hands. We have more milk than we can handle with those things. And I think I remember my mother saying that goat's milk was more tolerable to a young child than cow's milk. You can find out for sure when Sumner comes back to the camp in a day or two. In the meantime, with two babes on her hands, Willow might find a little extra nourishment could come in handy."

With that, he closed the door with a soft thud.

Leaving Charles more unsettled than ever.

Chapter Four

Charles had been gone for only a few minutes when Willow heard a soft tap at the door. She froze.

"Willow, it's me." The voice was distinctly feminine.

Hurrying to the door, Willow drew back the bolt, allowing Lydia to slip inside.

"What are you doing here?"

The other woman grinned. "I was helping to clean up in the cook shack after the evening meal, and I happened to see Charles head to the livery with Jonah Ramsey, so I slipped out the side door."

"Won't the Pinkertons realize you're gone?"

Lydia sniffed, eloquently offering her opinion of the men tasked with being their guards. "I'll be back before they know I've gone. Besides, Gideon Gault has taken the lead tonight, and it won't hurt for him to be brought down a peg or two."

Willow didn't comment on the fact that the head of the mining camp's Pinkerton unit seemed to rub Lydia the wrong way more than any of the other guards.

"Besides, I wouldn't be able to sleep tonight if I didn't have a chance to talk to you."

The woman's eyes narrowed as she studied Willow intently. "You are happy, aren't you?"

"Happy?"

"With Mr. Wanlass. You haven't been forced into anything against your will, have you?"

"No! I... Mr. Wanlass... *Charles* and I..." Willow didn't know what to say to reassure her friend, so she offered weakly, "We're in love."

The explanation tasted false on her tongue. Willow didn't have the slightest idea what "love" even meant. When she'd agreed to marry Mr. Ferron and serve as his helpmate and the mother of his children, she'd known that love had nothing to do with it. The two of them had shared a business agreement, nothing more, nothing less. If she'd ever had any dreams of romance, Willow had pushed them aside and consoled herself with the fact that the marriage of convenience would offer her the one thing she wanted: a family. Or at least the closest thing to a family that she was likely to get.

In that respect, the arrangement with Charles wasn't much different. Willow was still playing at being a wife and mother. The principal characters had just changed for the time being.

But Lydia was unaware of Willow's turmoil. The woman grasped her hands, squeezing them.

"I thought so, otherwise I wouldn't have interfered. It was my idea to bring the dress, the veil."

Willow's fingers slid from Lydia's grip to the pink ribbon at her waist. "Oh, you'll need your dress back. It will only take a minute to—"

"Stop it. I don't want it back. It's a gift. The other dresses that you wore were..."

"Awful," Willow blurted out.

Lydia laughed. "I honestly thought you were wearing them for religious reasons, or as penance or something."

"Lydia!"

"Okay, I'm exaggerating. But now that I know you have no objections to colors, I've got a few more gowns you can have."

Willow stiffened.

Lydia must have sensed her concern because she gave a dismissive wave of her hand. "Please, don't say no. My aunts insisted on an entirely new wardrobe for my speaking engagements. I headed for California with thirteen trunks—thirteen!" She grimaced. "Even Mr. Gault had something to say about such excess when the men finally managed to unearth the last of them. I refuse to continue my journey with more than three trunks—four at the most. Consider the new clothing a wedding gift. Most of them have never been worn—and it will take you a month of stitching to alter them to fit, so I'm inconveniently adding to your workload. But it would bring me such pleasure if I knew that they could be of use to you."

"I…"

"Just say 'thank you' and I'll consider this conversation finished."

Willow hesitated, but in the end, the temptation proved too much. The yellow dress she wore now was unlike anything she'd ever owned before, and she was discovering that the use of color and delicate fabrics made her feel…pretty.

"Thank you, Lydia."

Lydia offered a squeak of pleasure and clapped her hands.

"I'll sort through things tonight and drop by tomorrow with a selection. You don't have to take anything you don't like, but I think you'll have plenty to choose from."

She was reaching for the doorknob when Willow

blurted, "I thought you disapproved of marriage, Lydia. Isn't that what your speaking engagements are all about?"

Again, Lydia waved a dismissing hand. "My speeches are about females gaining a voice in government, standing up for their own happiness and relieving themselves of the tyranny of male domination. It's time women refused a subservient role and spoke out against inequality, abuse and the demonizing effects that an excess of hard spirits or gambling can have in any relationship. Just as importantly, men need to see that women are their partners, not their servants. There should be equal respect between the sexes, and an acknowledgment that some women are happiest as wives and mothers. But there are others, like Sumner, who have much to offer the world if they are allowed to pursue their dreams of a career."

"And what about you, Lydia?"

Her friend grinned. "I am not the marrying kind. I would much rather spread the Female Cause than wear a ring on my finger." She enfolded Willow in a quick embrace. "But even though I may never be a mother myself, that doesn't mean I don't want to be around children. So, I'll give you a day or two to settle in with Charles, then I'll be slipping away from the Pinkertons anytime I can for some cuddling of those twins, you hear?"

Willow laughed. "I'll be expecting you."

Then, with the squeak of the door and a rush of icy wind, Lydia disappeared.

It took Charles much longer than he'd thought to find Willoughby Smalls, then return to the long, narrow barn where some of the smaller animals were kept when the temperatures were low.

Since Willoughby's throat had been injured in an accident two years back, the man communicated by scrawling notes on whatever scraps of paper he managed to collect. Charles glanced down at a torn half of a weigh slip. According to Smalls's notation, he was to take a goat from one of the last enclosures. It needed to have one brown ear and one white. Smalls had assured him that the animal was a good milker and would stay warm enough in the lean-to behind Charles's house.

"As a newly married man, shouldn't you be with the little missus?"

Charles grimaced when he saw Gideon Gault watching him from a pile of feed sacks.

"You just about scared the life from me," Charles groused. He'd been gone from Willow too long. All these interruptions to his original errand were taking up too much time. "What are you doing here?"

"Lydia Tomlinson slipped out of the cook shack. And seeing that you'd left Willow alone, she headed over to your place."

Charles couldn't account for the relief he felt, knowing that Willow hadn't spent all this time by herself.

"Shouldn't you be hauling her back?" Charles grumbled, slipping the catch to the gate free and stepping into the goat enclosure. Immediately, the animals began shifting and bleating, clearly upset by the change in their routine.

"Not just yet. I don't want Lydia catching on to the fact that I've figured out how she's been sneaking away from the other guards, now and again."

"Then shouldn't you be watching her?" Charles offered.

"Oh, I've been doing that, too. Through the knothole in that wall over there. There's no sense freezing my fingers off just because she's of a mind to play hooky. Besides, I had another man circle around to the side entrance of your place, just in case."

Charles stepped into the midst of the milling animals, trying to find a goat with one brown ear and one white one. He'd never realized how many shapes, sizes and colors were possible in goats. There were big ones and little ones, goats with long fur and with closely cropped fur. There were goats with curved horns and some with spikes. But none of them matched Smalls's description.

"What *are* you doing, Charles?" Gideon said with a bemused grin.

"I'm looking for a goat. A milking goat."

"And?"

"And it's supposed to have one brown ear and one white."

Gideon searched the herd with his keen gaze and finally pointed to the far corner. "It's over there. Judging by its udders, it won't be long before it will need to be milked again."

"You see a rope anywhere?"

Gideon disappeared for a moment, then returned with a length of heavy twine. "Will this do?"

"Yeah."

Charles snagged the cord from the Pinkerton, then waded into the sea of goats, keeping his eyes pinned on his target.

"Hey, Charles. You got a good look at that woman's body, didn't you?"

Charles felt gooseflesh pebble his skin, but he didn't pause in his pursuit. "Yeah."

"Those wounds weren't an accident."

He nearly stumbled. Gault hadn't offered the words as a question.

"No. I didn't think so, either."

Chancing a glance at his friend, Charles turned to find Gideon staring at the far wall, his brow furrowed in thought.

"Who would do that to a woman? It's barbaric."

Charles gave up on his chase as a cold finger of foreboding trailed down his spine. "Yeah."

"A person's got to have a whole lot of anger to do something like that." Gideon's thousand-yard stare shifted, and he pinned Charles with a gaze that had the power to burn right through him.

"You take care of your little ones, you hear? And your wife. I've already doubled the guards around the brides until we know for sure what happened. But I can't do a whole lot for you and Willow without attracting Batchwell's attention. I'm counting on you to see to it that Willow stays indoors as much as possible. When I can, I'll have some men watching from afar, but it would be best if you both kept close to home as much as you can." Gault straightened. "You still got that rifle of yours?"

"Yes."

"Can you shoot?"

"Yes."

Charles didn't like to advertise his marksmanship, since he preferred to stay as far away from violence as possible. But he'd trained himself to be an expert shot. A body didn't come to the Territories with the naive idea that the rules of conduct peculiar to Bachelor Bottoms would extend to everyone. It was best for a man to be prepared.

"You might want to take it out of the cupboard and dust it off."

"I'll do that."

Gideon opened his mouth to say something else, but he must have seen a flutter of movement through the knothole, because he suddenly backed away.

"There she goes again. Good night to you, Charles."

"'Night, Gideon."

* * *

As soon as Lydia left, Willow wasted no time. After throwing the bolt home, she hurried to the cupboard, which Charles had referred to as "the larder."

There weren't many choices for their meal. She found a few staples—salt, pepper, sugar, flour—a bag of raisins, another of oats, and a crock of honey. Grasping a pot, she filled it halfway with water, then poured in a measure of oats, a pinch of salt and a handful of raisins. A bowl of porridge wasn't exactly a gourmet delight, but it would be warm and filling and hearty. Just the thing for a cold winter night.

Covering the pot with a plate, Willow made a mental note to send for her trunk as soon as she was able. Unlike most of the other mail-order brides, she hadn't traveled west with crates full of domestic items to set up housekeeping once she'd married. But she hadn't come to America completely empty-handed, either. She had a set of pots, some dishcloths, a few precious lengths of fabric and her mother's Blue Willow china.

How her mother had loved those dishes. There were times when Willow wondered if they were the reason for her own name. They'd been the one thing to survive the host of troubles that had besieged her family: her mother's death, her father's accident in the mills and their descent into poverty. When her father had been taken to debtors' prison, the dishes were meant to be sold. But unbeknownst to Willow, her father had packed them in a trunk and hidden them in one of the caves near their home. It wasn't until Willow had been sent away to the Good Shepherd Charity School that he'd written to inform her where he'd hidden the china. It was the last letter she'd received before he died. An unwitting dowry for Willow, who had seen becoming a mail-order bride to a widower with ten children as the only means to escape a life of destitution and menial labor. Granted, she would probably be exchanging one form of servitude for another, but at least it would be her choice.

But now, in an impulsive need to help a friend, all of those plans had gone awry. And who knew what would happen once her lie was exposed?

Once again, the spot between her shoulder blades seemed to burn with past punishments, but she pushed the sensation away. Since coming to America, she'd already faced obstacles that she might have once thought impossible. She'd learned to tamp down her fear and focus on the end goal—and things were no different now. She would concentrate on Jenny's children.

Since dinner was cooking and hot coffee waited in a pot on the stove, she returned to the tufted chair. She drew the basket close to her feet, where it would be warm enough to absorb the heat of the fireplace, but not so near that a stray spark might burn them. Pulling the blanket aside, she studied the two infants.

They were so small, so new. Their faces were still squinched and wrinkled, their little legs drawn tight to their bodies. She would wager that they were only a day old, perhaps two. So fragile.

So helpless.

No. Not helpless. Willow was here to protect them. And so was Charles.

One of the babies began to whimper, its fists balling up and flailing. Offering soft hushing noises, Willow reached to scoop it into her arms, only to discover that the baby was wet—which meant that now its clothes were wet and the blankets, as well. Thankfully, Willow had set the small stack of flannel nappies on a nearby table.

The infant settled somewhat once she had removed

its wet clothing and changed its diaper. *Her* diaper. The smaller baby was a girl. Willow would need to find some dry blankets or cloths. But first…

When the second baby began to fret, Willow changed his diaper, as well.

A boy and a girl.

As she swaddled him beneath the woolen cape beside his sister, Willow blinked back tears. Jenny must have been so proud. How on earth had she managed to deliver them on her own and keep their arrival a secret? She must have been incredibly frightened to have taken such measures—and even more alarmed to have left them behind.

Willow jumped when someone pounded on the door. But the noise was quickly followed by "Willow, it's me. Charles."

She hurried to let him in, then closed the door amid a swirl of snow. The weather grew more frightful by the minute. The walls seemed to vibrate from the force of the wind. By the time she was able to set the latch, a skiff of white had coated the floor with icy crystals.

Charles had gone out with one pail, but he'd returned with two.

"I brought the milk and some water for washing."

She took the buckets and transferred them to the wood range for heating. Then she helped Charles to shrug out of his coat and hat and hang them on the pegs by the door.

"It's getting pretty fierce out there," he said, brushing stray snowflakes from his shoulders and stamping his boots to rid them of a layer of ice.

"Sit by the fire."

"No, I'll help you with—"

She pulled on his wrist. "Sit. I'll bring you something to eat and drink, then we'll worry about the rest."

The fact that he nodded and sank into the chair gave credence to the effort it must have taken to slog through the drifts.

Willow hurried to scoop a mound of mush into his bowl. She filled a spoon with honey and set it atop the hot mixture. Then she poured coffee into a mug and carried them to Charles.

"Thanks. You were able to find everything you needed?"

"Yes."

When he didn't immediately eat, she shifted uncertainly. Had she somehow offended him with the simple fare?

When he spoke, it wasn't a complaint. Instead, he asked, "Aren't you going to eat with me?"

The thought hadn't even occurred to her. At school, she'd been forbidden to take her own meal until the rest of the adults had finished theirs. Oftentimes, there hadn't been much left and she'd been forced to go hungry.

"Go on. Get your food. I'll wait," he urged. "I suppose we could eat at the table, but the fire feels good. You can pull up that little crate there, and we'll use it to hold our cups."

Willow did as she was told, then collected her own food. By that time, Charles had drawn one of the kitchen chairs close to the fire.

"Here, you take the comfortable seat," he said.

"No. I couldn't possibly—"

"I insist."

Reluctantly, she settled on the edge of the tufted chair. After all he'd done, Charles deserved the cushions, in her opinion. But he seemed oblivious to her consternation as he sat.

"Shall I say grace?"

"Please."

"Dear Lord of all…for these blessings and those that Thou sees fit to send to us, we are truly grateful. Amen."

"Amen."

There was a beat of uncomfortable silence. Willow supposed that the pair of them were so accustomed to being alone, neither knew how to proceed.

Thankfully, Charles broke the quiet by reaching for his bowl.

"Oatmeal. One of my favorites."

Some of the stiffness left Willow's frame and she started swirling the honey into the mush with her spoon.

"With raisins, too," he commented.

She glanced up in sudden concern. Had she made herself too at home with his stores? Were the raisins reserved for some other purpose?

But Charles didn't look upset. Instead, he took a bite filled with the fruit, then made a soft humming sound and nodded. "It's good. Really good."

Willow wilted in relief.

"What? Were you thinking I wouldn't like it?"

"I—I didn't know if you were expecting something… fancier."

He gave a short humph. "I'm well aware of the shortcomings of my larder. And what true Scotsman doesn't like his oatmeal?" He offered a wink. "Especially with raisins."

Willow laughed, and the brittleness of the moment was broken.

"How are the wee ones?"

"Fine. I've no doubt they'll rouse soon. Unfortunately, while you were gone, they wet themselves clear through their clothes and their blankets. There were spare diapers, but not much else."

"We'll make a list of what they need tonight. The

company store opens soon after breakfast is served and the shifts change."

"Afterward, maybe you could…watch the children while I go to the Dovecote?" she asked hesitantly. When Charles regarded her questioningly, she said, "I'll need to fetch my clothing. And a trunk with some belongings."

"If you want to write a note to Sumner or one of the other girls, I'll hitch up the sleigh and fetch them for you myself. There's no sense going out in this weather if you don't have to."

Other than her father, Willow had never had someone put her comfort first, and the suggestion settled in her chest with a warm glow.

"Thank you. That would be very nice."

Charles set his empty bowl aside and reached for his cup.

"There's more oatmeal on the stove."

"Mmm. Maybe in a minute. Right now, it feels good to sit by the fire." He took a sip and then stared down at the children. "You're sure they're hale and hearty? They seem to sleep a great deal."

"They're only a day or two old. All that sleeping is normal for a newborn. Even so, we should probably have Sumner take a look at them."

"She'll be at the Dovecote in the next day or so. If she's there when I collect your things, I'll ask her to drop by. If not, I'll leave a message."

Willow hesitantly said, "We should give them names. As their parents…we would have named them."

"You're right." His expression became solemn in the firelight. "It seems wrong somehow…for us to do the honor. Their mother should have had the chance."

The soft luffing of the fire filled the silence.

"Did she mention possible names to you?"

Willow shook her head. "I don't think she anticipated

having twins. She rarely spoke about the baby itself, merely…her discomfort with her condition."

Charles met her gaze, his expression sober and intent. "Then the task falls on us."

As if understanding that they were the subject of conversation, the infants began to stir. Willow set her bowl aside and bent to touch the cheek of the littlest child.

"This one is a girl."

She stroked the dark tuft of hair on the other baby.

"And this one is a boy."

Charles bent closer. "A boy *and* a girl. Imagine that." He reached out a finger and the little girl reacted instinctively, clutching it in her fist. Charles half laughed, half gasped in astonishment.

"The first two children born in Bachelor Bottoms." His lips twitched in a smile. "Our own Adam and—"

"Eva," Willow interrupted. "Her name should be Eva."

Charles grinned.

Willow had grown so accustomed to seeing Charles Wanlass—a man the miners had nicknamed "The Bishop"—looking serious and reserved. She could scarcely credit the way that his expression made him seem young and boyish.

"Adam and Eva."

Charles touched each of the children on the top of the head with his broad palms. Then, before Willow knew what he meant to do, he closed his eyes, saying, "Dear Lord, we are grateful to Thee for these sweet children, little Adam and Eva. We mourn the loss of their mother and pray that, with Thy guidance, these infants will be happy, healthy and free from harm. Amen."

Willow's eyes pricked with tears. Other than her father, she'd never witnessed a man who was so tender and gentle.

Yet strong.

When he'd ordered Mr. Batchwell from his home,

Charles had made it clear that he would brook no interference with the infants he'd claimed as his own.

Or his wife.

His pretend wife.

Willow couldn't account for the stab of disappointment she felt in her chest. She thrust the sensation away before she could dwell on it.

She needed to remember that this was a temporary situation. Once they'd found the danger to the children and eliminated it, this entire charade would be over.

Then what?

She would return to the life that awaited her before the avalanche. She had agreed to marry Robert Ferron, a man in his sixties who had lost his first wife to consumption. Mr. Ferron was an invalid himself, having suffered a serious fall from the loft of his barn. He needed a strong, capable woman to care for him and his children. Willow would look after Mr. Ferron until his children had moved away to begin families of their own, and Robert had passed on. Then, as per the agreement of their marriage, Willow would be left a small settlement—enough to tide her over if she lived frugally.

She couldn't leave such a man in the lurch.

She'd given her word.

So why was she suddenly discontented with the arrangements she'd made months ago?

Her eyes dropped to Charles's broad hands. Now that his prayer had been uttered, he stroked the downy fluff on the tops of the twins' heads. The babies seemed to arch against that gentle caress, their eyes fluttering. As Willow absorbed the sight, she felt something in the pit of her stomach twist with an emotion she'd never felt before. One that felt very much like...

Envy.

Chapter Five

Charles glanced up in time to see a montage of emotions flash across Willow's features: curiosity, joy, sorrow. Then something that looked very much like regret. However, before he could ask what was wrong, the babies at his feet began to whimper.

Within moments, that whimper became full-fledged wails that filled the room.

"What did I do?"

Willow jumped to her feet. "Nothing. I think they need to eat."

She rushed to the box stove. From one of the open shelves she took a small bowl, which she filled halfway with goat's milk.

"Rock them for a few minutes while I try to figure out a way to do this."

Charles scooped both hands beneath the children, lifting them against his chest. The babies were so small, so slight, that it was as if he clutched little more than the fabric of Willow's cloak. But the cries made it clear that the makeshift blankets were far from empty.

He watched as Willow circled the kitchen, examined the contents of the only hutch against the far wall, then the open shelves. Finally, she seemed to settle on a course of action, taking a half-dozen dishcloths and placing them on the table, then returning to test the milk with her pinky.

"I think this will do. Carry them to the table, please."

Charles held the twins even more securely to his chest, then rose and joined Willow.

"Sit at the head, there."

She carried the bowl of milk to the table. Then she took one of the twins from his arms and cradled the child against her.

"I think if we dip the corner of the dishcloth into the milk, then allow it to drip into the babies' mouths, we can get enough nourishment in their stomachs to tide them over for an hour or two."

He watched as she proceeded to demonstrate, holding the soaked cloth against Eva's lips.

At first there was little progress. Eva continued to cry as the milk dribbled into her mouth and down her chin.

Sighing, Willow tucked another cloth around the baby's neck, then tried again.

The newborn continued to resist her efforts. Enough milk had dribbled into her mouth that the child made odd gurgling cries. Then, miraculously, she swallowed.

In an instant, the cries stopped and the baby blinked up at Willow in surprise. She quickly dunked the cloth in the milk again and returned it to Eva's mouth. This time, the child sucked on the pointed corner. The moment the milk stopped dripping, Eva began to whimper once more.

Seeing that Willow was having some success, Charles tried the routine himself. Adam was more resistant to the process and it took nearly ten minutes of trying—until Charles feared there was more goat's milk on Willow's cloak than in Adam's mouth. Finally, as his cries grew weary, the baby seemed to realize that the liquid being forced at him might be worth a try. Within seconds, he was latching on to the corner of the cloth.

"It's working," Charles murmured.

Willow caught his gaze and he could see the unchecked delight in her expression. Then she laughed, and the sound seemed to shimmer over him like sunshine.

"We did it, Charles. We did it!"

The two of them continued their efforts. At one point, Willow taught Charles how to pause and lightly pat the babies' backs in case they had air trapped in their tummies. Eva managed to offer a tiny grunt, while Adam closed his eyes and let out a belch worthy of a miner drinking up his share of Mr. Grooper's home-brewed Fourth of July sarsaparilla.

They returned to the milk-soaked cloths, but it wasn't long before it became apparent that the children were sated. At least for the time being.

"Do you have any blankets we can use?"

Charles nodded, setting Adam back into the basket. "Give me a minute."

He hurried up to his bedroom—the only room above stairs that he'd bothered to furnish. Truth be told, there wasn't much to be found there. A trunk with his belongings, an upended crate with his shaving kit, a nightstand with a lantern, and a narrow bed.

He quickly stripped the mattress of its blankets, then dug into the trunk. Inside, he had a half-dozen precious lengths of Scottish tartan, which he'd brought with him from Aberdeen. Since Charles had no idea of his true parentage, he'd picked the plaids for their colors. He chose one that was a bright cobalt-blue with narrow strips of red and gold, and another that was red and black and green.

After setting the lantern on the floor, Charles piled

everything into the crate and then took the steps two at a time back to the main floor.

When he stepped into the great room, he stopped, then stared.

Willow had returned to sit by the fire, where he was sure she'd meant to watch over the children in the basket. In the flickering light, he could see that her head lay against the back of the chair. Her chest lifted and fell in sleep.

She was so beautiful.

Unconventional.

But beautiful.

The firelight limned her auburn hair with molten gold. With everything she'd been through, the plaits were coming unpinned. Her skin was as pale as fine marble, but the spattering of freckles across the bridge of her nose made her approachable. She still wore the yellow dress she'd donned for their wedding, not that awful black gown.

After holding her in his arms, Charles knew her figure was slim and lithe. And strong. He'd never met a woman who could suffer the gamut of emotions that she'd experienced in a single day and still manage to move forward.

Charles carefully approached, trying his best to remain quiet. He'd never been a graceful man. His upbringing hadn't included the niceties. Left as he'd been on the steps of the Grottlemeyer Foundling Home at about the same age as the twins, what education he'd received had been an exercise in survival.

Setting the crate down, he used one of the tartans to make a soft nest in the basket, then used the second one to cover the twins. Then, not sure what else he should do, he settled into one of the kitchen chairs.

To watch.

Dear Lord above, is this really how You answer a man's prayers? So suddenly? So overwhelmingly?

Since the women had come into the valley, Charles had begun spending a few nights a week at the Dovecote, attending to their spiritual needs. Each time he stepped inside the dormitory, he'd been immediately enveloped in their warmth and camaraderie. They plied him with baked goods and enveloped him in chatter and laughter. He'd found their strength and spirituality contagious, which had made him even more aware of the masculine, rough and gruff existence of the mining camp.

Anyone who applied to work at the Batchwell Bottoms Mine did so knowing that it was an all-male environment. Before being hired, a man had to promise to adhere to a strict set of rules. He promised to forgo drinking, gambling, cussing and the company of women.

Many of the men who worked at the mine had been here for years. They'd grown accustomed to hard work and spartan living conditions. But there was no denying that things were beginning to change. The men were congregating in the cook shack and lingering at the Devotionals. They soaked up the softer atmosphere the women inspired whenever they were present.

Then, when they returned to the Dovecote, the camp felt…empty again. The miners congregated in the Hall to play darts or checkers, but their efforts to enjoy themselves seemed forced. Even worse, because Charles had permission to spend time with the women, he'd grown aware of a certain…separation between him and the other men. As if they felt slightly resentful of the way he was able to enjoy something that they'd been forbidden.

They couldn't know that, to Charles, it was a double-edged sword. Yes, his time with the women was something special. But it seemed to only underscore his solitary lifestyle. Since he'd been serving as lay pastor to the men of the mining community, he'd been given a row house to himself. This allowed him the opportunity for counseling if someone came to him for advice or help. But the nights were long and quiet, his surroundings stark. More often than not, he spent the evening poring over the Scriptures or on his knees, praying that the Lord might illuminate a means for him to banish the source of his…discontent. He'd asked God to help him see what else he should be doing to feel needed. Alive.

In that instant, Charles realized that he'd never felt more alive than he did now.

Was this what he'd been missing? In insisting that he was better off alone, had he closed himself off to the possibilities of something wonderful? Could it be that the scrappy orphan from Aberdeen was discovering that the Lord might have grand plans for his future?

The thought was at once terrifying and liberating. It was as if he'd asked the Lord for a few drops of rain, then had been given a deluge. Even so, he couldn't completely reconcile the fact that he'd appealed to his Creator for relief from his loneliness, and the Lord had seen fit to give him a wife and two children.

But not really.

The arrangement was temporary.

As soon as the pass was cleared of snow, Willow would ask for an annulment, and then be on her way to another life. And he would be alone again.

His gaze skipped to the basket.

Or would he?

He'd known about the twins for only a short time, but he feared that he was growing as attached to them as any new father. He couldn't imagine letting them out of his sight, let alone handing them over to the care of someone else.

Nevertheless, it would be madness to consider raising them himself. He was a dyed-in-the-wool bachelor. Even worse, his upbringing hadn't given him any clues on how to raise a family.

But if not him...who?

He looked at Willow again, absorbing how the heat from the fire had pinkened her cheeks. She looked so young, so innocent. She had to be at least ten years his junior. Yet she was already betrothed to another man— one with a houseful of children. Charles doubted that she could take the babies with her.

Did that mean the twins were destined for a foundling home?

Charles had spent enough years in such a loveless existence that he couldn't bear the thought of Adam and Eva ending up with the same fate.

Willow shifted and a frown came over her brow. The chair couldn't be very comfortable. She needed to stretch out in a real bed.

He stood and carefully approached. When she didn't wake, he dared to slide one hand beneath her legs and the other around her shoulders. She made a soft groan, but didn't rouse when he lifted her against him.

She sighed, resting her head against his shoulder. She was such a delicate creature. And all Charles had been able to offer her for supper was oatmeal.

Tomorrow, he'd go to the company store first thing. He'd stock up on food, blankets and a few lengths of fabric—although his choices would be slim in that area. Then he'd chop more wood, repair a few broken boards on the lean-to walls, head to the Dovecote to collect

Willow's things, summon the doctor to check on the children...

Tomorrow.

Charles liked the sound of the word, the promise it held. In the morning, when the sun rose—if they weren't plagued by more snow—he would awaken to the presence of a wife and two babies. Granted, they were a borrowed family.

But he'd never had any *family before. Borrowed or otherwise.*

Unable to help himself, Charles touched his lips to Willow's hair.

"Until tomorrow," he whispered. Then he carried her upstairs, laid her down on his bed and covered her with another length of plaid from his trunk. Afterward, he returned to the sitting room, the full weight of his new responsibilities settling over his shoulders. He crossed to a free-standing hutch and grasped his rifle, his cleaning kit and a handful of bullets.

Then he settled into the chair by the fire and began his watch.

Willow woke with a start at a touch on her shoulder. As her eyes flew wide, she fought to focus. Immediately, she was inundated with the need to protect.

The events of the previous evening came rushing back and she found Charles standing above her.

So tall.

So strong.

So completely out of her realm.

"I'm going to the company store and the Dovecote, then I'll come back and milk the goat again. Is there anything else you need that isn't on our list?"

Her brain seemed packed with cotton wool. Finally,

she remembered that, during one of the many feedings they'd had with the children during the night, they'd discussed what the babies would need.

"I wrote it down…" She frowned, trying to remember where she'd left the envelope and pencil she'd used. "I'll come find it for you."

He opened his mouth, probably to stop her from getting up, but Willow jumped to her feet and hurried downstairs.

She still felt guilty for using his bed. Charles had insisted that he would sleep on the cot in the spare bedroom. But as she rushed past where she'd dressed for her wedding only the night before, she could see that the mattress was still tightly rolled against the footboard.

Maybe he didn't have linens enough for the bed *and* the cot. If that was the case, she felt even worse about sleeping in his room. She could have easily taken the chair.

However, there'd been no talking him out of it. And if she were honest with herself, a day spent helping in the cook shack, then the shock about Jenny, the confrontation with Batchwell, and the rushed wedding ceremony had left her exhausted, and she hadn't had the strength to put up much of a fight. Tonight would be different.

Her heart seemed to clatter in time to her footsteps as she realized that, in order to make their charade seem real, she would be spending another night in this house with Charles Wanlass.

Her husband.

Annulment or not, the vows they'd said had been real. The signed marriage documents stowed in the hutch attested to that fact.

Even so, she mustn't forget that one day those documents would be only a memory.

She stumbled slightly, and did her best to cover up her unsteadiness by crossing to the table. Hours ago, she'd gathered up the remains of the refreshments, and the bowls and dishcloths from their latest feeding. To her surprise, the scratched surface was covered with tins of oil, stained cloths, brass casings and a fine dusting of gunpowder. When she glanced over her shoulder in confusion, Charles appeared slightly embarrassed.

"I was checking on my supplies—since I'd be heading to the company store, and all. Then, since I had things out, I decided I might as well clean my weapons. It's been a while since they've been used."

Her sweeping gaze took in the revolver on the corner of the cupboard, a shotgun leaning up against the wall next to the fireplace and a rifle propped against the hutch near the door.

"Has something else happened?" she breathed, almost afraid to ask.

"No!"

He tucked his thumbs beneath his suspenders. "No I happened to run into Gideon Gault last night when I went for the goat. He seems to share my opinion that what happened to Jenny wasn't an accident."

Willow remained quiet.

Finally, Charles offered, "He's worried. There's never been any real violence in Batchwell Bottoms. Now and again, a miner has lost his temper and a few fisticuffs erupted. These petty skirmishes end quickly. But for a murder to occur…"

"Does he have any idea of who it could be?"

"Not that he shared with me. Nevertheless, he's doubled the guards for the women at the Dovecote, just in case."

Willow's eyes bounced back to the weapons. Charles

had been preparing for the worst. He'd been intent on protecting *her*. Her and the children.

"Do you think all this is necessary?"

"Until we know who hurt Jenny and why? I'm not willing to take any chances."

The statement created a soft warmth in her chest.

"Do you know how to use a weapon, Willow?"

She nodded. "Da and I used to hunt for rabbits in the woods outside of town sometimes."

"Then I'll leave the shotgun here with you."

She opened her mouth to object. But when she thought of Jenny, then Adam and Eva…

She nodded. "Fine."

"Will you be all right while I'm gone? I can probably drop by the store and the Dovecote in an hour. Two at the most. Then I'll see to the goat. I ended up leaving it in the main barn last night. I was afraid it would wriggle through a few holes in my lean-to. It shouldn't take too long to make the repairs. Will that work for you?"

She straightened her shoulders. "I'll be fine."

"You're sure? Because I could come back with supplies and wait a while before going to the dormitory."

"I'll be fine, Charles. We have enough milk left for a couple of feedings. While the children are still asleep, I'll get a pail heating on the stove so that I can wash the dishcloths and launder the babies' blankets and diapers. Is there somewhere that I can hang them?"

Charles grimaced. "I've always taken my own things to the company laundry. Where's that paper we made up last night? Add string and some pegs to it, and I'll fetch them from the store, as well."

Willow found the tattered envelope and stubby pencil on the cupboard next to the dry sink. But when she returned to the table and settled into one of the chairs, she hesitated.

Already, they'd made a lengthy list. As she reread the notations, Willow felt heat seep up her neck.

She'd been six when her mother and two older brothers had died of influenza. Since the loss of income from their jobs had been a blow to their family, Willow had joined her father in the woolen mills. At the time, her tiny fingers had proved a valuable commodity, since she could rethread the looms with ease. Nevertheless, it had meant she had little to no schooling until her father's death, when the vicar and his wife had taken pity on her and had arranged for her to go to the Good Shepherd Charity School for Young Girls. She hadn't learned to read and write until she was nearly twelve. Looking down at her careful printing, she prayed that Charles wouldn't know at a glance that her education was rudimentary.

Rereading the words she'd written the night before, Willow wilted beneath another wave of shame. She had only a few coins left from her nest egg. Even once she'd retrieved her belongings, she wouldn't be able to help Charles pay for much, and the fact merely added to her guilt. She hated to be beholden to anyone—and she was already indebted to Charles Wanlass in more ways than she could count. It galled her that she couldn't buy an equal share of the goods. The night before, she'd tried her best to cross out some of the items, but Charles had insisted he had credit at the store.

"If you could wait until we gathered my things…" she said softly. She had five dollars at the most. She'd done her best to save every penny, but since she'd anticipated ending her journey in California, where Mr. Ferron would have met her at the station, she hadn't been too worried.

Until now.

Charles shook his head. "No, Willow. I told you last night that I'd take care of everything."

"But you quit your job," she whispered.

He snorted. "So what? I've lived simply for years, put plenty aside. There's more than enough to tide us through the winter. Besides, I have a healthy credit at the company store—and I can't take it with me once I go. So I've got to spend it now, while it can do us both some good."

"But you shouldn't have to shoulder all of the responsibilities for the children's welfare on your own."

She scrambled to think of a way she could offer more help. But she had nothing to sell. Nothing but her mother's china. Maybe one of the women at the Dovecote would be willing to buy it.

Before she could even suggest such a thing, Charles sank into the chair opposite her and then reached across the table to enclose her hand in his own sure grip.

"I'm not doing anything on my own. Don't you see? We're partners, you and I. We each have our own strengths and specialties. I have the ability to get the supplies we need. But, let's face it, you have all the skills to put them to work. You'll be stitching clothes for the children, making more diapers, cleaning, cooking and setting things to rights. I'll help in whatever way I can, but beyond setting my sights on washing a few dishes, milking a goat or burning a steak, I feel like a fish out of water in all this. If anyone's beholden in this arrangement, it's me."

Unaccountably, Willow's thoughts slipped back to the conversation that she'd had with Lydia the night before, to the way the woman had insisted that the best marriages were a partnership. Maybe Charles was right. Maybe it wasn't charity to accept the temporal goods that he was willing to purchase, if she would be offering her own time and talents, as well.

Finally, she gave a short nod. "Thank you, Charles."

He squeezed her hand. "No. Thank you. I don't know why Jenny left the twins with me. But if I'd been forced to take care of them by myself..." He offered Willow a crooked grin—one that lightened his usually sober features in a way she never would have imagined during her earlier encounters with Bachelor Bottoms's lay pastor.

As if he'd suddenly become aware of the way their hands were still linked, Charles let her go and sprang to his feet, so quickly that the chair skidded noisily across the floor.

"Don't forget the cord and pegs," he said gruffly, pointing to the list.

She obediently added the items.

"Check through things again, just to make sure. Once I get back, I'll stick close to home." He opened his mouth, shut it and then offered, "To help."

She pretended to read over the list again, even though she found it impossible to concentrate on the words.

"It's fine."

"And you've got another note for Sumner or one of the other women at the Dovecote? Telling them what you need?"

"Yes. I put that letter inside the envelope."

"Good." He shifted uneasily before saying, "You don't have to worry about the laundry just yet, you know. You could get some more sleep..."

This time, it was her turn to jump to her feet. In a rush, she became aware of her rumpled yellow gown—and her hair! The plaits had come loose and were beginning to unravel. Since she'd slept completely clothed, she probably looked like a cat dragged through a knot-hole backward.

But Charles hadn't seen fit to comment. Instead, he continued to watch her, his eyes quiet and curiously intent.

"No, I… I'd like to get a few things done." When he remained quiet, she quickly added, "And it would probably be best if I remain alert."

At that, the fierce protectiveness returned to his gaze, startling her with its intensity. She'd seen that look before, when he'd held the children or rocked them back to sleep. But she couldn't account for the way he directed it toward her.

Charles was still watching her intently. Then he murmured, "Even so, try to get a little more rest. The babes are sleeping soundly, but they won't stay that way for much longer. I'll be back as soon as I can gather your things."

Willow nodded, knowing that there weren't many things to gather. Her clothing and personal belongings could fit into a single carpetbag. Her only trunk held her precious Blue Willow dishes.

He lifted his hand, and her breath caught when it hovered in the air, as if he meant to stroke her cheek. After a moment, he reached for the revolver instead, shoved it into the back of his trousers, then shrugged into his coat and settled his hat over his hair. She saw the way he glanced toward the basket near the fireplace.

"Throw the latch in place behind me, then you can see to the bairns."

Chapter Six

Charles took the steps outside two at a time, then grasped the shovel propped against the lean-to. In a matter of minutes, he managed to clear the stoop, the boardwalk in front of the house and a path to the lean-to. After a soft word to the goat inside, a scoop of feed, and breaking the ice on the animal's water, he left the shovel inside the shelter and secured the door. Once he returned, he would repair a few broken boards so that the enclosure would retain as much heat as possible.

As soon as he turned, he hesitated. His gaze scoured the snow drifted up against the house.

When he'd milked the goat the night before, the wind-driven piles had been untouched and sculpted by the storm. This morning, however, he could see that something had disturbed the freshly fallen snow.

He moved closer, crouching to look at the impressions more closely, then used his glove-covered hand to push the fresher powder aside. There, the lower layers of sleet and slush had frozen, revealing the impression of a boot print.

Charles frowned. The mark wasn't entirely clear. The heel was distinct, but the rest was incomplete. Unfortunately, it was impossible to tell much in the way of size or detail, but Charles couldn't push his uneasiness aside.

Granted, there could be plenty of reasons for a boot print to be found in the snow next to his house, close to the window of the main keeping room. There were hundreds of miners at Bachelor Bottoms, and with a storm blowing, it wasn't uncommon for a man to walk between the row houses to avoid as much of the wind as possible. Judging by the amount of snow deposited on top, the print had probably been made late at night. It could have been someone walking home from the Hall. Or a miner leaving his shift early to retrieve something from his home.

Or...there could have been someone watching them last night.

His gaze flew to the window a few feet away. From here, he had a clear shot of the kitchen table and chairs. It wouldn't have been at all difficult for someone to stand here in the darkness, watching them as they fed the twins.

Charles circled the house, looking for other telltale marks. If a miner had been on his way home—and had paused for a moment to catch a peek of the twins—there would be more prints heading on to the other houses. However, he could find no evidence of anything else being disturbed.

He backed away, hurrying in the direction of the store. He needed to gather supplies as soon as possible—chief among them, some fabric that could be used to cover the windows. And more ammunition for his revolver.

As soon as she'd flung the bolt in place, Willow shot a quick glance toward the children who slept in their basket near the fireplace. Then, she ran upstairs, knowing that she wouldn't have much time to tend to her ablutions. She poured icy water from the pitcher into the bowl in

Charles's room. Meeting her reflection in the mirror, she squeaked in horror when she realized the extent of repair needed to her hair. She looked like Medusa come to life.

She quickly washed her face, hands and neck, ruing the fact that she had no soap and cloth of her own—and somehow, using Charles's seemed far too…intimate. Seeing no other alternative, she unwound the plaits from her wedding coiffure and used his comb to get rid of the worst of the snarls. Then she wound her hair into two braids, which she crisscrossed over the top of her head, fastened in place with hairpins, then folded into a knot at the back of her head.

She was just finishing when she heard one of the babies beginning to snuffle. It would be time to feed them again.

She charged downstairs again, stoked the range and placed the last of the goat's milk in a pan on one of the burners.

She was just collecting a set of dishcloths when she heard a soft rap on the door.

Willow whirled, peering that way as if she could see through the boards. It was far too soon for Charles to have returned with everything they needed.

"Willow, it's Lydia!"

She rushed to let the woman in—only to discover at least a dozen more women waiting outside in the cold.

"I hope you don't mind," Lydia said, as she hurried in. "We brought you some breakfast from the cook shack. We figured you wouldn't want to be taking the babies outside in this weather."

"And we knew you'd be needing some meals on hand, so we brought you provisions," Iona offered, setting a large covered basket on the table.

Behind them, Myra and Miriam struggled to carry in a trunk.

"Here's your dishes."

"And we found a satchel to carry your clothing and personal things."

Behind the Claussen twins were other inhabitants of the Dovecote, each carrying something else to contribute.

Emmarissa Elliot and Marie Rousseau placed packages wrapped in brown paper on a nearby chair.

"We raided the laundry for extra toweling and face flannels."

"And here are a few larger pots and pans for melting snow, or washing and bathing."

Greta entered, giggling. "Cookies!" she exclaimed, brandishing a large tin. "More cookies."

Behind her, Stefania Nicos gave an answering chortle. "Because a man can always be influenced with sweets."

The last two women struggled to bring in a hip bath. "Where do you want this?" Millie Kauffman asked, panting.

When all eyes turned in her direction, Willow finally suggested, "Upstairs in the spare room?"

As the girls carried the tub upstairs, Lydia and Iona scooped the twins from their basket. Other women were already gathering pails of snow from the drifts outside. By the time they had placed them on the range and poked the coals into a raging inferno, the door opened to admit their Pinkerton guards, who carried a trunk larger than any Willow had ever seen.

"Where do you want the dresses, Willow?" Lydia asked.

Willow hesitated. She hadn't explored the house enough to know if there was a wardrobe or dresser large enough to store that many items of clothing. However, before she could speak, Lydia waved the question aside. "Put the trunk in the spare room, as well. She can sort through everything later, after she's had time to take a nice, long soak."

Before Willow quite knew what had occurred, the female army was already hard at work. Although Charles's home was fairly neat and tidy, they attacked it with the brooms and mops they'd brought with them. Soon the floors gleamed and the counters shone. Then the women eliminated the smallest speck of dust and polished the wooden surfaces with enough beeswax to make the place smell like a hive.

At long last, when they'd cleaned the house to their satisfaction, Myra and Miriam used scissors to apply a decorative edging to lengths of brown butcher paper. Then they lined Charles's open shelves and began unpacking Willow's china, arranging the pieces in a way that was both decorative and functional.

"You've done enough to help us," Iona said, shooing Willow toward the staircase. "We can manage the little niceties on our own and take care of the children. You go upstairs and have a hot bath. Everything's been laid out for you."

Since it became apparent that it would be impossible to refuse, Willow reluctantly complied. When the door to the spare room closed behind her, she discovered that the cot had been made with fresh linens and a quilt that smelled faintly of lavender. A carpetbag lay on the floor by the bed. On the dresser there were towels and flannels, a new bar of soap, and Willow's own brush, comb and hair box. A few feet away, Lydia's trunk had been propped open, revealing garments that hung suspended from an iron bar and metal hangers, like a portable wardrobe.

Willow's eyes prickled with unshed tears at the kindnesses that had been shown to her by the other women. She had made more new friends after being stranded here than she'd ever had in school—perhaps because the charity school had not encouraged relationships. Instead, the girls had been given fundamental instruction in reading and writing, then were trained for service, and sent out into the work force as soon as possible. The more incorrigible cases—those who learned too slowly or were considered to have "improper temperaments" for service—would be employed by the school. Willow had fallen in that category due to her "incorrigible shyness."

The thought made her sigh. But since the children were downstairs, and Charles would be returning soon, she didn't dawdle. Instead, she took advantage of the hip bath, donned clean undergarments, her corset and a petticoat. Then she stood in front of Lydia's trunk in indecision.

When she'd agreed to accept the gift of a few dresses, she hadn't realized that Lydia would send her so many. She'd assumed her friend had been exaggerating about the excesses of her wardrobe. There had to be at least a dozen gowns inside, if not more—and except for one set of drawers, there was no place to keep them.

Until now, Willow would have supposed that no one other than royalty would have so many pieces of clothing to wear. She couldn't possibly accept them all.

But she didn't want to offend Lydia by giving them back, either.

In the end, Willow decided that she would explain to Lydia at some later date that she had been far too generous. Until then…

She closed her eyes and reached out. Her hand fell on an ivory cotton day gown printed with brown fern fronds.

She quickly dressed, using the same pink ribbon as the day before to secure the waist, then smoothed a hand over her hair and stepped into the hall.

The house seemed strangely quiet. Willow frowned, wondering if the women had all left.

The babies.

She rushed down the staircase. But when she reached the bottom, her breath left in a rush. The women were there—seated at the table or by the fireplace. Someone must have gone to the cook shack to retrieve more chairs, because everyone had managed to find a seat. Drinking fragrant cups of tea, they spoke in low murmurs, probably in deference to the sleeping babes held by Myra and Miriam.

"We found the milk, the bowls and the dishcloths, and cobbled together how you've been feeding them," Myra whispered.

Emmarissa reached to squeeze her hand. "Don't worry that you don't have milk enough. Not all women are able to nurse. My own mama had sixteen children, and she had some she could feed herself, and some she couldn't."

The whisper could have been heard halfway across the camp, but the children remained oblivious.

"Sit right here," Lydia murmured, patting a spot at the table. "Oh, and this came for you."

She gestured to a package wrapped in brown paper and tied with a ribbon.

"What is it?"

Lydia shrugged. "We heard a knock at the door, but when we answered, there wasn't anything but that package sitting on the stoop. We assumed that it was a wedding gift from one of the miners."

Willow felt her heart bump against her ribs. Could a person ever get used to receiving so much attention?

She carefully removed the silk ribbon. A green one, much like the one Jenny had often worn. When she removed the paper, an ornate silver baby rattle fell into her hands.

"How precious!" Lydia exclaimed.

The other women clamored for a closer look. Only Willow seemed to feel unsettled.

She'd seen this rattle before. With Jenny's things.

The women's chatter washed over her like a wave, seeming to become muffled and indistinct, and Willow warred with her thoughts.

Had the rattle been found at the Dovecote and brought here by one of the brides? If so, why hadn't the person come in to visit?

But if it hadn't been left on the doorstep by someone Willow knew...

Who had been going through Jenny's things?

And why had the rattle been brought here?

As a gift?

Or a warning?

"Too bad the twins are asleep. We could have seen how they liked their new toy."

Realizing that the other women were looking to her for an answer, Willow quickly pinned a smile on her face. "Yes. You're right. But they're probably too small to play with it yet, anyway. I—I'll just put it over here for safekeeping."

She crossed to the shelves and hid the rattle inside a covered vegetable dish. Then, even though her hands trembled, she returned to the table.

The other women seemed bemused by her behavior, but they quickly resumed their chatter.

"Come along," Lydia said. "We've warmed up your breakfast, so eat." She shot a disapproving glance at the two dark shapes outside the window. "We've already been warned that we're getting close to overstaying our welcome, at least by Mr. Batchwell's standards." She sniffed in open disapproval. "But I suppose we can give you and the children a little bit of *quiet* time." She grinned. "At least until the supper shift at the cook shack. Then who could fault us for taking a little detour to come see the twins again?"

The hush in the room dissolved beneath a wave of laughter and chatter, and Willow sank into her chair, feeling unsettled. But as the familiar camaraderie surrounded her, she drew strength from the companionship, knowing that, in the group of women around her, she had a wealth of knowledge and experience that could come to her aid should she need it. More important, with so many women and so many eyes, someone, somehow, must have clues to Jenny's disappearance and murder. If Willow were subtle, she could ply them all for information, one by one.

But for now...

She would forget about the rattle, forget about the gooseflesh that still peppered her arms, and enjoy her meal and the company.

Charles waited impatiently as Marty Grooper, the head clerk at the company store, gathered the requested supplies and began packing them into an empty dynamite crate.

"I hear tell you an' the little redhead got married last night," the man said, peering at Charles over his spectacles.

Charles wasn't sure how to answer. According to the story he'd told the bosses, he and Willow had married months ago in England. He didn't know how the other miners in the camp were going to take the news. He supposed that to some, it was neither here nor there. But others might resent the fact that Charles was currently living with his bride, while they had been forced to live apart from their own loved ones.

"We, uh, restated our vows. Yes."

"Lucky man. She's a pretty little thing. A bit on the quiet side, but judging by what I've tasted at the cook shack, she can sure make her some hot cocoa." He cackled in delight, then leaned forward to whisper conspiratorially, "I put some o' the cocoa I order special for Creakle an' a few o' the men in a bag, and tucked it in a corner of the box. I'm sure yer missus will be wantin' somethin' sweet one o' these nights. It's a little gift from me an' the boys who stock my shelves."

"Thank you, Mr. Grooper."

"Don't you be getting formal on me. It's Marty. You know that. Just cuz Batchwell forced you t' resign ain't no reflection on all the good you've done fer us, so don't think you need to treat none of us no different than you did before."

"Thank you, Marty."

The wizened man winked and moved to one of the rear bins to begin ladling flour into the center of a large square of brown paper that he'd set on the scales. As soon as he reached the proper amount, he folded the paper into a neat package and secured it with twine. Then he reached for a wheel of cheese and began the process all over again.

"You don't need to be buying your own supplies, Charles."

Charles glanced behind him to find Jonah Ramsey at his shoulder.

"I'd be more than happy to send someone over from

the cook shack with a meal for you and Willow both. Or you could stop by and get it yourself. We've used the same arrangement for the other marooned families."

Charles stiffened slightly. He'd always been a man who worked for his living, and he wasn't about to take anything for free now.

"I'd rather take care of myself and my own."

Ramsey eyed him carefully. "I can't find fault with that. But keep in mind, you've only been out of work, so to speak, for a few hours. I'm doing my best to find a way to get you reinstated. I can't afford to have my blasting foreman off the job—and I'm sure Smalls will need your help shoeing the mules. It might take a little time…" Jonah's eyes crinkled ever so slightly in the corners. "But I hope to have something worked out by the time your…honeymoon is over."

Before Charles could speak, Ramsey held up a hand. "In the meantime, if you insist on accounting for everything, feel free to use the cook shack anytime you want. You can give Marty a tally of the meals you use, and I'll have him deduct them from your credit. The arrangement might come in handy, with a couple of babes rearranging your schedule."

Jonah placed a penny near Marty's receipt book and reached over the counter to take a half-dozen horehound drops from a glass jar. "Marty, I've left you some change for the sweets," he called out.

"Thank you kindly, boss man. You be sure t' give the doc my regards."

"I'll do that, Marty. And pass on my fond regards to your family in your next letter."

The bell over the door jingled as Ramsey stepped outside, but just as quickly, Gideon Gault came in. Since he was without his Pinkerton blues, Charles surmised that he was off duty.

"Hello, Charles."

"Gideon."

"I thought I'd let you know that there's no need to rush through your errands."

Charles grimaced, wondering when his every move had become the main entertainment of Bachelor Bottoms. "Why's that?"

"Well, the girls brought an extra large contingent to the cook shack this morning. But rather than all of them working on the food, half of them peeled off to your place. Near as I can tell, they enlisted the help of my men to help bring Willow's belongings to your house. Right now, it looks like they're giving your place a thorough cleaning, so you might want to avoid all the ruckus for a while."

Gideon gestured toward the door. "How about you join me at the cook shack? I haven't eaten yet. If you have a minute, I've got a thing or two that I need to discuss with you."

Charles was ready to insist—again—that he didn't need to be eating anything provided by the company. But Marty waved him away. "This is going to take me a bit of time, Charles. You go on ahead and I'll start a tally for your meals, just like Mr. Ramsey said."

One last time, Charles opened his mouth to object, but a glance in Gideon's direction made him realize that the other man's features were carefully schooled. Clearly, the invitation hadn't been completely social.

"Thanks, Marty. I'll be back in a few minutes."

"Take your time. I'm going to have to go to the storehouse to collect the flannel you need. I'm plumb out here at the store. Give me at least a half hour or more."

The bell jingled hollowly as Charles and Gideon headed into the cold. Thankfully, it looked like last night's storm had blown itself out, at least for the time being. With the shifts at the mine well underway, the offices, barbershop, laundry, cook shack and company store were open for business, and the foot traffic had picked up. A crew of men were clearing the boardwalks of snow, while a miner pushed the drifts from the main road with a metal grader hitched to the back of a converted wagon frame drawn by a pair of mules.

The two friends walked the few yards to the cook shack. Inside, the air was moist from the warmth pouring from the box heaters and the cooking area at the far end of the building. Joining the line, Charles and Gideon filled their plates with fried venison, grits, biscuits and gravy, then used a finger to "hook" a mug of hot coffee from those waiting at the end of the counter.

Charles fielded greetings and congratulations from some of the miners, then from the women who circulated the room with pots of hot coffee. For a month now, many of the brides had volunteered their services at the cook shack as a means to thank the miners for rescuing them from the avalanche and sharing their supply of foodstuffs with their unwitting guests. In Charles's opinion, it was the miners who needed to be offering their thanks. Before the women had taken over, their meals had been prepared by a bunch of cantankerous men, and the food had been all but inedible. Now, the employees of Bachelor Bottoms couldn't wait to see what delicious items would appear on their plate—and which pretty, smiling females would be there to serve them.

"Let's go into the private room."

Charles's brows rose slightly at the suggestion. The private dining area was reserved for Ezra Batchwell,

Phineas Bottoms and occasionally Jonah Ramsey, as a means to combine eating with company business. Charles could count on one hand the number of times he'd been asked to join such events.

He entered the room, expecting to see the table covered in mining documents and littered with the remains of the bosses' breakfasts, but the women had apparently adopted this domain, as well. The area was neat as a pin. A striped cloth had been laid over the scarred table and places were set with real silver, rather than the cheap tin utensils used in the main dining hall.

"Have a seat."

Charles took a chair on the far side, then realized that the place setting included a napkin. When was the last time he'd eaten with a napkin?

"Will you say grace?" Gideon asked.

Charles bowed his head, offering thanks to God and asking that the miners and the food be blessed. Then, when Gideon murmured his own "Amen" and settled his napkin on his lap, Charles asked, "So what's on your mind?"

"Pass the salt, would you?"

Charles handed it over, a part of him noticing that it wasn't a simple saltcellar, but a bona fide cut-glass-and-silver piece. Then, realizing that Gideon wasn't about to talk until he'd at least tasted his food, Charles split open his biscuit and slathered it with butter, then passed the crock on to him.

"I spent a few hours last night and this morning retracing that woman's footsteps."

"Jenny's?" Charles's food was instantly forgotten.

Gideon nodded. "It took me a while, especially with the storm. But I was able to find her path." Although they were alone, he leaned forward and said quietly, "She came from the direction of the last block of row houses to the north."

"The ones being used by the other avalanche survivors?"

"Yeah. Actually, there are six houses on the block, three on each side. In that section, four aren't being used by miners. One of them quarters the crew from the train, another the salesmen and farmers who got stuck here, and the other two are being used by the Wilmott family and the Hepplewhites."

"Mrs. Hepplewhite is pregnant, as well. Not as far along as Jenny, but there's no hiding it. Maybe Jenny went to her for help?"

"I thought of that and had a word with both the Hepplewhites and the Wilmotts, but none of them saw or talked to Jenny—and both families have been sticking close to home on account of the weather and the fact that they have young children. Their meals are being brought to them by miners who live on the same block. They're on shift right now, so I'll have a word with them later tonight."

"You think one of our own men could be involved?"

Gideon's eyes became a dark, impenetrable blue. "I don't want to think anyone was involved. I'd love to find out the whole thing was an accident. But I can't rule anything out."

The Pinkerton grew silent as he ate a slice of venison, then a mouthful of grits. He offered thoughtfully, "The thing is, that woman had no business being near any of those houses. But she was gone from the Dovecote…how long? Two days? Three?"

"I'll ask Willow for sure."

"In that time, she had to have shelter. It's been below zero since Christmas. Which means…"

"She's been living in one of those houses."

"Or she's been staying somewhere we haven't figured out yet."

Charles sat back. "I can't wrap my head around why anyone would want to hurt that girl. Especially in her condition."

Gideon stabbed another piece of venison with more force than was necessary. "I learned during the war that we humans can do some horrible things. But those injuries… I'd bet my money on the fact that she knew her attacker. I can't see her turning her back to a stranger—and I'd bet the one to the rear of her head was the first blow."

Charles poked at his food with the tines of his fork. "So, it has to be someone she knew well…"

"Or someone she recognized enough to trust. And that could have been any number of men who've been in and out of the Dovecote." Gideon took a bite of his biscuit, then shook the remaining half in Charles's direction. "See what Willow can remember. I think she'd be the best person to recall who interacted with Jenny."

"I already spoke to her about it. She said she'd sit down and make a list sometime today."

"Good. In the meantime, keep your ear to the ground. I have no doubt that the women will be traipsing in and out of your house on a regular basis. I'm not asking you to break a confessional session or anything—"

"I never took confessions. I've only served as a lay pastor."

"Well, whatever you do, you don't need to break any confidences. But if you hear even a peep of something that might point us in the right direction, let me know."

Chapter Seven

It was nearly two in the afternoon before Charles returned home. His tardiness wasn't due to his errands; he'd finished them hours before. No, what delayed his arrival was the fact that, since there were Pinkertons posted at his door, that meant the women hadn't left yet. Therefore, he'd decided to wait until the visiting females departed before going inside.

With nothing else to do, Charles had spent the afternoon at the company store, sitting by the stove and playing checkers with the off-duty miners. He'd positioned himself facing the window so that he had a clear view of the front stoop, and he'd kept an ear trained for any stray bits of gossip circulating about Jenny. Finally, he'd seen the Pinkertons snap their rifles into position and the door open. Within seconds, the women emerged in a whirl of bright colors, flounced skirts and pretty bonnets.

As they hurried through the snow, laughing and giggling among themselves, Charles realized yet again how much the women had managed to change the mining community's atmosphere in the few weeks since they'd been here. His memories of winter in Bachelor Bottoms always seemed to be colored in shades of gray—the overcast skies, the icy river, the blackness of the mines. But somehow, the women had brought watercolors to the area. The sky between storms was a crisp, cool blue, some of the windows were hung with brightly painted feed sacks, and the cook shack was adorned with deep green bunches of holly and pine.

Juggling the box of supplies, Charles hurried home. But when he pushed inside, he discovered that two of the women still remained. The older widow, Iona Skye, and Lydia Tomlinson, the self-proclaimed suffragist who had organized the cook shack crews into a formidable team.

"Mr. Wanlass, how nice to see you," Iona murmured, as she wrapped a scarf around her neck. She bent to press a kiss against Willow's cheek. "We'll see you tomorrow, dear. I'll do my best to keep the thundering hordes from the Dovecote away. I know they're all anxious to see the twins, but I'll convince them to wait a little while." She seemed to rethink her statement and added, "If that's at all possible."

Lydia was the next to hug Willow. For a moment, she gazed down at the baby Willow held—little Adam—and smiled. Then she looked up at Charles.

"Will you be speaking at the Devotional tonight, Mr. Wanlass?"

Charles opened his mouth, closed it, then chose his words carefully. "I've resigned from the mine, Miss Tomlinson."

She blinked at him for a moment, then said, "Perhaps. But I don't remember your resigning from God. I've enjoyed your words, Mr. Wanlass, and I think that most of the camp would agree with me."

Charles couldn't be sure, but he thought she winked at him.

"Still, I suppose that, as a new father, we can't expect you to be back quite so soon. Nevertheless, we'll be looking forward to the moment you resume your duties."

After a few more waves and goodbyes, the women hurried out the door and shut it firmly behind them.

This time, when quiet settled over the house, there was no awkwardness, no need to fill the silence. As he set the crate on the table, Charles's eyes slipped to Willow.

Her head was bent toward the baby she held, and the light from the nearby window gilded the braids she'd wound into a knot at her nape. For a moment, Charles was struck by the sweet, rapt expression on her face, the cornflower-blue of her eyes, her pale skin and those beautiful freckles. In the foundling home where he'd been raised, one of the matrons had a painting over her desk of a sleeping child being protected by a ghostly woman who hung in the air above him. When Charles had asked about it, Matron Bedelmeyer had launched into a long explanation about Realism and art and the familiar motifs of death and the afterlife. She'd expounded on the use of color and shadow and perspective, but Charles hadn't listened much. He'd been too entranced by the specter hovering over the child with her arms outstretched. In the end, he'd decided that ghost was the child's mother, protecting him from beyond the grave.

Since Charles had believed that his own mother must have died—else why would he be left at the foundling home?—he'd felt a special connection to the picture.

Gazing at Willow, he was struck by how much she looked like the woman in that painting. The light shining from her eyes made Charles realize how important it was that he save the twins from a fate like his own. No child should ever have to grow up without seeing their worth shining from their mother's eyes.

"The women took me by storm soon after you left,"

Willow murmured. Her voice adopted a slightly singsong quality, as if she intended to woo the heavy-lidded baby into succumbing to sleep.

"I gathered as much," Charles said. Then, unable to help himself, he shrugged out of his hat and coat and crossed to sit in the chair nearest Willow and the basket at her feet. "How are they?"

"Their tummies are full—" again, she seemed to sing the words "—and they've been bathed, changed and wrapped in fresh blankets."

When she looked up, her eyes were sparkling with something akin to joy.

"The women brought all sorts of things for us to use—fabric and toweling and flannel for more nappies. They've set a hip bath upstairs in the spare room, brought me my trunk and my belongings. So you can have your own bed tonight, and I'll take the cot."

"No, I'll take the cot."

She made a soft *tut* with her tongue. "Nonsense. All my things are already in that room and yours are in the main bedroom. The cot will be just fine." Her voice dropped. "Won't it, Adam?"

The baby was fighting so hard to stay awake. Willow reached out a finger and stroked his forehead—and just like that, his eyes shut.

"They also brought my dishes." She tipped her head toward the open cupboards in the kitchen and Charles noted that the shelves had been filled with plates, bowls, cups and platters. "And my pots and pans."

She bent, placing the baby in the basket by his sister. Then, after stroking each baby's cheek, she straightened, grinning. "Louise Wilkes stopped by a few minutes ago and brought her tabletop sewing machine." She pointed to a wooden case on the far end of the table. "So I'll be able to make the layette pieces in a fraction of the time."

And curtains. She needed to make curtains.

Charles opened his mouth to tell her about the footprint under the window, but stopped himself. Not just yet. He couldn't bring himself to shatter the mood so quickly.

"I guess I'd better head outside and milk the goat. She's probably bleating something fierce."

When he would have stood, Willow quickly said, "No need. Greta took care of that hours ago. The women saw the milk and dishcloths from yesterday and assumed that I wasn't able to feed the twins."

He watched her cheeks flood with pink, and the sight delighted him no end.

"Anyhow, they've set everything to rights in a single morning." Her face suddenly fell and she said, "Oh, my. You probably need something to eat!"

Charles reached out, catching her hand and pulling her down again.

"I ate in the cook shack with Gideon Gault. Jonah arranged for us to use my credit should we decide to take advantage of the women's cooking."

"Oh. I don't mind cooking."

"I know. But there might be a day when the children have kept you busy or you want to join the women for a meal. Either way, we won't have to worry."

She beamed. "That's wonderful. Thank you, Charles."

Despite the fact that he'd hoped she would linger in her chair, she jumped to her feet and moved to the shelves. She fiddled with the dishes for a moment before returning with something in her hand.

"This was left on our doorstep today."

He looked at the rattle lying in her outstretched palm

and whistled softly under his breath. He picked it up, examining the intricate silverwork.

"Who would leave such a thing? This is worth more than a month's wages."

He looked up to find Willow's eyes clouded with worry. "I've seen that toy before. It was in a bag that Jenny used to hold her stockings."

"Maybe one of the other girls brought it."

Willow shook her head. "I don't think so. If any of them had brought it, they would have done so openly. This was done...on the sneak."

Charles's fingers tightened around the rattle.

"That means someone has either been going through her things..." Willow paused. "Or they knew one of Jenny's hiding places. She had some jewelry, a few pairs of gold bob earrings and a garnet ring that she kept in the same bag, rolled up in one of her stockings."

Willow returned to the counter and snatched up an envelope covered in her neat printing. "While the women were here, I had them make a list of anyone they remembered having any contact with Jenny." Her brow furrowed. "I didn't give them any details of her death, I just told them we were trying to piece together where she'd been for the last few days."

She handed Charles the list and he fought the urge to groan when he saw that there were at least two dozen names.

"So many."

Willow grimaced, scooting her chair close so that she could see the list, as well. Not for the first time, Charles became aware of the sweet scent of violets that lingered in her hair.

"I tried to make a notation next to each name if the women could remember why they were at the Dovecote," Willow said. "Mind you, these names are only from a week or so before Christmas, when we moved into the dormitory. When we were at the hall… I know we all had contact with the Pinkertons, Mr. Creakle from the office and Mr. Smalls from the livery. But I'll have to see if anyone remembers seeing someone else."

Charles nodded. "This is a good start, Willow. We'll go through these together and see if we can come up with any theories." He hesitated, then said, "In the meantime, I'll put all the supplies from the store away. I, uh… I brought you everything we thought we'd need, as well as some muslin. Maybe, before you start on clothes for the bairns, you could…make some curtains for the windows."

When she eyed him with blatant puzzlement, he said slowly, "When I shoveled the walks this morning, I found a set of boot prints near that window there." He pointed to the panes opposite the kitchen table. "I think someone might have been trying to watch us last night."

Since the incident with the rattle had unsettled her, Charles had been expecting Willow's cheeks to pale. What he hadn't imagined was the way she jumped to her feet, her hands balling into fists. In an instant, her expression changed from sweet protector to angry mother bear as she stalked to the window in question. Her eyes narrowed, and studied the alleyway to the left, to the right, then right below to the spot where the faint outline of a heel impression could still be seen.

"Oh, no," she murmured, her tone laced with anger. "No, that will not happen tonight." Then she whirled, her hands on her hips. "Show me where you put the muslin, Charles. I've got some window coverings to make before dark."

Willow blinked against the light pressing in upon her eyelids. Stretching, she focused on the far wall and the window—one completely covered by a set of muslin curtains.

There were eight windows at the Wanlass house.

And she had made eight sets of curtains.

It had taken most of the night, but...

Dimly, she became aware of pounding coming from below and she frowned. What on earth?

But when her eyes fell on the small clock she'd set on her nightstand, she immediately bolted upright. It was nearly ten thirty!

Too late, she realized that daylight had broken some time ago and the twins had decided to sleep more than three hours at a time. But now, afternoon was swift approaching, and Willow was still abed.

Reaching for her wrapper, she bounded for the door to the spare room. Where had Charles gone that he hadn't bothered to wake her first?

She dodged into the hall, then backed into the spare room again when Charles appeared from the main bedroom. A giggle burst from her lips when she noted that he'd pulled on a pair of trousers and looped his suspenders over the top of his union suit. For the first time she could remember, the man wasn't completely neat and groomed. His hair was mussed and a shadow of stubble glinted from his jaw. Even his feet were adorably bare.

"Back!" she whispered. "I'll answer the door. You get dressed, make up the beds and bring the children down." Charles had kept the children near him at night, since his room had a small fireplace.

He nodded, retreating into his room.

Willow quickly dragged her arms into the sleeves of her wrapper, hurrying barefoot down the stairs.

"Who is it?"

"Willow, it's me. Sumner."

Willow nearly stumbled on the last step. She'd been hoping the unknown visitor would be someone she could instruct to come back at a later time. But if she didn't open the door for Dr. Ramsey, Sumner would think that something was horribly wrong.

"Just a minute!"

As she raced past the mantel, Willow glanced at her reflection in the peering glass and groaned. Her hair had come loose from her braid and curled riotously around her head like a lion's mane.

She'd always hated her hair. It was too bright, too thick, too curly. And this morning, it made her look like a child.

Smoothing the waves as best she could, she tightened the tie to her wrapper and took a deep, calming breath. Then she cracked the door open a few inches.

Immediately, she noted that Sumner carried her bag and had donned her physician regalia—somber skirt, high-necked blouse and dark woolen coat. If it weren't for the jauntiness of the fur on her collar and hat, she would have appeared quite staid. But Sumner somehow managed to wear the severely tailored garments with flair.

"Hello, Doctor. Are you making your rounds?"

"I came to see you." When Willow didn't move, she added, "And your babies."

Knowing that any more attempts to stall would fail, Willow opened the door and waved her friend in.

Thankfully, Sumner didn't comment on the fact that Willow had clearly just roused—at a shockingly late hour, no less. Instead, she flashed a bright smile.

"You could have knocked me over with a feather when Jonah came home to tell me that you were married to Charles Wanlass." Sumner laughed. "You are a dark horse."

Not knowing how she should respond to that comment, Willow helped Sumner remove her coat, hat and scarf, then impulsively pulled her close for a quick hug.

From the moment their train had been hit by an avalanche, Dr. Sumner Havisham—now Ramsey—had helped Willow to make a place for herself in Bachelor Bottoms. After so many years in a strict charity school, Willow had found it difficult to adjust to the open camaraderie of the other mail-order brides. And since modesty had been demanded at the Good Shepherd Charity School for Young Girls, Willow had been taken aback when it had become clear that communal living would involve a lack of privacy for washing and changing.

Sumner had found a way to make a secluded changing area for all the women who felt uncomfortable. Then she'd included Willow in many of the daily tasks, allowing her to grow more confident as she made friends.

But there was a risk to their close relationship now. As Sumner drew back, she studied Willow with those keen brown eyes.

"So, what's this I hear about you marrying Charles months ago?" she asked, her gaze dragging over Willow from tip to toe. "And you've given birth to a pair of twins, as well?"

Willow cringed, knowing she'd never be able to lie outright to her friend. So she took Sumner's hand and drew her near the fireplace.

"Sit down for a minute while I poke up the coals. I spent the whole night making curtains, so… I'm afraid I overslept."

Sumner didn't seem inclined to follow her, so Willow hurried to lay kindling on the grate, then blew softly on the glowing embers until she could add twigs, then sticks, then finally a log. Through it all, she couldn't seem to stop herself from chattering.

"Louise loaned me her tabletop sewing machine, which made all the difference. I finished in no time. I think if I had a machine of my own, I could take in orders for sewing myself. The headmistress at my school, Mrs. Owl—that was her real name—always said I was a tolerable seamstress. I used to make and repair the uniforms for the new girls and—"

She broke off when Sumner's brow knitted in concern.

"Would you like some tea? Or cocoa?"

Sumner looked as if she would refuse, but she finally relented. Tugging the kid gloves from her fingers, she said, "I'd love some tea. Do you need help?"

"No! No." Willow gestured to the chair. "Just…sit. I want to welcome you to my home properly. Even if…" Her hands smoothed the folds of her wrapper—a beautiful calico one that Lydia had included with the dresses she'd given her. Willow had dithered for hours about sending it back, knowing that the garment was finer than anything she had ever hoped to own—and completely feminine and frivolous. But then she'd realized that, if she meant to live in a house with Charles, she would need something to cover her nightclothes.

"I'll just…tea…"

She headed to the kitchen, quickly stoking the range in much the same fashion as she'd done with the fireplace. In no time at all, she had the teakettle simmering, cups and saucers laid out on a tray, as well as some leftover scones from the batch the women had brought the previous day.

"How is Jonah?" Willow asked innocently enough as she carried the tray into the other room. Setting the tea things on the overturned crate that she and Charles had been using for such a purpose, she settled into the straight-back chair.

"He's fine. Willow, what is going on here?"

Before she could say anything, a clatter of boots came from upstairs. Both she and Sumner watched as Charles hurried down the staircase. Just before reaching the last step, he seemed to become aware of Sumner and his gait slowed.

"Dr. Ramsey."

"Mr. Wanlass."

Willow was relieved to see that Charles was completely dressed—worn boots, wool trousers, suspenders, dark maroon linen shirt. His jaw was freshly shaved and his hair had been so recently combed that she could still see the tine marks like furrows branching out from a severe side part.

His pale eyes skipped from Sumner to Willow, then back to the doctor. "Have you come to see the babies?" he asked.

If anything would keep Sumner from asking too many questions, it would be the twins. Willow had noted that when the other mail-order brides had visited, one glance at the wee little things had reduced the grown women to mush. Even Iona, practical, matter-of-fact Iona, had begun to coo and prattle.

"Of course I want to see the babies."

Sumner's features instantly softened as Charles approached and set the basket he carried at her feet.

"This is Adam," Willow murmured, pointing to the larger twin with the waves of dark hair.

In the scant time he'd been with them, Adam was making his personality known. He wanted to eat when he wanted to eat, and there was no putting him off. He preferred to be held face out, so that he could survey the room, and he would perk up at the sound of conversation. But he wouldn't sleep unless his little sister was near.

"And this is Eva."

Eva was daintier, with only a wisp of hair. Unlike her brother, she was patient, slow to fill her stomach, and preferred to snuggle beneath Willow's chin. She liked to be wrapped tightly in her blanket. She despised being left bare to the cold, even to change her diaper. Once she began to cry, she found it difficult to stop unless Willow or Charles rocked her. And if her brother was near, she tended to fling out a hand to touch him, as if reassuring herself that he was there.

"Oh, my," Sumner breathed, her expression softening. "It doesn't matter how many infants I've taken care of in my short career, I'm always so surprised at how small they are." She reached for the blankets. "May I?"

"Of course. I was hoping you'd check them over. Make sure they're healthy."

Sumner took Eva first, laying the baby in her lap. As if sensing she was the center of attention, the little girl stretched, arching her back. Her eyes opened, then she yawned and closed them again.

"Sweet thing." Then, just like every other adult who'd come into contact with the children, her voice became melodious. "And aren't you the little princess, hmm, poppet?" Sumner chanced a quick glance at Charles. "I bet you have your papa wrapped around your little finger, don't you?"

Charles shifted uncomfortably, and Willow thought she saw a hint of red touch his ears.

"But I do believe Miss Madams has a wet nappy, don't you, love?"

"Oh!" Willow jumped to her feet. "I'm so sorry! I should have known, since they slept so late—"

But Sumner waved aside her frantic apology.

"Sit, sit. I'll want to undress them anyway to give them a proper examination." She adopted a wide smile—one that was completely guileless, but which Willow recognized as her "do what I say" expression. "Charles, why don't you go get some fresh water for the twins? Since we'll have them undressed, we may as well give them their morning baths, don't you think?"

He sighed softly. "Yes, ma'am."

"What have you been feeding them?" Sumner asked, turning to Willow.

"Goat's milk?" she offered hesitantly, worried that the doctor would chide her for doing the wrong thing.

Instead, Sumner nodded. "Nothing wrong with that." Again, she speared Charles with a look that brooked no argument. "While you're out getting water, you could tend to the goat, as well."

It was clear that Charles didn't want to go, but he didn't really have an option if he wanted to avoid creating a scene.

"Fine. Anything else you need me to do?"

"I left a crate at the Dovecote. I managed to gather up some of the leftover bottles and baby things that I brought with me from my last posting. I left them on the table in my examination area, if you'd be so kind as to retrieve them."

Willow watched Charles walk to the door. He slowly donned his hat and coat, then looked over his shoulder as if he hoped Sumner had changed her mind. But she was busy putting the baby back into the basket.

"Is there anything you need, Willow?" Charles asked softly.

She shook her head, wishing that she could think of a logical reason for him to stay. But she also knew that if Sumner was determined to have a private word with her, she'd have it. One way or another.

"I'll be back then. Soon as I can."

He closed the door quietly behind him. The latch had barely clicked into place before Sumner stood and walked calmly across the room to throw the bolt. Then she turned, folded her arms and asked sternly, "Now then...what on earth is going on?"

Charles was still standing bemusedly on the stoop when he realized that he'd forgotten the pails. It wouldn't do him much good to go for water—or milk—if he didn't have a container to put them in.

Low laughter sifted through the air and he glanced up to find Jonah regarding him with amusement from where he slouched against the lean-to. The man removed a pocket watch from his vest and checked the dial.

"Six minutes. I'm amazed that she got you out of the house that quickly. It has to be a record."

Charles scowled. "I have no idea what you're talking about."

"Sure, you do. She's had a bee in her bonnet since she heard that you and Willow married on the sly over a year ago. I've been trying to keep her at our place as long as I could, but today she threatened to snowshoe into Bachelor Bottoms if I didn't bring her here myself." He straightened, then sauntered toward Charles. "It seems she's in mother hen mode. She's been worried that, since you and Willow kept so quiet about your courtship and all, you might have forced Willow into marrying you."

"What?" Charles turned toward the door.

"It won't do you any good," Jonah warned.

Too late, Charles realized that he'd been locked out of his own house.

Jonah grinned. "What did she say to get you to leave?"

Charles hesitated, wondering if he should pound his fist against the rough wood or make a tactical retreat.

"She asked me to get some water and to milk the goat."

Again, Jonah chuckled. "And what are you going to carry it all in? Your pockets?"

Charles glared at the man, but Jonah merely tipped his head toward the center of town.

"Come on. We'll go to the cook shack and get you some breakfast—or maybe lunch. Then, we'll borrow some pails from the back room where they prepare the food. Maybe, if the brides are baking today, we can even snag some cookies to take back to our wives. I know I've grown quite fond of the gingerbread men."

Feeling a little numb—and a wee bit cowed—Charles reluctantly fell into step.

"Do you like gingerbread?" Jonah asked companionably.

"Aye. But I'm fonder of the oatmeal cookies. The ones with the raisins."

"I can understand that, you being a Scot and all."

"How long do you suppose this is going to take?"

"It could be all day, knowing Sumner."

Chapter Eight

The indistinct male voices had barely faded into the distance when Sumner asked again, "Willow? The truth, now. What on earth is going on with you and Charles Wanlass?"

Willow couldn't meet Sumner's eyes. Instead, she bent to fuss with the twins' blankets.

"I don't know what you mean," she offered blithely. The words sounded hollow, even to her own ears.

"Willow Granger, those children are no more yours than they are mine. And if you think I believe that you married Charles Wanlass last spring when he was collecting mine equipment in Newcastle, you may as well claim I can sprout wings and fly!"

Willow's eyes immediately filled with tears and her body was inundated with a flood of panic unlike anything she'd ever known before.

"You mustn't tell!" she whispered. "Please!"

The sternness dissolved from Sumner's features and she rushed to Willow, sitting on the chair again. She reached out, taking her hands, then began chaffing them as if Willow had a chill.

"Willow, honey, I'm not mad. I'm concerned. You do

realize that the exchange of vows Batchwell insisted on was legally binding, don't you?"

Willow nodded, sniffing. "I don't care. I—*we*—had to do something." She broke free, scrubbing at the tears that continued to fall. Although she'd known that her actions might one day incur the disapproval of the rest of the inhabitants of Bachelor Bottoms, she couldn't bear it if Sumner thought less of her. "Don't you see? These are Jenny's babies!"

Sumner exhaled. "I figured as much."

"She left them in that basket, here in the keeping room of his house. There was a note pinned to the blankets that said 'Please, please protect my little ones and keep them as your own. They are in more danger than I can express.'"

Willow had thought about that note so many times that the words seemed to have been carved into her heart.

"When Batchwell stormed in, Charles and I...we reacted instinctively. We couldn't let them be taken away or given to...*strangers*!" She sobbed. "Don't you see? When we realized that Jenny had been murdered..."

"I told them not to say that."

"You mean she wasn't killed?"

Sumner's eyes gave her thoughts away.

"You suspect it, too, don't you?" Willow pressed.

"Yes, but I didn't want the gossip to get out any sooner than necessary." She looked down into the basket. Her lips thinned for a moment, then she met Willow's gaze head-on. "But *marriage*, Willow?"

"It was the only way. Charles has told me that, when this is all over and we've found Jenny's killer, we can get things annulled if we want."

Sumner still didn't look convinced.

"Please tell me you'll help us. It was Jenny who chose

Charles to be the protector of her children. But he can't do this alone." She could see that Sumner was weakening. "Please. Jenny was my friend."

"Very well. But only until we can determine who did this to poor Jenny."

Willow felt a puff of relief burst from her throat. "Thank you!" She hesitated before asking, "And you won't tell Jonah, will you?"

Sumner shook her head. "Something tells me that ship sailed long ago—probably about the same time you and Charles exchanged vows."

Charles's stomach was growling by the time he and Jonah collected their meals—bacon, pancakes, eggs and fried potatoes. As the rich scents twined up from his plate, he knew that he wasn't the only miner in Bachelor Bottoms who would rue the day when the mail-order brides were banished from the valley and Stumpy resumed his job as master chef.

Except now, Charles had more to mourn than the loss of the home cooking they'd been enjoying for a month now. All too soon, his bride would be forced to leave, as well.

Either that, or Charles would have to find a new place of employment.

Jonah led him into the private dining area, shutting the door with his shoulder. "We miss you down in the mine," he stated, as they settled into their places and draped the cloth napkins over their laps.

Cloth napkins.

Charles had seen the use of more napkins in the last few days than he had in his entire life. The Grottlemeyer Foundling Home had struggled to put enough food on the table. There'd been no extra coin for such niceties as china teacups, cut-glass saltshakers or finely hemmed linens.

"We've been trying to make some headway on that new tunnel, number nine. But the announcement of your marriage has left me without an experienced blast foreman."

Under normal circumstances, Charles was sure that he would have felt a pang of guilt. But when he thought of what might have happened if he and Willow hadn't agreed to Batchwell's marriage ceremony...

No. He'd done the right thing.

They both had.

"What in the world were you thinking, Charles?"

Charles had been about to take a mouthful of egg, but when he looked up, his eyes met Jonah's.

He knows about the lies.

For long moments, his fork hung suspended in the air, the yolk dripping, before he set the utensil down with great care.

As he held Jonah's stern gaze, he knew there was no sense trying to lie any further.

"How long have you suspected the truth?"

Jonah's lips twitched at the corners. "Let's see...from the moment you opened your mouth and insisted those babies were yours."

"What gave me away?"

Jonah half laughed, half sighed. "The fact that you insisted those babies were yours."

Jonah uttered the words in a way that made it clear the answer was obvious.

"Let's face it, man, I've known you a long time. If you'd married Willow while you were on a business trip—or you'd received word that you were going to have a child—I would have known about it from day one." He leaned forward, tapping the table with his index finger. "You never would have kept anything like that a secret. Ever. You would have been owning up to your responsibilities and hotfooting it back to England."

Too late, Charles realized that his friend knew him much better than Charles knew himself.

"Who else knows?"

"Sumner, I'd wager."

"You haven't said anything to her?"

"I was pretty sure I didn't have to. Willow? Pregnant? With twins? Come on. The girl might have been wearing those horrible tent-like dresses of hers, but she was never pregnant." Jonah leaned back again, spearing a potato with his fork.

"Do you think anyone else noticed?"

Jonah shrugged. "You might get away with it. Willow has always done her best to stay in the background. She's always happiest when she isn't being noticed." He took a bite of food, chewing thoughtfully. "So, what are you planning?"

"What do you mean?"

"About Willow? You, uh, intend to stay married?"

Even a day before, Charles was sure that he would have offered an immediate "No!" But right now…he couldn't bring himself to utter the word aloud, so he said instead, "I don't know."

For some reason, that made Jonah smile. "You like her?"

"Of course I like her. I wouldn't have let things get this far if I didn't think she was a fine woman. An… honorable woman."

Jonah's eyes narrowed and he shook his fork in Charles's direction. "I don't have to tell you that what you've done can have lasting consequences."

"We are both well aware of that. I've told Willow that, in the future, if she wants an annulment, I'll see to the matter myself."

"And in the meantime…how do you plan to protect that girl's reputation? You know how this community talks."

Charles could feel his ears begin to heat. "We have separate bedrooms and a pair of babes to take up all our time."

Jonah didn't seem convinced.

"When the time comes, I'll make a full confession, tell everyone how we came to be in this predicament and why. Considering the fact that Jenny was killed and her babes were threatened…that should lend some weight to our explanations. If Willow wants to end things between us, I'll do whatever it takes."

Again, Jonah seemed to regard him like an insect pinned to a board. "What about you? Do you want an annulment?"

"I don't know," Charles finally admitted.

"And those twins. Are they Jenny's?"

"We think so, yes. Someone left them in a basket in my home with a brief note. Jenny was afraid the children were in danger."

Jonah seemed to mull over those words. "Judging by what happened, I'd say her fears were well-grounded."

"Willow and I have decided—by mutual agreement—that the children will remain with us until we're sure they're safe. One way or another, we intend to find out who killed Jenny Reichmann."

Thankfully, Jonah didn't argue the point. Instead, he set his fork down and reached into his pocket. "Then you'll be needing this."

He held out a ring, dropping it into Charles's outstretched hand. As he studied it, Charles could tell by the size that it was most likely a man's. It was well-worn, the gold filigree worn away in spots. The stone—an acidy yellow-green peridot—was scratched. Inside an inscription read: *Love Always, D.*

"What is this?"

"Isaac Zimmerman, the undertaker, took on the job of laying Jenny out this afternoon. He found that clutched in Jenny's hand, along with a few strands of dark brown hair."

Charles returned to find the door unlocked. Carrying the pails of water and milk inside, he set them on the floor and called out, "Willow!"

From above, he heard the sound of quick footfalls. Then Willow rushed down the steps.

She'd changed from the frilly wrapper she'd worn this morning to a pale green gown—one that made her skin seem porcelain fine and her eyes even more blue. Her hair had been combed into a thick braid that hung down her back. Charles wished that she'd left it loose. He loved the way it had tumbled around her face and shoulders this morning.

She came to a skidding halt in front of him.

"Sumner knows."

"Ramsey knows."

They'd blurted their confessions at the same time.

Charles laughed, shaking his head. "You first."

"Sumner's pieced it together since the beginning."

"Jonah did the same." Charles dug into the pocket of his coat and removed the ring Jonah had given him. "Have you seen this before?"

Willow took the ring, regarding it from every angle. "No. Sorry. Whose is it?"

"That's what we have to find out. Ramsey said it was found clutched in Jenny's hand."

"So maybe it belongs to the killer."

There was a snuffling noise from the basket by the fireplace and Willow handed the ring back to Charles, then rushed to scoop Eva from the basket. As she tucked the infant beneath her chin, the baby blinked at Charles with wide, blue eyes. Then she rooted around for a more comfortable spot and yawned, content to be held.

"Sumner brought us a few types of baby bottles to try. She says the twins look healthy, but that our dish towel method probably won't last for much longer."

"I think she's right. Adam is already demanding his food faster than we can give it to him."

Charles set the ring on the table, then shrugged out of his hat and coat. "When did you feed them last?"

"Only an hour or so ago. Sumner was still here, so we made short work of what milk was left."

Charles moved the buckets closer to the range. "I'll leave the milk alone for now and just heat the water, then."

He placed the pail on the stove, then grabbed the buckets he'd forgotten to take with him. He dodged outside for a few minutes, packing them tight with snow and hurried back inside, setting them on the stove next to their mate.

"There. That should be enough for washing and cooking. As soon as that snow is melted, I'll get some more."

"Thank you, Charles."

He sniffed appreciatively. "Something smells good."

"With all the supplies the brides brought me, we have enough food for an army. I made a stew for our supper and baked some bread. I told the girls that I'd be happy to do some of the baking for the cook shack, but they wouldn't hear of it."

Hearing Adam beginning to stir, Charles paused to squeeze Willow's shoulder before moving to the basket.

"I don't think it's a reflection on your abilities, Willow. They know you're busy with the twins."

That seemed to mollify her somewhat.

"It won't be long before they're sleeping a little less every day," he added. "Soon, we'll have our hands full."

"I suppose so."

The baby at his feet offered a snuffling cry, and Charles saw that Adam had inadvertently pulled the blanket over his face.

"Hey, little man," Charles murmured. "Can't see what your mama is up to?"

He scooped the baby up, marveling at the way the child nearly fit in one of his broad palms. He was still so tiny, even though Charles was sure that he was growing a little heavier each day.

As soon as Adam was out of the basket he stretched— arms flung high, legs pushing against the blanket that still bound him. Then he settled into the crook of Charles's arm, his forehead growing wrinkled and serious as he seemed to fix his gaze on Charles's face.

"There's a fine fellow," Charles murmured, stroking the boy's cheek. The baby's skin was so soft and velvety, Charles worried that the calluses on his finger might scratch him, but Adam leaned into the caress.

"Come look what we did."

Willow motioned him back to the table. There, she unfolded a large piece of brown paper covered in penciled notations.

"This is the list of men you and I were gathering," she said.

To Charles, the tally seemed even longer now that it had been written down.

"We're assuming that Jenny was killed by a man," he offered.

"I thought of that. But when I asked Sumner that same question, she said that the wounds would have required a lot of strength, so she figured it was unlikely a woman was responsible."

"Which means we've narrowed our suspect list by fifty some females. That leaves only two hundred males to go."

To his utter delight, Willow pulled a face. "Don't be a doubting Thomas. We've only just begun." She pointed to another list of names. "These are the men Sumner remembers being injured in the avalanche and staying in the Miner's Hall those first few days."

Charles scanned the looping script. "So, we've got most of the crew from the train."

"Yes. Sumner and I crossed out Mr. Creakle and Mr. Smalls, who spent a few afternoons in the hall with us the first week. Their contact with Jenny was minimal, and frankly, we couldn't see either one of them being our culprit."

Charles had to agree. Creakle was getting on in years and was plagued with rheumatism. As Ramsey's right-hand man, he had a logical reason for having contact with the brides when they'd arrived. But he was so tongue-tied around them that Charles doubted he'd ever harm them. Willoughby Smalls was a gentle giant. An injury in the mine had crushed his throat, leaving him mute. Charles knew for a fact that the man doted on the women, even though he tended to blush beet red any time they were near.

"This is the interesting bit that Sumner was able to give me." Willow pointed to a line she'd drawn across the bottom of the paper. Above the line were times and dates.

"We came up with a timeline of Jenny's movements from our point of view. Sumner is joining the brides in the Dovecote for dinner tonight, so she's going to subtly get more information. But this is what we've pieced together so far."

Eva began to make soft grunting noises of distress, but somehow, Willow managed to rock back and forth and point at the chart at the same time.

"We both remember seeing Jenny on New Year's Eve and New Year's Day. Neither of us recall her seeming particularly upset or ill." She slid her finger to the next notation. "But Sumner remembers examining Jenny on January 3. She said Jenny wasn't feeling well and seemed listless and weepy, so she told her to remain in bed for the next few days. But when she went to check on her later in the day, she couldn't find her in the Dovecote."

"Was that unusual?"

"For Jenny, yes. She usually stayed in her room or walked near the tree line, where everyone could see her." Willow shrugged. "Let's face it, even with the move to the Dovecote, the constant presence of the Pinkertons has caused some of the brides to get a little...creative."

Charles allowed Adam to grasp his finger. "Meaning?"

"Let's just say that a few of the women are able to slip past their guards to do a little exploring."

Charles opened his mouth, then closed it again. Granted, Gideon Gault had stated that he was aware of Lydia Tomlinson sneaking away from time to time, but Charles wondered if he knew about the others.

"But Jenny hadn't done that before?"

"Not that I know of. Like I said, she tended to stay in our room in the Dovecote."

Since Willow had shared a room with the girl in the

dormitory, then Charles supposed she would have the best insight.

"Although..." Willow's brow furrowed.

"Yes?"

"Since the brides started working in the cook shack, and there were men injured in the second avalanche *and* when the tunnel collapsed in the mine just before Christmas..." She shrugged. "We were all pretty busy in other areas of the camp. Who's to say what she was doing when most of us were gone?"

A shiver ran down Charles's spine. He looked at the chart again. "So, what's this?"

There was a star next to "January 5, 9:00 a.m."

"That's the last time either of us could remember seeing Jenny."

"But that's over a week ago! You didn't notice that she was gone that long?"

Willow sadly shook her head. "Don't you remember? We had three men injured when there was a fire in the machine shop. During that time, Iona, Lydia and I volunteered to help with the nursing duties at the infirmary every night so that Sumner could go home. When I came back to the Dovecote in the morning to sleep, and Jenny wasn't there, I assumed she was spending her time elsewhere in the building so that I could get some rest." Guilt tinged her gaze, making her eyes a cloudy blue. "I should have asked. I should have sought her out. But I didn't."

It pained Charles to see Willow so upset over something that was not her fault, so he wrapped his free arm around her shoulder and drew her close.

"You couldn't have known, Willow."

"But I could have tried to find her to ask how she was feeling or...or something..."

Unable to resist, Charles bent to place a kiss against

her hair. "You can't blame yourself. There were nearly fifty other women in the Dovecote, and none of them realized anything was wrong, either. It seems to me that Jenny *wanted* to slip away—and maybe she'd done it countless times before. If she was that determined, you couldn't have stopped her."

Willow drew back slowly. "But where did she go?"

"That's what we have to find out."

Chapter Nine

Charles checked the door to the lean-to to ensure that the latch had snapped in place. Peering up at the moonless sky, he could see that the clouds had dropped low and snow was already beginning to fall. Thankfully, there didn't seem to be much wind with it, which would allow the temperatures to remain a little warmer than the night before.

Grasping the pails he'd packed with snow, Charles headed toward the house, whistling softly under his breath.

He couldn't account for the sense of contentment that settled in his chest. Nothing had changed. He still had no job, no clear idea of his future, no comprehension of who could have harmed Jenny or threatened the children. But there was a sense of "rightness" to his present situation that he found inexplicable, yet reassuring. In the past, when he'd encountered such sensations, he'd felt as if the Lord had stepped in and taken the helm of his life in order to make a slight adjustment. After some time in the lean-to on his knees, Charles had decided that he would trust in his Creator and have faith. Perhaps one day he would know why God had offered him this challenge. Until then, he would do his best to protect those in his charge.

Sniffing against the cold, he smiled to himself when he caught the delicious scents of dinner in the air—the savory tang of cooking meat, the comforting aroma of beans and an earthy warmth. Cornbread, perhaps? The girls in the cook shack couldn't hold a candle to Willow, in his opinion. She'd shown Charles well enough that she could make a banquet out of only a few ingredients.

His steps quickened as he rounded the corner of the house. But when he saw several dark shapes near the stoop, he came up short. Too late, he realized that he'd come outside without his rifle.

How could he have been so careless? After everything Willow had told him in the last hour, he should be on his guard more than ever. But he'd been so sure he could feed the goat in just a few minutes, and gather the pails of snow for washing, he hadn't thought much further than to grasp the buckets.

One of the men rapped on the door.

Quickly, Charles counted the figures, which were barely visible in the dark and the veil of snow.

One on the stoop.

One on the steps.

Three near the road.

"Is there something I can help you with?" Charles's voice emerged too forceful, but he didn't bother to school it. For all that the camp knew, Charles and Willow were newly reunited and living together under the same roof. That should denote a honeymoon, of sorts. Any miner worth his salt would have known not to come calling unless it was an emergency.

"Charles?"

Willow's voice came from the opposite side of the door.

Good girl. She'd kept it closed.

"I'll be inside in a minute, dearling!" Charles called out. "No need to fret."

He closed the distance to the house and set the buckets in the snow. Then he stood with his feet slightly braced, his arms at his sides.

Luckily, the door remained shut. Even so, it didn't completely dispel the tension that seeped into his body. Charles could feel his heartbeat quicken and the muscles of his spine and legs tighten. Old emotions—emotions that he hadn't felt since he was a boy—quickened his breathing.

Fight or flight.

A part of him acknowledged that he was probably overreacting. But that fact didn't seem to calm him. Embers of distrust and suspicion from his days at the foundling home flared in his gut. For a moment, he was that scrawny kid trying to survive on the streets of Aberdeen, enduring the taunts and epithets being thrown his way, sensing a possible threat from a mile away. He'd been wily enough to protect himself then, and he was more than able to protect his family now.

The man on the stoop must have noted Charles's stance, because he quickly held up his hands. "Whoa, there! We didn't mean to startle you!"

From inside the house, Willow stepped to the window. The curtains parted and a beam of lamplight slid onto the snow.

The man on the stoop quickly stepped into the light, dragging his hat from his head so that his features were clearly visible.

Not a miner.

But Charles recognized his face.

"I'm Rosco Beamon. I was first porter on the train."
He gestured to the gangly fellow on the step below him.
"This is Clancy Midgely, our stoker."

Midgely couldn't have been much more than nineteen.

"And this is Bobby Callahan, second porter, Noah
Offenbach, our conductor, and Ed Niederhauser, our engineer."

The men touched their hands to their hats. Since the
contingent seemed alarmed by Charles's challenging posture, he forced himself to relax.

"Gentlemen. What brings you here?"

Beamon still held his hands up in a calming gesture.

"We were on our way back from evening Devotional,
and we just wanted to pay our respects." He slowly descended the steps, Clancy behind him. "See, we feel
kinda responsible for the women being stranded here. If
we'd come through that pass a little slower…not blown
our whistle…checked the slopes a little better…maybe
that avalanche wouldn't have happened."

Charles willed his fists to unclench and his posture
to ease. He wasn't sure if it was the timeline that Willow
had shown him or the appearance of the rattle, but he'd
obviously overreacted.

"Anyhow," Beamon continued, "we heard about the
babies and how you and the missus renewed your vows
and…we just wanted to give y'all a gift."

Maybe the rattle hadn't been the ominous gesture that
Willow and Charles had supposed.

*Even though it had been obtained by rifling through
Jenny's belongings?*

Beamon eased toward Charles as if he were a bear
about to charge. Then he held out a drawstring bag.

"It's not much. The company store didn't have much
in the way of baby items." He laughed nervously. "Heck,

it didn't have anything at all along those lines, this bein' Bachelor Bottoms an' all." He stopped, cleared his throat uncomfortably, then added, "Anyhow, we took up a collection among us instead. We thought you could tuck it away in case the kiddies need somethin' when they started school…or somethin'…"

What muscles had remained on alert in Charles's frame finally relaxed. "That's very kind of you, gentlemen. I don't know if I should accept, seeing as how—"

"Don't say no," Callahan—the second porter?—interjected hurriedly. "We're all fathers. Well, all of us but Clancy. So's we know how expensive the little tykes can be."

The other railway employees gave a round of weak laughter.

"Like I said," Beamon offered. "We feel awful that it was our train that put these women in the fix they're in. We're just glad that at least one family has had a happy ending."

In Charles's mind, he and Willow were still at the beginnings of their relationship. Nevertheless, that wasn't something he intended to admit to anyone, so he thanked the railway crew again, shaking each man's hand in turn. Then he watched them disappear down the road in the direction of the row houses to the north.

The drawstring bag felt heavy in his palm, even though he could distinguish only a few coins inside. As the men disappeared into the gloom and the falling snow, shame tugged at his shoulders. With everything that had happened, he'd been so quick to think ill of them. He'd allowed the old anger and distrust—emotions that he thought he'd abandoned years ago—to surface long before common sense.

He couldn't go back to being that person again.

He had to be careful.

Deliberate.

Controlled.

He couldn't allow his worries over Willow and the children to cause his character to regress to what it had once been. He had to guard against solving his problems with harsh words and his fists, or lashing out at people for the slightest provocation.

Please, Lord, help me.

Help me to be the man I need to be.

"Charles?"

He turned to find Willow peeking at him through a barely opened door.

"What was all that about?"

His breath emerged in a swift gust. "A group of railway employees stopped by for a visit. They brought a gift for the babies."

She bit her lip, and he hurried to reassure her. "They took up a collection among themselves. I...didn't know how to refuse."

She opened the door wide. "Come in out of the cold, Charles."

Willow couldn't have known how, in that moment, Charles felt an alternate meaning to the words. In that instant, with the lamplight behind her, the aromas of a meal spilling into the darkness, and that shy smile flitting about her lips...

He felt her warmth like a palpable thing.

Until now, his life had been ever so cold. He'd been living alone—*existing* alone. But he hadn't been happy. He hadn't even been content. Instead, he'd stumbled hollowly through his usual routines, drawing upon his faith and his work to see him through each day. Then the next. And the next.

But until now, he hadn't really known how much he'd been missing. He honestly couldn't remember the last time that anyone had cared about his well-being. Oh, sure, he had friends who wouldn't want anything to happen to him.

But he'd never had anyone who seemed so determined to envelope him in true caring and affection. And he'd certainly never felt this way before—like a parched man being led to a spring to quench his thirst. Every moment in Willow's presence seemed to make him feel more alive.

"Come on, Charles. We'll tuck the money away for now, start a little nest egg for the children. But we can talk about that later. You'll catch your death out there."

The last of his unsettling thoughts skittered away and he grasped the pails and called out, "You will, too, lassie. Look at you, standing in the doorway waiting for your fool husband to come in."

In the next few days, Willow noticed a change in Charles. He seemed quieter than usual, more apt to linger around the house. She oftentimes found him reading his Scriptures, or holding one of the children and studying the chart that they'd tacked to the wall. More than anything, he appeared…careful. His words were measured, his actions deliberate—as if he feared that a hasty reaction could cause the world to crash down around him.

At first, Willow thought she was the one to blame. She knew it couldn't be easy for him. He'd been a confirmed bachelor before she'd stumbled into his home and claimed to be the twins' mother. He must have been used to a particular schedule, certain foods, an abundance of quiet time. Now, his life had been turned topsy-turvy by

crying babies, a wife who was a stranger, a cantankerous goat, and an endless number of chores. And yet…

He didn't seem unhappy.

Merely…cautious.

She supposed that she should comfort herself with the
fact that Charles seemed as intent as she was on solving the mystery of who had killed Jenny. But even that
thought brought its own host of fears.

Was he so eager to get rid of her?

But, no. She wouldn't think that way. She *couldn't*.

"Willow, come look at this."

He stood in front of the chart again, frowning, Adam
cradled in the crook of his arm. He'd tucked the stubby
pencil behind his ear so that Adam could grasp his forefinger. Charles looked so deep in thought that she doubted
he realized the way his body swayed from side to side in
deference to the child.

"What is it?"

She'd been sewing tiny layette gowns and flannel undervests on Louise's sewing machine. If she finished the
batch, she'd have nearly a dozen on hand—about half of
what she figured she would need to keep the children
clothed between changes and allow enough time for laun-
dering and drying. For the most part, the clothing was
basic and serviceable—hardly anything to crow about.
But the women of the Dovecote had promised to help her
embroider some of the garments for those times when
the children might be seen in town.

Would that day ever come? Would they ever catch
Jenny's killer so that the children could go with her to
the Dovecote or evening Devotional? Or perhaps to the
cook shack, so that she could lend her hand with the
baking again?

Willow arched her back, then rubbed the back of her

neck. How long had she been hunched over the sewing machine? Three hours? Four?

Charles frowned. "You're working too hard. Do the twins really need so many clothes?"

She grimaced. "They wet through their gowns at least once or twice a day—and then there's the mess from the goat's milk if they spit up. With the weather the way it is, I sometimes need a day to soak them, and another day to wash and dry them."

He grimaced in turn. "I could help with wash duty."

She grinned. "I've seen the way you wash—by carrying your laundry into town to have it done there. Somehow, I don't think Mr. Grimaldi would know what to do with a basketful of diapers and undervests."

Charles laughed, and oh, how she loved that sound. A low, deep rumble that lightened his features and chased the shadows from his eyes.

"You are correct once again, Mrs. Wanlass."

She stopped beside him, peering at the chart. "What am I supposed to be looking at?"

He gently pulled free from Adam's grip and pointed to the timeline.

"I've been able to add a few more details here. We thought that Jenny was last seen on the fifth of January, at nine in the morning. But one of Gideon's men saw her walking along the tree line around the Dovecote a little after ten. According to Gideon, the man's sure about the time because he'd been on duty all night and most of the morning, and he was hurrying to the cook shack before the girls stopped serving hot breakfast and put out the cold meats for lunch."

He paused, pointing to yet another comment he'd written in his looping cursive.

Willow bit her lip, wondering if she should confess

to him that she had no way of fathoming what the words said. In her years at Good Shepherd, she'd never learned to write in script, let alone read it.

But that wasn't something she wanted to admit. Not yet. At the Good Shepherd, they'd made it quite clear to her that her inability to learn to read and write at the speed of the other children revealed a flaw in her moral character.

"Around one, Stumpy was sure that he saw Jenny in the woods."

"The woods!"

He nodded. "Ever since the women took over the meals at the cook shack, Stumpy and his men have been using their time to hunt."

Willow was well aware of the fact. That's why the women had volunteered to help in the first place. The brides had feared, with so many new mouths to feed after the train had become stranded, that the company's food supplies wouldn't last the winter and the men would resent their presence all the more. But with a hunting party able to work full-time, the concerns had been eased.

"Is he sure?"

Charles nodded. "He said she was circling through the trees to the riverbank. But when she saw Stumpy and his men, she dodged back into the pines again."

"Where was this?"

He pointed to a rough map of the area that he'd drawn on the upper right-hand portion of the chart. "She must have come from the Dovecote…" His finger touched a large square. "But rather than following the track west to the main road, then north into town, she went east through the pines and aspens here near the river, then headed north."

"But why? There's no shelter nearby, is there?"

Charles shook his head. "Nothing but trees and scrub and the river—which is pretty much frozen this time of year."

"What's on the other side of the river?"

"She'd have to scramble up some steep bluffs, but even then, there's nothing but snow and open fields until she'd hit the opposite side of the valley. During the summer, that area is used to grow feed for the mules and livestock."

Jenny, what were you doing?

Charles pointed to the long column of suspects they'd made only the day before. Already, the list had been substantially cut down.

"Gideon was able to clear a few more men, and Jonah another three. That brings our suspects down to eighteen."

Charles seemed to sense her disappointment, because his hand wound around her waist to pull her close.

"Don't be discouraged. We've crossed off a lot of suspects since we started."

She nodded. Charles was right. They'd been living together as man and wife for little more than a week, and the children were still safe. By chipping away at Jenny's movements, they were adding more and more information to her whereabouts just before she'd disappeared.

"If she was last seen the afternoon of the fifth…" Willow's eyes widened. "Wasn't that about the same time the fire broke out at the machine shop?"

"I think you're right. We came barreling out of the tunnels to help with the blaze, and we couldn't have been on shift that long." He frowned. "You know, Ephraim Zanata was sure there was something wrong with that fire. He said it was burning too hot and too fast to have been caused by a spark from his blast furnace—and the fire seemed to start on the outside wall of the building, which didn't make a whole lot of sense at the time."

Willow bristled at the thought that her friend might have been responsible. "No. Jenny wouldn't have done such a thing." She gestured to the map. "And if she was seen in the woods—"

Charles stilled her protests with a squeeze of her waist. "I'm not saying Jenny did it. But what if it was a diversion?"

"What do you mean?"

"You and I both know the minute that alarm bell rings, the entire town comes running. Just look at the way you women at the Dovecote came rushing to help when the tunnel collapsed and Jonah was injured."

Charles's eyes grew troubled, like storm clouds piling up against the jagged mountaintops above the mine.

"What if the fire was the killer's attempt to isolate Jenny at the Dovecote? Alone."

"She wouldn't have come running," Willow whispered.

"Not in her condition."

"But if Stumpy was right, and she'd already left the Dovecote…"

"Then Jenny knew she was in trouble."

Chapter Ten

Willow and Charles were sitting down to bowls of stew and cornbread when a rapping at the door signaled yet another visitor.

"I don't think I've had so many people wanting to talk with me in my whole life," Willow said. "But now that you and I have married, we seem to have become the social hub of Bachelor Bottoms."

Charles couldn't help but smile. She had a point. Even he couldn't remember having so many callers drop by his house—which worried him, since they still had no clue who might have harmed Jenny.

"Just be careful about answering the door if I'm not around," he warned.

Surreptitiously, he settled a revolver on his lap, covered it with his napkin, then nodded to Willow.

"Who's there?" she called next to the door.

"Mrs. Wanlass, ma'am. It's Mr. Creakle and Mr. Smalls come to talk to Mr. Wanlass, if you'll beg our pardon… Mrs. Wanlass…ma'am."

Willow grinned and quickly unbolted the door, swinging it wide. "Come in, gentlemen."

The two men were silhouetted against falling snow, short and tall, wizened and bullish.

"Thank you, ma'am."

Creakle carefully pounded his feet on the stoop to clean his boots as much as possible, then stepped inside, dragging a rabbit skin hat from his head. Immediately, his white hair stood up in a ring around his balding head, giving him the tufted appearance of an owl.

He made room for Willoughby Smalls, who did the same.

"Let me take your coats."

"Oh, no, ma'am. We can do it."

Smalls, who was wearing an enormous greatcoat made of what looked like a bear skin barely minus the bear, was the first to shed his outer coverings. Willow staggered beneath the weight of the garment as she hung it on the pegs beside the door.

Creakle seemed to be having more trouble with his coat—so much so that Smalls finally grasped the garment by the cuffs and lifted them straight up. Willow could have sworn that Creakle's boots left the floor before he was unceremoniously dumped free.

Hiding a smile, Willow hung his coat next to Smalls's.

"Would you gentlemen like to join us for dinner? We were just about to have some venison stew and cornbread."

Smalls's lips slid into a wide grin and his eyes jumped to the table a few feet away. But Creakle, his constant companion—and most days his voice—offered a tentative, "No, my mama always told me not t' interrupt folks' dinners. We can come back…"

His words might decline her offer, but there was no heart to them, so Willow made a dismissing gesture with her hands.

"Nonsense. Have a seat. You may as well eat here—and my mam, before she left us, God rest her soul, was adamant that no one should ever leave her home hungry. Sit, sit!"

The two men nearly knocked each other down scrambling for a seat, and Willow made a mental note to invite them to dinner more often. Creakle, as Ramsey's assistant, had probably had more contact with the mail-order brides than any other miner in the camp. And since he and Willoughby were friends, Smalls probably came in a close second.

Willow gathered up two more place settings of her precious Blue Willow china and the mismatched silver, which had been hidden along with the china. She set them in front of the men, then gestured to the pot she'd placed on a folded dishcloth in the middle of the table.

"Help yourselves, gentleman."

As she settled into her own place, she could have sworn that Creakle muttered to his friend, "One foot on the floor at all times, and if somebody touches somethin', they've laid their claim. Them's the rules."

The men quickly filled their bowls, then began to eat—and despite Creakle's explanation of "Boarding House manners", the sight of them fighting like little boys over who would be first to get a piece of cornbread nearly caused her to laugh outright.

For several long minutes, they all ate in silence. Through it all, Willow would have been the first to admit that the warm room, the glowing lamps and the appreciative company made the food taste even better than before.

"So, what brings you both here?" Charles asked after they'd all had a chance to take the edge off their hunger.

Creakle looked up, his spoon poised halfway to his

lips. His eyes, pale with age but wise beyond their years, blinked for a moment. Then he seemed to remember.

"Oh, Mr. Ramsey said they're having a hard time with blasting that new tunnel. Number nine? He wondered if you'd stop by the office some time tomorrow morning."

"The main office?"

"No, the one in the mine."

Willow saw a muscle working in Charles's jaw.

"Do Batchwell and Bottoms know he's asked me to come in?"

Again, Creakle blinked, his expression becoming blank. But Willow sensed that, like the barn owls that nested in the tree near the Dovecote, he could swoop into action at the slightest hint of a threat.

"No?"

Charles chuckled at that. "So, Jonah didn't bother to confer with them?"

Creakle's head swung from side to side.

Charles thought for several minutes. "Fine. Tell him I'll meet him right after the early bird shift reports for duty."

Creakle grinned at that, sitting a little taller in his chair. "See, Smalls, I told you he'd help the boss."

Smalls frowned and nudged Creakle with an elbow.

"Oh! I almost forgot. They've been askin' fer you up at the Meetin' House. Everybody's wonderin' when you'll be comin' back t' give yer sermons."

Willow felt rather than saw the way Charles became still. "I don't know that I'll be coming back, Creakle. Not as the company's lay pastor, anyway."

Both Creakle and Smalls regarded him with their mouths agape. In unison, they lowered their spoons to their bowls.

"But why not?" Creakle asked.

Again, that muscle flexed in Charles's jaw. Willow felt a tinge of guilt, realizing that she was part of the reason he didn't feel he could resume his duties. If she hadn't claimed that the children were hers, if they hadn't allowed Batchwell to force them into marriage…

Her thoughts slammed to a halt at that point.

What other choice did they have?

Rather than explain himself, Charles said, "Currently, my duty is to my family."

Creakle and Smalls exchanged glances. But Charles's response must have satisfied them because they resumed eating.

Willow decided that it was her turn to probe for information. "Mr. Creakle, you and Mr. Smalls were at the Dovecote quite often. Did you ever speak with Jenny?"

Creakle's brow creased. "No. I can't say that I did. She kept to herself most the times I was there. But…"

Willow felt a flutter of hope. "Yes?"

"She had a fondness for gingerbread men."

Just as quickly, the hope wilted.

"I know this, cuz the boss has a fondness fer them, too."

He glanced at Smalls, who urged him on with a nod of his head.

"There was a couple o' times me an' Willoughby saw her. Late at night it was, after most folks had gone to bed. Me an' Smalls even walked her back t' the Dovecote a time or two—just t' make sure she got home all right. See, she was havin' a hankerin' fer the gingerbread…" he dropped his voice to a barely audible whisper "…what with her bein' in the family way an' all."

Smalls nodded to corroborate Creakle's pronouncement.

"You're sure she was going to the cook shack?" Charles asked.

"Seemed like it t' us. Each time, she had a little bag of food with her."

Willow's gaze met Charles's. Had Jenny truly been searching for a means to ease her cravings? Or had she been gathering food, knowing that she meant to go into hiding?"

Smalls punched Creakle in the arm, making a soft grunting noise.

His friend grimaced, rubbing the spot. "Knock it off. I'm getting t' that part."

Charles leaned forward. "What part, Creakle?"

"Well, there was a couple o' things strange about those nights we saw her. First, she didn't have none o' those Pinkertons with her, so's we know she was sneakin' away without 'em seein'. Then, when we happened upon her, she t'weren't comin' from the direction of the Dovecote. She was headin' inta town from the direction of Rock Creek Road."

Willow looked to Charles, but the news seemed significant to him.

"You're sure?" Charles said with a frown.

"Sure as I can be. Didn't you think so, too, Willoughby?"

The gentle giant nodded mournfully.

"Rock Creek Road?" Willow finally asked, when no one seemed inclined to explain.

Charles offered, "It's not really a road, more a trail that heads north out of the camp. It follows the river for about a mile, then opens into a meadow where there's an old trapper's cabin." His gray eyes seemed to darken to flint. "It's in the same direction Gideon traced the blood trail."

* * *

Willow stood on the stoop, her arms wrapped around her body as huge flakes fell around her like ash, coating the stairs, the road, and piling up against the windows.

"Maybe you shouldn't go alone," she said. There was a tremor to her voice—and Charles knew it didn't have anything to do with the cold.

"I'll be fine." He finished adjusting the cinch. Then, holding the reins, he climbed the steps to the door one last time.

She looked so small, so sweet, so worried for him that he couldn't resist tucking one of those fiery tresses of hair behind her ear.

"I'm going to meet Jonah at the mine, see what's on his mind. Then I'll ride out to the trapper's cabin and nose around. I won't take any more time than necessary."

"But—"

"I've got my revolver and my rifle. I'll be fine. You, on the other hand, need to be careful today. Stay in the house, keep warm and watch over our children."

Our children.

He wasn't quite sure why those words had slipped from his mouth. For the past few days, he'd referred to them as "the twins," "the bairns" or "the wee ones." But this morning, he found himself claiming them as if they were his own blood. *Their* own blood.

But that's how he felt. With each day that passed, this…arrangement seemed more natural to him than breathing. It felt *right* to come home to the warmth of a helpmate and children. He was comforted in some inde-scribable way by the sight of wee clothes hanging from the drying cord he'd strung over the range. He loved the feminine frippery that had invaded his home—curtains and lace and Willow's precious china. And, inevitably, the moment he entered, his gaze would seek out his wife and his bairns.

As if the scene of familial bliss was real.

Willow studied him with worried eyes. "You should wait and take Jonah or Gideon with you."

He shook his head. "They both have work at the mine to do."

"Then take someone else!"

"It would take too much explaining." Unable to resist, he gently grasped her shoulders. "I won't be at the cabin long—and it's not that far away. It's you who needs to be careful. I don't want you opening the door for anyone other than your friends from the Dovecote, Jonah or Gideon."

She nodded, but he could feel her shiver beneath his hands. Unable to resist, he drew her into his arms, closing his coat around her shoulders. For several long moments, he merely held her that way, allowing his body heat to sink into hers, absorbing the sensation of...*belonging.*

Was this what he'd been missing all this time? He'd been so sure, after a miserable childhood in a foundling home and a hardscrabble youth, that he was destined to spend his life alone. He'd even signed up for a job with Batchwell and Bottoms knowing that he would be sealing his fate in that regard.

You never knew what you were missing.

Until now.

Knowing he couldn't delay any longer, he placed a gentle kiss on her forehead.

For a moment, her eyes fluttered closed—as if she wanted to savor the contact. Then she looked up at him, her eyes blue as a summer sky.

"Be careful," she murmured.

"I'll be back by lunchtime."

He felt her hands, small and delicate, clutch at his waist. "Promise?"

"Promise."

Unable to help himself, he bent again, this time kissing her briefly on the lips. Drawing courage from the flare of wonder he saw in her eyes, he forced himself to back away.

"Make me some cookies?"

"What kind?"

"Oatmeal?"

"Deal."

Then, knowing that he wouldn't be able to go at all if he didn't leave now, he jumped over the steps to the ground and swung onto the horse. He quickly jammed his hat more firmly on his head and turned the mare in the direction of the mine.

When he dared to glance over his shoulder, Willow was still on the stoop watching him.

For some reason, that fact warmed him from within.

Charles felt unaccountably self-conscious as he entered the mine and made his way down to what had once been tunnel one. There, a shack of sorts had been built to serve as an on-site office.

He was at home here. Unlike the first mine he'd worked in as a boy, the Batchwell Bottoms Silver Mine was primarily cool and dry, smelling of earth and a lingering hint of gunpowder—probably from the blasting that Jonah had been doing in tunnel nine. Here at the entrance, the walls and ceilings were wide, and lined with timber to shore them up. Safety lamps had been set at regular intervals, casting golden puddles in the darkness. Two sets of iron rails ran down the middle of the earthen ramp, stretching side by side until they forked into different tunnels a hundred yards away.

As Charles closed the office door behind him, Jonah looked up from a table lined with schematic drawings.

"Thanks for coming in this morning."

"Not a problem."

"Come and look at this."

Jonah pointed to a drawing of the various passageways branching out from tunnel one. The last corridor, tunnel nine, was little more than a penciled doorway, like a sawed-off branch of an elaborate tree.

"What's the problem?"

"Getting through that bedrock is the problem."

It hadn't been a fortnight since Charles had been in the mine, yet if felt like years. Where once his world had revolved around the job, now it seemed like a secondary concern.

"I thought we were planning on blasting there. I drew up the plans a few days before I resigned."

Jonah sighed, resting his hands on his hips. "They've gone missing. No one has been able to find them since you left."

"My men should—"

Jonah's lips twitched. "Your men are refusing to work without you. They're claiming that it's not safe for them to set the charges unless you're there to oversee things."

The pronouncement took Charles aback. He couldn't remember the last time anyone had staged a protest in the mine.

"I'll have a word with them, if you want."

Jonah shook his head. "Nah. I kind of like things the way they are. It can't hurt for Batchwell to see how invaluable you are to this operation. And your men. But…" He pointed to the map again. "What little progress we've been able to make has revealed a thick layer of bedrock, here." He traced a line with his finger. "And there's a seam of silver running behind it, here." He looked up. "Think you can draw up another plan for where to set the dynamite?"

Charles nodded. "I could do it tonight."

"Good." Jonah rolled up the map, secured it with a piece of string, then handed it to Charles. "I'll put you on the payroll as a consultant." He drawled the last word with something akin to glee.

"Consultant?" Charles echoed dubiously. "Batchwell will get one look at that and cross my name off the books in record time. You don't have to pay me, Jonah. I'd be happy to do it. Especially since the original plan went missing."

Jonah shook his head. "No, I already looked through the company charter. Seems that the mining superintendent, which I happen to be, has the authority to hire a consultant for 'special projects.'" Jonah gestured to the map. "You've got yourself a special project."

"I'll have it done by tomorrow."

"You misunderstand. I'm not just talking about drawing up the schematics. I'm assigning you as special consultant to tunnel nine. It's your baby. I want you to get it up and running. You'll be in charge of your men from the blasting gang, and two more crews assigned to clear away the debris."

For several long moments, Charles wasn't sure what to think. Only a few days ago, he would have jumped at the opportunity. But now...

He worried about Willow being alone at the house. Opening a tunnel would mean long hours and careful supervision.

"Before you say no, I've thought a lot about this. I

know you want to stick close to home for the next little while." Jonah's eyes glinted with rich specks of green and blue and brown. "So I've spoken to Gideon about getting a pair of men stationed outside your house while you're on shift. He's shorthanded for the next few days, but he can adjust schedules by the end of the week. In the meantime, I've assigned some assistants to help you until you can return to us full-time. They can be your eyes here at the mine, or you can keep them at home to watch over Willow."

He glanced beyond Charles to where a window looked out over the tunnels, and lifted a hand, beckoning with his fingers. Almost simultaneously, the door to the office flew open and outlined a pair of shapes in a puddle of lamplight: one wizened and small, the other as bulky as a bull.

"Howdy, boss man number two," Creakle said with a cackle.

Beside him, Smalls offered his best grin and a quick salute.

"What will you be wantin' us t' do fer you today?"

Willow felt as if she were forever being summoned to the door. She'd already had a quick visit from Iona and Lydia. Sumner had sent word that she would be stopping by later in the afternoon. And now there was another knock. She'd been hoping to finish baking the cookies, then finish up the children's layette gowns before Louise needed her sewing machine back. But with all the interruptions, Willow hadn't made much progress.

"Who is it?"

"Mrs. Wanlass, ma'am, it's Creakle and Smalls. Yer husband sent us t' sit with you till he could get back. We're to see t' it that no harm comes t' you or the babes."

Willow couldn't help smiling. Charles had promised to be back by lunchtime, but he'd still sent the pair of men to guard them. In her opinion, he was being completely overprotective of her and the children. Since the rattle had appeared on the doorstep, there'd been no more unsettling activity. Maybe Jenny had been wrong to think that the children were in danger.

"One moment."

She wiped her hands on a dish towel. As promised, she'd made a batch of oatmeal raisin cookies for Charles, and she was just about to put the first sheet in the oven. No doubt Creakle and Smalls could be persuaded to join her for a cup of tea and some refreshments.

Truth be known, she was getting a bit stir-crazy being cooped up in the house. Maybe, just maybe, the two men could watch the babies for a few minutes so that she could take a walk around the block and clear the cobwebs from her mind. She would have to steer clear of the main office, where Batchwell might see her, but...

Setting the cloth on the cupboard, she hurried to the door and slid the bolt free. But when she opened it wide, she stood rooted to the spot, all thoughts of a walk skittering out into the snow.

Both Smalls and Creakle had come to the row house prepared for any eventuality. Smalls wore a bandolier brimming with ammunition. A pair of holsters sported pearl-handled revolvers, and she could see one, two, *three* knives tucked into his boots. Creakle was similarly attired, sporting one of the largest Bowie knives Willow had ever seen.

The two men stepped into the house and shoved the bolt home. Then they each dragged a chair to the two windows in the keeping room and moved the curtains ever so slightly with the barrels of their revolvers.

"Can I get you anything?" she offered weakly. For the past several hours, she'd managed to talk herself into believing that the worst of the danger was past. But with the two men taking her safety so seriously, she couldn't help but feel the first pricklings of unease—and she chided herself for growing lax.

"No, ma'am. You just keep on with whatever you were doin'. Me an' Smalls will take over the watch until the boss man gets home."

"Boss man?"

"Yes, ma'am. Mr. Wanlass done got his job back—or thereabouts. He's been promoted and we've been assigned to help him."

Charles had his job back? Her heart leaped at the idea. She'd been so worried when he'd been fired. He must be so relieved to be able to go to work.

But on the heels of that thought came a strange disappointment. If he was heading back to the mine, they would no longer share their days and meals together. Nor would they be able to study their chart of suspects and share theories of what to investigate next. She would be on her own for most of the afternoon—and even though she'd been alone most of her life…

She felt more bereft than she had a right to feel.

Chapter Eleven

Charles carefully maneuvered his horse through the snow, keeping his mount to the portion of the trail that butted up against the mountain. Here, the drifts remained in shade and stayed frozen and firm. The last thing he needed was for his mount to stumble in the loose powder and come up lame.

He'd been riding for several minutes, going slowly, his eyes sweeping the path ahead of him, looking for the slightest sign that Jenny had come this way.

The chances of finding anything were slim. It had snowed several times since the night of her murder, and the winds had been strong. Even now, a veil of flakes fell in front of him, allowing only a few feet of visibility.

Grimacing, Charles hunched deeper into the collar of his coat and jammed his hat more firmly on his head.

If he'd thought things through, he would have waited until the weather cleared. The wind was growing sharper, stronger, driving the snow against his cheeks. Beneath him, his horse grew skittish and kept tossing her head as if to tell Charles that they were going the wrong direction.

"I know, girl. I know," he murmured, patting the animal on the side of her neck. "We'll just look inside the cabin and then head for home."

Home.

For the first time in his life, Charles felt an inner glow at the word. Willow and the twins had definitely done that. They'd taken the cold bachelor's quarters and made them feel like a haven.

How was such a thing possible? He really didn't know much more about Willow than he had before they'd married.

No.

That wasn't quite true. He might not know the exact place of her birth or her favorite flower, but he knew the important things. She was loving and gentle, resourceful and brave. She was the kind of woman that any man would be proud to claim as his own.

And she was his wife.

At least for the time being.

He squinted into the storm until, at long last, Charles could see the dim outline of a structure up ahead. Veering his mount in that direction, he urged the beast to hurry. If Jenny had left any kind of trail to track, it was buried now. The only way to check out his hunch would be to look inside the building itself.

He waited until the mare had stepped beneath the roof's overhang, then he swung to the ground, his limbs jolting from the drop. Charles hadn't realized how cold he'd become. His joints seemed to creak from the low temperatures and his extremities were already growing numb.

Just a few more minutes. Then he could go back.

He looped the reins around the branch of a scrubby pine tree. Then he gazed around him. He wasn't sure if it was the wind, the snow or the thought that this could have been the last place Jenny had come for shelter, but the spot between his shoulder blades prickled with uneasiness.

He touched a hand to the holster he'd strapped to his hips, then slid the rifle free from its scabbard. His eyes roamed what little of the landscape he could see—the craggy slope of the mountain to the left, the icy gray-blue sheen of the river to the right.

Charles wasn't sure what he was looking for. He simply felt the overwhelming need to be cautious.

Get in there, look things over, then get out of here.

Slowly, he levered a bullet into position and walked closer to the door.

The old wood was swollen and caked with ice and snow, the drifts on the covered porch extending up past his calves, so Charles was forced to bang his shoulder against the rough panels. Once. Twice. Then the door burst open.

It took a moment for his eyes to adjust to the dimness—and he rued the fact that he hadn't thought to bring a lantern with him. But after several seconds, he was able to see an old glass lamp on a rickety table. Offering a quick prayer that it had oil, he reached for the iron match holder hung a few feet above. The recess was thick with dust, but there were two matches inside. Hopefully, they weren't so old that they wouldn't light.

He rasped the head of one against the holder, and a burst of flame leaped into view. Working quickly, he set his rifle against the wall, lifted the glass chimney and touched the match to the wick.

For a few moments, Charles fiddled with the wick until the flame grew, curling and writhing against the chimney like a living thing. But a glance at the reservoir and what little kerosene remained reminded Charles that he didn't have much time.

Turning, he held the lamp high, letting the glow seep into the corners. Instantly, he found what he'd been looking for. There were blankets piled in the corner, fresh wood stacked neatly by the fireplace. On a table near a rusty box stove were tins of food, some of them full, some opened and empty. Beside them, incongruously, was a woman's hairbrush.

Charles moved to pick up the brush. It was a pretty thing. Made of silver, the back had a design of ornate curlicues with a fat cherub in the middle. Captured in the bristles were a few strands of dark hair.

He tucked the brush into his pocket. Willow would be able to tell him if it belonged to her friend, even though Charles was pretty sure he'd found the place where Jenny had gone to find shelter.

Who was she hiding from?

A burst of wind slammed the door against the opposite wall. Snow began to whirl into the cabin.

He turned in a slow circle, looking for any evidence of a comb or mirror. But there was nothing. Except...

He frowned when he saw a stick in the corner. No, not a stick. The wood was carefully shaped, polished. As he crept closer, Charles could see that it was the handle to an ax, most likely. The head was gone, but the groove that had once held the blade in place was still there.

Even then, it wasn't the broken tool itself that drew his attention. It was the dark smear that stained the wood.

A cold finger seemed to trace down his spine.

Was he looking at the murder weapon?

Charles crouched to examine the piece more closely, just as a shot rang out and something slammed into the far wall.

Flattening onto the floor, Charles realized, too late, that he'd left his rifle leaning against the door jamb. He tried to belly crawl toward the weapon, but another shot rang out, piercing the floor next to his hand.

Instinctively, Charles rolled to the right, out of the range of the open doorway, then scrambled to his feet. After drawing his revolver, he pulled back the trigger.

He scanned his surroundings, knowing that he was in a sorry position. Judging by the second shot, the gunman was closer this time. Charles had only seconds before he was cornered. Then it would be a simple matter to pick him off.

In a flash, a dozen images raced through his head—Willow wearing her wedding veil, the twins in their basket, his wife's hair curling wildly down her back.

No. He was going to keep his promise. He'd said that he would be home by lunchtime, and he would. One way or another.

Briefly closing his eyes, Charles offered up a quick prayer.

Lord, help me in my hour of need. Help me to return safely to my wife. My children.

Then, without another thought, he ran full tilt the breadth of the room and dived through the window.

As the glass shattered around him, he rolled in the snow in an attempt to absorb some of the impact. Then he was pushing to his feet, running toward the trees that grew next to the river.

The sound of his escape must have alerted his attacker, because Charles saw a shape moving around the side of the house, saw him lift an arm.

Bam!

Charles veered hard to the right just as a pine branch exploded beside him.

Only a little farther now. Once he reached the trees, he would have some cover.

He veered hard to the left.

Bam!

A puff of snow signaled that the gunman was beginning to anticipate his moves.

Charles launched himself into the air. Then he was falling, rolling, sliding past the cover of the trees to the river beyond. He skidded across the ice, moving far out into the center.

Cra-a-ack.

He scrambled to find his footing, to crawl back to the safety of the shore, just as a figure loomed out of the trees. Judging by the size and shape, it was a man. But just when he lifted his arm one last time to fire...

The ice imploded and Charles went down into the murky depths.

Willow was removing the last batch of cookies from the oven when she was suddenly overcome with a feeling unlike any she had ever encountered before. A dark heaviness settled over her...

She dropped the baking pan and stood rooted to the spot, trying to push the sensation away.

There was nothing at all to inspire such a reaction. Mr. Creakle and Mr. Smalls were still at their posts. The babies were lying on a quilt she'd spread out on the floor. Beyond the walls of Charles's house she could hear the usual midafternoon bustle of Bachelor Bottoms—deep male voices, laughter, the muffled thud of hooves in the snow, the hiss of sleigh runners.

Her gaze skipped to the mantel clock. It was only half past noon. A little later than Charles had thought he would be home, but not so late that she should worry.

Nevertheless, as she chided herself and reached for the spatula, her hand trembled.

Needing to reassure herself, she hurried to kneel beside the twins. They slept soundly, Eva with her fist pressed to her mouth and Adam's lips twitching as if he were sucking on an imaginary bottle.

Fine. They're both fine.

Not knowing why, she moved to the door, unbolted it and threw it wide.

Both Creakle and Smalls eyed her strangely.

"Is somethin' wrong, Mrs. Wanlass, ma'am?"

"I... I don't know."

She stood for long moments, her ear cocked, expecting to hear the warning bell for the mine begin to toll.

The afternoon was peaceful, with gusts of wind whipping at the falling snow.

Was it the sound of the wind whistling across the chimneys and through the alleys that had disturbed her? It sometimes made a keening whine.

Even as she tried to isolate the sound, her eyes kept scanning the street, and the sensation did not waver.

"Mr. Smalls. I wonder if you'd be so kind as to find Mr. Wanlass. Ask him if he'll be much longer..."

It was a weak excuse at best. But since the babies were safe, she knew that she wouldn't be able to relax until she knew that Charles was on his way home. She had an overwhelming need to study him, from the golden waves of his hair to his scuffed boots. Just to make sure he was all right.

"Beggin' yer pardon, ma'am. But he's not all that late," Creakle stated.

"I know. I just..."

Since she had no other explanation for this...over-

whelming urge to check on Charles, she turned beseech-
ingly to Mr. Smalls.

"Please?"

The word emerged as little more than a rough whisper,
but Smalls must have sensed a portion of her urgency,
because he rose and reached for his greatcoat.

"He was going to the trapper's cabin just beyond the
mine. Do you know where that is?"

Smalls and Creakle exchanged glances, then Smalls
nodded. Reaching for his hat, he jammed it onto his head.

Creakle must have finally begun to feel a portion of
her worry, because he stood, as well. Instinctively, he
grabbed the rifle he'd leaned against the wall and held
it diagonally across his chest as he joined Willow at the
door.

"Go to the livery and hitch up the sleigh," Creakle said
to his friend. "You know how Mr. Wanlass is punctual to
a fault. Maybe he's had trouble with his horse."

Smalls nodded, then dodged into the storm. He'd gone
only a few yards when he stopped, cocking his ear in the
direction of the mine.

Without warning, a horse plunged out of the swirling
snow. It ran riderless in the direction of the livery, its
reins whipping behind it.

"Catch that horse, Smalls!" Creakle bellowed. Then
he turned to Willow. "Get inside. Lock the door. That's
Mr. Wanlass's mount!"

Willow stood leaning against the panels of the door,
panic assailing her.

What could have happened?

Where was Charles?

She tried to tell herself that a horse coming back alone
to the camp wasn't a catastrophe. The animal could have

been spooked by a rabbit and bucked Charles to the ground. Or Charles could have tied the animal up and the wind could have startled the mare.

Nevertheless, the dread she felt didn't ease.

Closing her eyes, she bowed her head and offered a quick heartfelt prayer.

"Please, Lord, watch over Charles and keep him safe. Help him to know that help is on its way, and help Mr. Creakle and Mr. Smalls find him." Her throat grew tight, but she added, "And please, help me to know what I should do. Amen."

She opened her eyes, barely seeing her surroundings. Instead, she took deep breaths to calm herself, then sorted her whirling thoughts into a logical order.

No matter what had happened, Charles would be cold.

Willow ran to the stove and stoked the fire, adding another log so that the flames wouldn't go out.

Water.

She checked the reservoir in the range, topped it off, then grabbed a pail. She filled it to the top with snow, then returned, bolted the door and set the pail on the range to heat.

Pressing a finger to the spot between her brows, she closed her eyes.

What else?

Her mind skipped back, to the day when the second avalanche had occurred and many of the miners had been injured. What had Sumner done to prepare for their arrival?

Unfortunately, Willow couldn't send for the doctor herself. Sumner hadn't come to Bachelor Bottoms that day. Lydia had mentioned it when the woman stopped to cuddle the babies for a few minutes during the morning shift in the cook shack. But if Willow could remember what steps Sumner had taken when the catastrophe had occurred...

Hot bricks.

Heated blankets.

Her eyes flew open. Running upstairs, she gathered the quilt and blankets from her own cot, then draped them on chairs near the stove and by the fire.

Bricks.

She didn't have any bricks! And the ones that Sumner had used were locked up in the infirmary.

Rocks. There had been some smooth river rocks piled next to the lean-to. They'd probably been left over from the foundation when it was built. Charles had warned her to step carefully if she ever went outside to tend to the goat, since the drifting snow sometimes obscured them.

Heedless of the storm, Willow ran into the cold, her lashes blinking against the whipping snow. The pile of rocks was all but buried beneath a drift, but she dug with her hands until she found the first stone.

It took nearly all of her strength to wrench it from its bed of ice. Staggering beneath its weight, she carried it inside and set it on the hearth, as close to the flames as she could. Then she returned twice more, before the ice surrounding the stones made it impossible for her to retrieve any more.

Bolting the door again, she laid several of the babies' flannel diapers on top of the stove. They were the perfect size to wrap the stones and—

She suddenly became aware of the jingling of sleigh bells. Running to the door, she flung it wide just as Creakle and Smalls skidded to a halt in front of the stoop.

"He's cold, missus. Deathly cold. Near as we can tell, he fell through the ice in the river and barely had the strength to get out. We found him shivering on the bank."

Creakle jumped from the sleigh and ran to hold the skittish horse while Smalls climbed into the box. Bending down, he flung Charles over his shoulder, then staggered toward Willow.

"Take him upstairs to the bed, Mr. Smalls. Start undressing him as quickly as you can, then cover him with the blankets. I'll be up in a few minutes with more."

Smalls nodded, and headed inside for the staircase.

"Mr. Creakle, when you've seen to the horse, I've set three stones on the hearth to heat. There are some flannel squares draped over the stove. Wrap one of the stones with the flannel, then carry it upstairs. We'll take turns putting the hot stones next to Charles's feet to help ward off frostbite."

"Yes, ma'am."

Since Creakle had been one of the men injured in the latest avalanche, he knew better than most how important—and how painful—it would be to warm Charles as soon as possible.

"Don't you fear none, Mrs. Wanlass. Charles is a strong man. A *good* man. The Lord will bless him."

Willow prayed that he was right. Because if anything happened to Charles, she didn't know what she would do.

Ants.

He was covered in fire ants, being stung a thousand times until his whole body was on fire.

But cold. So cold.

Charles groaned as the dark oblivion that wrapped around him like a thick fog began to dissipate and fade. With it came the pain.

Unable to bring back the blackness, he fought the heaviness invading his body and tried his best to open his eyes. The most he was able to manage was a mere slit. Even then...

Had he died?

He seemed to be surrounded in a golden glow that flickered and danced. He vacillated between being warm and shivering uncontrollably.

His gaze fell upon a field of brightly colored flowers that enveloped his body. The blooms were oddly shaped, like something out of a dream.

A quilt. The blanket had been tucked so tightly around him that it bound him in place, preventing him from lifting his arms.

Even if he'd been able to find the strength to do so.

As he marveled at the warmth, the glow, the too-bright colors of the quilt, a shadow moved above him.

No. Not a shadow.

It was the ghostly mother again, the one from Headmistress Bedelmeyer's office. This time, rather than regarding her child with rapt attention.

She was looking at him.

The glow seemed to grow brighter the longer he looked, illuminating her silhouette with an aura of red and gold. And then she spoke.

"Charles."

She knew his name.

"Charles, you're safe now."

He didn't feel safe. Warm, yes.

But safe?

His extremities were still bedeviled by a thousand demons poking him with pins. And his shoulder...

It burned as if it had been branded.

She touched him then, resting her hand against his forehead. That touch stilled the rapid beat of his heart.

He felt the coolness of her touch stealing through him like spring water.

As if she'd read his mind, she asked, "Would you like something to drink?"

He thought he nodded—he *hoped* he nodded. Because his mouth felt dry, sticky.

She reached behind him to tip his head up, then pressed a tin mug to his lips. As soon as the liquid hit his tongue, he gulped greedily, fearing that there would never be enough water in the world to quench his thirst. But after only a few swallows, she took the mug away again and lowered his head.

"Not too much. Not yet. After a few minutes, I'll give you more. Then, when you're feeling better, I've got some broth heated and waiting."

He frowned. The more she talked, the more he seemed to…know her.

Her hand returned to his brow again and he swallowed against the horrible dryness.

"Wh-what happened?" His voice emerged as an awful croak, but she seemed to understand him.

"Mr. Creakle and Mr. Smalls found you on the riverbank. You were soaked clear to the bone and the ice had broken in the center. They think you fell in."

He closed his eyes, trying to remember. But it wasn't the ice he recalled. Instead, images burst into his consciousness.

A dingy cabin.

Hair brush.

Ax.

Blood.

The crash of a window.

A shuddering crack.

In that instant, the pieces of the puzzle began to form a moving picture.

He remembered riding up to the trapper's cabin. Going inside.

Yes, it was all there now. He could see the dusty interior that someone had tried so hard to make clean. There had been cobwebs hanging from the rafters, but the floor and the nest of blankets in the corner had been neat. A stack of logs had rested near the fireplace and tins of food waited on the table. And then…

He squeezed his eyes shut, forcing his mind to picture the rest.

A brush.

Yes. He'd found a silver hairbrush lying in the middle of the table as if it had been carelessly set aside, but still waited patiently for its owner. He remembered looking for the companion pieces…

And finding the bloody ax handle instead.

Then someone had shot at him.

"The brush —" He tried to rise and found himself hampered by the tight blankets, the trembling of his limbs and a bolt of lightning that raced from his shoulder to the base of his spine.

"Shh."

She pressed him down onto the bed.

Willow.

His wife.

"You need to stay put. You nearly died from the cold. If Mr. Creakle and Mr. Smalls hadn't found you when they did…"

He watched her throat move convulsively. A sheen of moisture pooled in her blue eyes.

Cornflower blue.

Forget-me-not blue.

"I don't want you pulling your stitches loose."

Frowning, he tunneled his hand through the blankets until he could gingerly touch his shoulder. Rather than skin, he encountered soft linen.

"It's a good thing I watched Sumner stitch up those miners after the cave-in." She offered him a smile that was more of a self-deprecating grimace. "I'm not saying that I did as well as she could have done. But my head-mistress always said I was a passable seamstress."

"What?"

"You were shot." She pointed to the fleshy part of her own shoulder near her neck. "There's a bullet hole in your coat to prove it. It made a furrow through your skin. I could have waited for Sumner to see to it tomorrow, I suppose. But we couldn't stop the bleeding. And when Creakle volunteered to sew you up, I figured you might want someone with a...more delicate hand."

Charles had to agree with her there. Before Sumner had come to the valley, the mining community had been without a doctor for several months. Creakle had stepped in on occasion to set bones and stitch up gashes, but his work was far from pretty.

"Thank you."

The words seemed completely inadequate, but Willow beamed at him as if he'd handed her the moon.

"I want you to sleep now. Your body has had quite a shock, so you'll need your rest."

She scooped up a tray from the bedside table and Charles could see a basin of water and a red-stained cloth.

His blood.

She was at the door before he remembered what he needed to ask her.

"Willow?"

"Yes?"

She turned, and he loved the way the lamplight slid over her silhouette like a river of gold.

"I found a hairbrush. Did it…did I…"

"We discovered it wedged into the pocket of your coat." Willow's features were filled with sadness. "I recognized it immediately. It belonged to Jenny."

Chapter Twelve

It was late that night when Sumner heard Charles stirring again. She filled a bowl with hot broth, slathered butter onto two thick slices of bread, then filled a mug with hot tea laced liberally with sugar.

As she walked into the keeping room, Mr. Creakle looked up.

Willow couldn't think of anything more endearing than the sight of Creakle and Smalls—the most unlikely of nursemaids.

Smalls held little Eva in the crook of one arm. He'd been entertaining her for several minutes by pulling the most elaborate faces. Judging by Eva's fascinated expression, she was thoroughly entranced.

Creakle, on the other hand, had been spinning an elaborate yarn about a pair of intrepid miners. Judging by the improbability of his tale, he was making things up as he went along, but Adam's eyes tracked his every move.

"I'm going to take some soup up to Charles," she said.

"You go right ahead. Me an' Smalls have got the little ones all taken care of, so don't you fret."

Although Willow had insisted that the men could go home, they'd both refused. As far as they were concerned, the boss man had been shot, and his missus needed some-one on guard.

She felt a little guilty since, other than the cot in the spare room, she had no place for them to sleep. But when Creakle had insisted they'd pull up a piece o' floor and wrap themselves in a blanket, she'd been secretly re-lieved. She was still feeling rattled after stitching up Charles's wound.

She pushed the bedroom door open with her shoulder, only to find that Charles was sitting up in bed. She was glad to see that he was wearing the nightshirt Creakle had found amongst his things. After all he'd been through, she didn't want him catching a chill. Even though there was a small fireplace in the bedroom, the area around the window was drafty. She would have to see if she could find some newspaper to plug the chinks.

"You're looking more alert."

He stroked his chin and frowned at the stubble.

"I don't need to be in bed."

She set the tray on his lap.

"Yes, you do. For one thing, it's nearly midnight. For another, we don't have a lot of chairs—and at the mo-ment, Creakle and Smalls are using most of what we do have to dry out your clothing."

Charles frowned again, but thankfully, he didn't push the point.

Willow grabbed the napkin from the tray and tucked the corner into the neck of his nightshirt.

"Would you like me to feed you?"

"I can feed myself."

The muttered reply sounded so much like a little boy insisting he could take care of himself that Willow nearly laughed. The cantankerous edge was another good sign of his recovery.

She shuddered when she remembered how he'd looked after Smalls had laid him out on the bed. He'd been so cold and gray and...lifeless.

"You had a close call," she murmured.

He nodded, seeming to stare into the depths of his soup for long moments. Then he reached to take her hand, and bowed his head.

"For this nourishment and for the safety that Thou hast provided, we are eternally grateful. Amen."

When she opened her eyes, Willow regarded her husband in wonder. He'd never taken her hand before when he'd said grace. She'd heard of the custom, but never experienced it herself. But the thought of his hand in hers, strong and callused and *warm* as he'd offered his prayer, had made communing with God that much more special.

She felt the backs of her eyes prickle with inexplicable tears. Hoping that Charles wouldn't see them, she urged, "Now eat. I want to warm you from the inside out."

Thankfully, he seemed eager to comply.

Willow waited until he had nearly finished his broth before asking, "So Jenny was staying in the trapper's canyon?"

He nodded, chewing the bread with more care than was necessary. "It looked like she'd prepared well. She had blankets, firewood, tinned food."

"I should have known she was gone," Willow whispered.

Charles reached to hold her hand again. "You can't blame yourself. Judging by what happened to me, Jenny was in real trouble. Going to the trapper's cabin may have been her only option."

"Why didn't she come to one of us for help? The women of the Dovecote would have rallied around her. Sumner would have appealed to Jonah."

Charles shook his head. "We'll never know for sure. But…" He set his bread down on the tray only half-eaten, then sighed. "I'd wager that she was killed in the cabin. I found…an ax handle. I think that's what was used to hit her."

Willow bit her lip, focusing on Charles, on the quiet, somber gray of his eyes rather than on the images that sprang to mind.

"She must have brought the children here, then gone back to the cabin for some reason—maybe to gather the rest of her things." Charles's fingers tangled with Willow's. "Judging by the note left with the twins and what happened to me, Jenny knew that someone meant to harm her."

"Did you see who shot at you?"

He shook his head. "I didn't even realize I'd been shot. The gunman cornered me in the cabin, and I knew that I didn't have many options. I crashed through the window and ran for the trees on the riverbank." His features tensed. "I tried to look back, but with the wind and the snow, I couldn't see anything more than a shape. Then he raised his rifle. I tried to dive into the bushes, but I hit the slope instead and slid into the center of the river. Before I knew it, the ice broke beneath me and I was crashing through. The gunman must have decided that the cold water would take care of me, because I don't remember much after that. I vaguely recall hoisting myself out and crawling toward the shore."

"You said gunman. You're sure it was a man?"

He nodded. "If I had to hazard a guess, I'd say he was six feet or so. Broad in the shoulders." Charles sighed. "But everything was happening so fast that I saw little more than a silhouette. The man was probably wearing a coat…"

"But he was tall."

"Yeah. I'd say he was at least Jonah's height, but not quite as tall as Gideon."

"Well, that helps a little, doesn't it?"

He squeezed her hand. "You're right. It gives us one more piece to the puzzle."

"Did you hear a horse? A sleigh?"

Charles considered that point carefully. "I don't think so, but he couldn't have been on foot. Not with as quickly as he left the scene."

"So, that means it's someone who has access to the livery."

"Smalls was with you today. Anyone could have gone into the stables and borrowed a horse."

"Oh." She brightened. "But someone may have seen a horse and rider coming out of the livery. That's where we'll start tomorrow. I'll have a word with Lydia. She and the girls could ask a few subtle questions while they're circulating through the cook shack."

Charles laughed. "You're pretty smart, Mrs. Wanlass."

She loved the way the words sounded as they left his lips. Warm. Intimate. With a hint of a Scottish burr.

"I'm so glad you're all right." The declaration burst from her unbidden, but she wouldn't have called it back even if she could. He needed to know that she cared for him—cared about him. He was her friend.

Her friend and more.

She suddenly began to tremble, the events of the day crashing around her and leaving her inexplicably exhausted and vulnerable and weepy. Knowing that she couldn't bear to burst into tears in front of him, she jumped to her feet and gathered up his tray.

"I'll leave you to sleep. It's so late…and you've been through so much…"

But once again, he stopped her at the door. "Good night, Willow."

The words were innocuous.

But there was something in his eyes—something warm and rare and oh, so sweet—like the heat of the sun slipping down the mountain slope.

"Good night, Charles. Pleasant dreams."

Because of his injuries, Charles stayed home, but for only a few days. It didn't seem to matter what arguments Willow offered for why he should allow himself to recuperate for at least a week, the moment that the whistle blew for the early bird shift, he was dressed and ready to go.

"I've packed a lunch for you. There's biscuits and cheese and cold meats."

"Willow, the company provides our meals."

"I know." She clutched her hands in front of her. "But I don't want anyone saying that your wife doesn't care enough to make a meal."

Charles couldn't keep his lips from twitching. Unable to help himself, he reached out to cup her cheek in his hand—and she leaned into it.

"There's no doubt that you care for me, Willow. The fact that you saved my life proves that."

Her eyes grew wide. It didn't seem to matter how many times he told her that he was feeling fine, she didn't believe him. He wished he could think of a way to banish the worry from her gaze, but they both knew that any reassurances he might offer her were hollow. After the incident at the trapper's cabin, the threat to their little family had become more real.

"Lock the door behind me."

"I will."

"I've already taken care of the side door and I've put braces on all the windows so they can't be opened from the outside."

"I know."

"You've got the weapon I gave you?"

She pointed to the revolver on the table.

"I want you to keep it within arm's reach at all times."

"I will."

"When will the other women be here?"

When Jonah and Gideon had dropped by to check on Charles the day before, he had asked if a few of the women could spend the day with Willow so she wouldn't be alone.

"Lydia and Iona will be here after they finish in the cook shack. Sumner will be a little later."

"Creakle and Smalls will sit with you when it's time for the women to go."

She placed her hand over his. "We'll be fine."

"I—" The words lodged in his throat. How could he tell her how much he'd grown to rely on her calming influence? All his life, he'd struggled with his temper and the temptation to lash out. He'd grown used to tamping down his emotions so deeply that he believed, sometimes, as if he didn't feel anything at all. He'd built a wall around his heart and his head that no one had ever been able to penetrate fully.

But with Willow, those defenses were tumbling, brick by brick. And rather than feeling exposed…he felt *free*.

Free to be the man she thought he was.

"Willow… I hope you've been happy with me the last few weeks."

The comment seemed to take her by surprise, but the smile she gave him was so open, so honest, that it nearly took his breath away.

"Of course I have."

The words had the power to burn in his chest in a way that no others ever had.

"Willow, could—" Charles's throat seemed to close around the question he'd meant to ask.

Could you ever consider making this arrangement official?

Would you stay with me, as my wife, as my family, even after the spring thaw?

But before he could force such sentiments past the desert dryness of his tongue, one of the babies began to cry.

Charles would know that wail anywhere. Eva had a pitiful, heart-wrenching sob, where Adam's was lusty and full of impatience.

"I—I'd better go. The bairns are upstairs and…"

"I know."

Even though Eva's cries seemed to pull at Willow like an invisible string, she hesitated.

Did she sense what he'd been about to ask her? And could he bring himself to say the words aloud? After all, Willow was doing him a favor by pretending to be his wife. She spent each day taking care of him and the twins. Nevertheless, she had her own plans, her own dreams. She'd come thousands of miles, endured months of travel, only to be marooned in a mining community that she'd probably never heard of before the avalanche. It wouldn't be fair for Charles to presume that she might be willing to change those plans.

But maybe she would.

For the children, of course.

And for him.

Eva's howls became even more heart-wrenching.

"I have to go," Willow whispered.

"I know, I—" Charles shook his head.

There wasn't time for a conversation, let alone one of this magnitude. So he forced himself to take a step back, then another.

"Forget the meal you made for me. I'll see if I can break away for a few minutes at lunchtime. We can eat together."

He was sure he saw her eyes flare with something akin to pleasure.

"I'd like that."

She smiled, and for a moment, her expression held such infinite joy that he was able to convince himself the light shining from her gaze was for him.

All for him.

He grasped his hat from the peg, then opened the door. Even so, he couldn't prevent himself from turning back. Before she could do anything to dissuade him, he bent and brushed a light kiss on her cheek.

"See you soon," he murmured.

Then, before he could gauge her reaction to his impromptu farewell, he hurried into the cold, slamming the door behind him.

Willow stood rooted to the spot, her cheek tingling from the unexpected caress. As her mind reeled, her hand lifted to touch the spot.

As if by placing her palm there she could make the frisson of delight last that much longer.

Unfortunately, Adam chose that point to join in with Eva's displeasure, and Willow raced up the stairs.

"I'm sorry, little ones," she gasped as she rushed into the spare room. The twins were swiftly outgrowing their basket, so at night they slept in a nest of blankets on the floor. Thankfully, the twins were still small enough that she could scoop them both into her arms. Cradling them against her chest, she offered them soft shushing noises as she hurried to the window overlooking the street.

She parted the curtains ever so slightly. Below her, she could see Charles striding forcefully past the other row houses on his way to the mine entrance.

He must have felt her gaze. Just before heading out of sight, he turned.

Even at this distance, she could see his smile—and she was struck with the fact that, in all the Devotionals she'd attended, she had never seen him smile.

She parted the curtain even more, waving to him.

He paused, throwing her a quick salute.

Then he was gone.

Willow bent to place a kiss on each of the twins' heads as they calmed and subsided into hiccuping sighs.

"Daddy won't be long," she murmured against Eva's downy head.

It should have felt wrong to refer to Charles in that way. After all, this arrangement they shared was temporary.

Wasn't it?

It would have to be. The only way Charles could permanently stay with the mine was by annulling their marriage.

But hadn't he been given his position back? As a consultant?

Her brows creased in thought.

Sumner and Jonah were married. And Jonah had kept his job.

But Jonah had property outside the mining community.

So, could Charles and Willow be a family? A real family, if they moved off company property?

Would Charles even be open to the idea?

Adam rooted against her, making soft baby grunts that she knew signaled his hunger. She rubbed his back. If she already felt this overwhelming...*rightness* whenever she held Adam or Eva in her arms, how would she ever find the strength to leave them? As much as she might want to make them hers, she couldn't expect Mr. Ferron to take on the added responsibility of two more children. Especially since he had so many offspring of his own.

Then again...did she even want to finish her journey?

Willow shook her head to rid it of such thoughts. More than anything, she had to remember that her time with Charles was temporary. If she allowed herself to entertain any other ideas...

The inevitable parting would be unbearable.

Stiffening her spine, she pushed such thoughts away. She wouldn't think about that now. Not today.

"Today, you're mine," she whispered to the babies in her arms. "And if that's all I will ever have, then it will have to be enough, won't it?"

Neither of the children were capable of answering. But she took comfort in the way they burrowed against her.

So when she backed away, she nearly didn't see the shape below. It was only in the last second that she saw the figure of a man striding quickly between the houses on the opposite side of the lane. The man was tall, broad, well over six feet.

A frisson of gooseflesh skittered up her spine.

Someone had been watching them.

The women arrived less than an hour later, bursting into the house with a wave of laughter and chatter.

"Get your hat and coat, Willow!" Lydia called out as she slammed the door behind them.

Willow blinked at them uncomprehendingly, rocking Eva in her arms, even though the child had fallen asleep long ago.

"We're taking you and the children for a walk," Lydia announced. "We've already spoken to Sumner about it—in fact, it was her idea. The sun is out and she recommends that you and the children get some fresh air. We thought you could come with us to the Dovecote, have some tea and gossip with the other women."

"But... I promised Charles that I'd have lunch waiting for him."

"We'll get you back in plenty of time for that."

"I don't think it's a good idea. I don't have anything warm for the children or—"

Iona dropped a basket on the table. "We've taken care of all that. Don't you worry."

She removed a hand-knitted baby sacque. The thick jacket-like gown had been fashioned from navy wool with a drawstring at the bottom to ensure that the baby's feet stayed warm.

"The women have been knitting and crocheting for days. There are sacques for each of the twins, two wee hats and two pairs of infant stockings. I also have a couple of sturdy infant blankets for wrapping them up."

Willow couldn't prevent the way her mouth gaped. "How did you manage all this in such a short amount of time? And with so few provisions? I hope you didn't use up your precious hope chest items."

Emmarissa laughed. "We didn't need to—although we would have been glad to do it. But as soon as the miners heard about the babies, we started getting donations. We unraveled a sweater for yarn for the jackets and made the blankets by cutting up a larger quilt. All of the women helped. They've tried to give you and Charles enough time to settle in, but they're anxious to see the twins, and I don't think we can hold them off any longer. If you don't come, they've threatened to storm the Pinkertons."

Willow laughed, still hesitant. But when she thought of the figure she'd seen watching the house...

Wouldn't she be safer in the Dovecote, surrounded by Pinkerton guards?

"I'll get my things if you'll bundle up the children."

"Deal," Myra said, reaching for Eva.

Willow raced upstairs, where she took a moment to rebraid her hair, tighten the laces on her boots and take off her apron. Then she grabbed her cape, her bonnet and her gloves and clattered down the steps again.

She found the twins bundled up to their noses. Only their eyes were visible as they blinked curiously at the commotion that surrounded them.

For a moment, Willow hesitated. "Are you sure this is a good idea? The weather has been so bad the past little while..."

"It's warmer today. Promise." Lydia took her hand and drew her toward the door. "Besides, we have another surprise for you."

"But the babies will need—"

"We've already gathered their things," Emmarissa interrupted, holding up the basket that Iona had brought with her.

Since Greta and Iona already had a firm grip on the twins, Willow allowed herself to be pulled outside where, as promised, a brilliant sun glinted painfully off the newly fallen snow. The fringe of icicles hanging from the eaves pounded out an irregular tattoo onto the melting ice below.

It wasn't until Willow stepped into the street that she realized more of the women waited outside.

"Ta-da!" Millie called out with a flourish of her hand.

She and Marie moved aside to reveal a miniature version of Mr. Smalls's sledge. The long wooden box had been painted a bright green and a tiny version of the bench had been painted red. Red sleigh runners allowed the conveyance to slide easily across the snow, and the tongue portion had been fitted with a handle for pulling. On the side, someone had painted the Batchwell Bottoms Mine logo along with a flowing script that read Miner Training Program.

"Oh!" Willow's hands flew to her mouth.

"Isn't it sweet? Mr. Ramsey made the sledge and Sumner did the painting."

Willow felt tears prick at the backs of her eyes. The tiny sleigh must have taken hours of work.

"We've lined the box with warm bricks and a blanket. We'll bundle the babies inside and cover them with another quilt and they'll be right as rain."

Iona and Millie made short work of tucking the babies inside. Then Greta grabbed the handle, calling out, "*Kommen*, ladies. Come!"

Chapter Thirteen

The sound of the women's laughter and chatter soon enveloped Willow like a warm, familiar hug. Because of their large group, they eschewed the boardwalk and made their way down the center of the street, their retinue of Pinkerton guards trailing along behind them. This time of day, there weren't many wagons, just a few men on horseback, or pulling handcarts full of tools, and it was easy to avoid them. As they passed, the miners tipped their hats and called out their own greetings.

"Mornin', ladies."

"Mighty fine breakfast today!"

"Good day t'all y'all."

Willow tipped her face to the sun, enjoying the warmth upon her cheeks. She couldn't remember the last time she'd been forced to remain indoors for such an extended period of time. Perhaps when she'd worked in the woolen mills as a child? At school, once the teachers had despaired of her catching up with her peers, she'd been banished from the classrooms and put to work instead. She'd been told that she was being trained for service, but Willow hadn't been fooled. They'd needed someone to clean and fetch and carry.

At the head of their group, Emmarissa and Marie had begun to sing "Onward Christian Soldiers" at the tops of their lungs, and Willow didn't miss the smiles of the men who tipped their hats at them from the stoop in front of the barbershop.

Although being outside with the other women was as heady as a trip to a summer fair, Willow couldn't prevent the way her gaze scanned the onlookers. If she studied the men hard enough, would she be able to recognize the figure who'd been watching the house this morning? Even more importantly, would he give himself away?

"The children are beautiful, Willow. You must be so proud." Essie Esposito walked backward as she made the comment.

"I am."

"I think they're already beginning to grow," Miriam said warmly. "Their cheeks are filling out."

"Yes. The goat's milk seems to agree with them."

There was nothing suspicious about the men waiting outside the barbershop. They watched the women for a moment, then turned back to their own conversations. A few doors down, two men came out of the cook shack. But after lifting lazy hands to the women, they walked in the opposite direction.

A wagon appeared at one of the cross streets and the driver pulled up, waiting for the brides to pass. He tipped his hat and offered, "Howdy, ladies." But other than a broad grin, he didn't seem particularly interested in the group.

Willow started when a hand took hers. Looking up, she found Lydia by her side.

"You seem preoccupied," her friend murmured in a voice that would not carry to the others.

"I…"

Lydia squeezed her hand. "I knew this might make you nervous, leaving your house. But I hoped with the Pinkertons present that you could enjoy yourself."

Willow felt heat seep into her cheeks. Was she that transparent? If so, she wasn't going to make a very good detective.

"It's understandable," Lydia continued. "We're all a little on edge since Jenny was…"

Lydia seemed to find it hard to say the word.

Killed.

Murdered.

"For the first time since Batchwell insisted we have a guard, the women are actually taking the Pinkertons seriously. The past week or two, they've stayed close to home. Even when they leave the Dovecote for a walk around the meadow, they take one of the men along."

"Except for you," Willow said wryly. "You still slip their net to come visit me."

Lydia's brows rose. "I can take care of myself. I learned long ago not to venture anywhere without a derringer tucked into my corset."

Willow's eyes widened. "You don't!"

"I *do.* And oftentimes, there's another one tucked into my boot top, as well."

Honestly, Willow would never have thought that Lydia—the personification of high society femininity—would be armed to the teeth.

"You need to be careful, as well, Willow."

"I am. Charles has left a weapon with me whenever he leaves the house."

"Good."

There was a beat of silence between them. Two. They were nearing the Dovecote. Willow could see sunlight glinting off sparkling clean windows. Smoke rose from the chimney, and if she weren't mistaken, the scent of baking bread accompanied it.

"I doubt you've heard it yet, since the plans were only set this morning, but…they'll be holding Jenny's funeral tomorrow."

Willow felt her stomach lurch at the thought, even though she'd been expecting as much for days.

"When?"

"Right after the morning meal has been served in the cook shack."

Willow's eyes skipped over the glistening snow in the lane, the towering pines, the dull sheen of the frozen river in the distance.

"Where will they bury her?"

"I'm not sure yet. Sumner accompanied Jonah to the mine office to help finalize all of the plans. But I thought you should know."

"Yes. Yes, thank you."

"I'm sure that you'll want to attend, since you were Jenny's closest friend. Iona and I could watch the children for you. Surely Batchwell wouldn't begrudge us that much."

"But you'll want to attend the funeral yourself."

"It's more important that you feel comfortable leaving the children for a few hours."

Willow's brain skipped from Lydia's confession of a derringer tucked into her corset, to the figure she'd seen in the alley, to the sight of Charles soaked and chilled to near death.

"No, I…"

Her brain seized on Creakle and Smalls, to their fierce determination as they went hunting for Charles and their sweet devotion to the children.

"No. You should go to the funeral. I have a couple of baby minders in mind, and they're armed to the teeth."

Lydia smiled. "That sounds perfect."

Charles straightened from where he'd been examining the failed charges from the previous blasting of tunnel nine.

"Any ideas on what went wrong?" Jonah asked.

"Yeah. Half of these charges were dummies."

"What?"

Charles reached for a set of dynamite that hadn't exploded. The charge had been fashioned from six sticks lashed together. The center portion of dynamite held the blasting cap.

He tugged the cap free, then took a knife from his pocket and cut the cords that bound the bundle. "None of my men would be fooled by these. They've been at this too long."

To most people, the units of explosives might look identical. They were all the same length, the same width, and wrapped in the same red label. But to a blaster, the weight alone was enough to give things away.

"This one's real," Charles said, handing it to Jonah. "The rest are not." When he passed him another stick, the man's lips thinned.

"Who would do such a thing?"

Charles squinted, looking at the rock face of the tunnel. "I'd vouch for my men. They've got nothing to gain from this kind of sabotage."

"Sabotage?" Jonah echoed.

"I'm not accusing anyone. But that would be my take on things." He reached out to feel the blackened portions of the wall where soot and residue clung to the rock. "Looks to me like whoever did this intended for the blasting cap to be inserted into the one real stick. That way, you get a nice boom and some rubble, but not enough power to do the job." He pointed to the units that Jonah held. "I think he got careless and put the cap in the wrong stick on this one."

Using his knife again, Charles sliced open one of the dummy charges. A trickle of white powder dribbled out. He leaned down to sniff it, then rubbed the substance between his thumb and forefinger.

"Flour."

A muscle worked in Jonah's jaw.

"Any of the blasters would have found the switch as soon as they picked it up. I'm not saying that it's impossible that one of them is involved, but I've been working with them a long time. I can't imagine any of them doing it."

"So, someone came along afterward and changed things."

"Aye. And even worse...that means someone out there has a stash of stolen dynamite."

Willow had missed the hustle and bustle of the Dovecote. From the moment she and the children appeared, they were welcomed inside, and ushered to a spot in front of the fire. Soon, she was being plied with cups of cocoa and a hot breakfast.

She hadn't realized how vigilant she had become, always listening for a sound out of place or a shadow at the window. But here, she was among friends, and her guard dropped. Before she knew what had happened, the children were whisked away from her and passed from one woman to another.

"You must still feel shaken after Charles's accident," Iona said, taking a seat nearby.

Willow lowered her eyes. It had been impossible to keep the news secret about his plunge into the river. But they'd managed to pass it off as a freak occurrence.

Iona reached to squeeze Willow's hand. "I can't imagine how frightened you must have been when they brought him home."

Again, Willow nodded.

Lydia dropped into a chair. "The Pinkertons said they'd be happy to escort you back before lunch, so you can relax and enjoy your visit."

Iona patted Willow's hand. "There, you see? We'll all have a wonderful morning with you and the babies."

It wasn't until an hour later that Willow was able to slip away. While the other women were engrossed with the twins, she made an excuse to go to the kitchen, then took the back stairs to the upper rooms. If Jenny's belongings hadn't been boxed up, maybe she could see if someone had rifled through her things.

Knowing that some of the floorboards creaked, Willow kept to the side of the corridor until she reached the room that she and Jenny had shared.

For all she knew, the room had been assigned to someone else. Willow's belongings had long since been moved to Charles's house, and with Jenny gone, there wouldn't be much sense in keeping the room empty.

Thankfully, as she slipped inside, she was able to see that all her friend's belongings were there. Even though…

Someone had been here. She was sure of it.

Willow examined the things on the dresser, taking in the mirror and comb that belonged to the same set that Charles had found. Jenny had been very particular about her belongings, always arranging them in the same order. Willow doubted that anyone else would have noticed, but many of the items had been moved.

She supposed there could be a logical explanation. The objects could have been shifted during cleaning, or when the girls had picked up Willow's belongings.

But when she bent to open Jenny's trunk, it was obvious that it had been searched. The contents were jumbled and pushed to the side. A pot of powder had been spilled over her Sunday-best gown, and letters and papers had been torn from their envelopes.

Willow had difficulty deciphering the script on the pages, so she carefully folded them again and put them on Jenny's bed. Her cheeks grew hot when she realized that she would have to ask Charles to read them, and in doing so, he would understand the limits to her education...

She thrust that thought aside. There was no room for pride where the twins' safety was concerned.

She took a few more minutes to go through the trunk. Just as she'd thought, the woolen stocking where Jenny had hidden some of her valuables had been dumped out. The earrings and coins that had been stashed in the toe were still there. Only the rattle was gone.

Saddened, Willow neatly folded Jenny's clothing and placed the garments back in their places. As she did so, she tried to decide if anything else was missing.

She couldn't think of anything. Like Willow, Jenny had come to the American Territories from England. She'd brought only the necessities and some hand-sewn items, most of which had been completed on her journey as a way to pass the time. The only other thing that had ever occupied her leisure had been her...

Her journal.

How could she have forgotten the woman's journal? Each evening, Jenny had made a careful entry in the leather-bound book. Willow had watched her friend with envy as she'd filled page after page with her elegant script, sometimes spending hours on the task. She'd told Willow that it was a way for her to think things through, to savor the good times and overcome the bad. She'd even pressed mementos between the pages—hair ribbons and blossoms, her ticket stubs and itineraries. Here in Bachelor Bottoms, she'd collected things from her walks: pine needles, holly leaves, a feather from a hawk.

Someone else must have remembered the book, either to uncover clues surrounding her murder...

Or to destroy something that Jenny had written.

"Please let it be here," Willow whispered, digging down below the stacks of clothing in the other woman's trunk. The tip of her finger felt carefully, finding the spot where one of the corners had a piece of missing wood.

To anyone unfamiliar with Jenny's habits or her trunk, the tiny imperfection would probably have gone unnoticed. Willow might well be the only person in Bachelor Bottoms who knew that the plank was actually a false bottom that could be lifted up and...

Her breath escaped in a slow whoosh. In the narrow space, she could see that all Jenny's treasures were intact. A fob watch that had belonged to her mother, a sack with a half-dozen gold coins.

And the journal.

Willow snatched up the book, setting it on the bed next to the letters. Then she quickly settled the bottom back into place and straightened the rest of Jenny's belongings. Only when she felt like everything had been given the attention it deserved did she stand.

For a moment, she paused, pondering her next course of action. She didn't have much time. At any moment one of the other women could come looking for her. If someone did, how was she going to explain why she had taken Jenny's things?

"Willow?"

The faint cry came from downstairs and Willow panicked. She didn't have a reticule with her or even a coat pocket.

Acting quickly, she shoved the letters into the journal, then tucked the book into the waistband of her petticoat. The dress she wore was just loose enough at the waist to hide the book as long as she was careful.

She was shaking her skirts out when the door suddenly opened.

"I wondered if you were up here," Lydia said. "You gave us all a start when we couldn't find you."

Willow feared the smile she summoned looked as shaky as she felt. "I just wanted to…"

"Visit the last place you saw Jenny?"

Willow nodded, hoping that the heat seeping up her neck wasn't noticeable. She'd never been much good at getting away with a lie.

"You must miss her, what with all the time you spent together."

Not trusting her voice, Willow nodded again.

"That's why none of us have packed up her things. It seems somehow…disrespectful to move someone else in here. It's too…soon."

Willow wrapped her arms around her waist to hold the journal more securely. "Yes."

"One of these days, you and I will pack up the little bits and pieces she has scattered around the room. I'm sure that Jenny would have wanted you to keep her things."

"No, I couldn't! I…"

The words died in her throat. Willow might not have felt comfortable taking them. But someday, when the children were grown, wouldn't they want something of their mother's?

Lydia must have sensed some of Willow's chaotic emotions because she stepped forward to enfold her in a hug. Willow squeezed her eyes shut, praying that the other woman wouldn't sense the hard shape of the journal or the pounding of her heart. But when Lydia drew back again, her pale blue eyes were full of understanding.

"There's plenty of time to decide all that. It's still months away from spring. In the meantime, none of Jenny's things are going anywhere. They'll stay right here, in this room where they belong."

In the end, it proved impossible for Charles to break away during the middle of the day—and he rued that fact. He'd wanted to check on Willow and the children.

But with the possibility of sabotage in the mines and nearly a case of missing dynamite, he'd stayed in the tunnels, looking for any clues that might lead to the culprit. Charles was still preoccupied about the dummy charges when the whistle blew, signaling the end of the shift.

Normally, he would join the tide, follow the other men from the mine to the Meeting House, where evening Devotional would be held, then from there to the cook shack for their meal.

But since he'd confessed to being a husband and father, he hadn't stepped foot in the Meeting House. It didn't feel right to gather for worship with the other men when he continued to mislead them. Even if it meant the safety of two wee bairns.

"Will y' be comin' with us, Charles?"

He looked up to find one of his crew members lingering at the end of the tunnel.

Not knowing how he should respond, Charles offered noncommittally, "You go ahead. I'll follow along in a minute."

Hal Groberg nodded. "We sure do miss your sermons, Charles. It's just not the same without y' there."

The man left, sparing Charles from having to come up with a comment. What could he say? Truth be told, he missed the Devotionals himself, not so much for the words he'd imparted, but for the fellowship of the men. It strengthened him to be with others who pushed their worldly cares away twice a day to focus on their spiritual paths.

Gathering up the last of his schematics, Charles headed to the tunnel office, where he stowed his equipment and the drawings.

For several moments, he stood in indecision, reluctant to leave until the others had filtered into the Meeting House. As his gaze scanned the office, he saw the small desk where Creakle generally tallied up the hours for the payroll.

Charles crossed to the desk and spread open the ledger, quickly rifling through the pages.

The mine had strict safety rules, as well as a means of tracking the men while they were below ground. A guard station was set up at the head of the two main tunnels. A pegboard held a series of numbered brass badges that were assigned to each miner, and each miner had two badges. One remained on the pegboard. The other went into the miner's pocket. A man couldn't go in or out of the tunnel without taking or leaving a badge. As soon as he did, the security officer would make a notation in the log.

Charles ran his finger down the page. He doubted that the charges could have been tampered with during the shifts. There were too many men going about their business. More likely, it would happen between the early bird shift and the hoot owl shift. Whoever had switched the dynamite could have let the other men go ahead, then made the changes while the other miners went to Devotional—much like Charles was doing now. The culprit could have had an hour. Two, if he worked while the rest of the camp was getting their evening meal.

Charles flipped the page.

January 16.

There were two entries leaving the mine later than the others. Theo Caruso and…

Charles Wanlass.

What on earth?

He squinted, sure that he'd read things wrong. The penmanship in the ledger came from someone with an illegible scrawl, and a few of the entries required some deciphering.

But, no. Written in a jagged script was his own name, along with his assigned badge number, forty-seven.

Perhaps the badge had been given to another worker when Charles had resigned, and the man at the checkpoint had used Charles's name out of habit.

But even that didn't make sense. When he'd returned as a consultant, he'd continued to use his old identification. The only time he'd been away from the mine since then were the three days he took to recover from his plunge into the river.

"Boss man?"

Charles started, slamming the book shut. He was reaching for his hat and coat when Creakle poked his head in the door.

"If'n yer about done here, yer missus sent me t' tell you that yer supper is hot and on the stove."

"Thanks, Creakle. Why don't you and Smalls head on to Devotional? I'll be going straight home."

"Thank ye kindly. I hear tell it's stew fer dinner at the

cook shack tonight, so's me an Smalls will be wantin' to find a seat by the door so's we can clip out right after the closing prayer."

Creakle offered a wink and Charles laughed.

"Don't let me keep you then. Go do what you need to do."

"'Night, boss."

"Good night, Creakle."

Charles waited until he'd disappeared, then returned to the ledger on the desk. If he hurried, he'd be able to see how many of the men on their suspect list had been in the mine the day Jenny had been killed. Since she'd been discovered after the evening Devotional, and her body had already grown cold, Charles felt that it would be safe to assume that she would have been killed before the shift ended.

"So let's see how many of you were off duty or left before the whistle, shall we, now?"

After her visit to the Dovecote, Willow's day had taken a turn for the worse. From the moment she'd stepped inside Charles's home, something had felt wrong. As if someone had been there. But try as she might, she couldn't find any evidence to support her misgivings. Nevertheless, as she moved from task to task, she couldn't keep her mind focused. She grew jumpy. Out of sorts.

Willow ran to move a cast-iron skillet from the stove before the sizzling bacon could burn, only to blister her hand when she forgot to use a hot pad. By the time she grabbed a cloth and shifted the bacon, the scent of charred meat stung the air. Lifting the lid to the pot at the rear, she groaned when she discovered that the beans had boiled dry and were now a caked, scorched mess.

"Oh, no," she whispered.

Ever since Charles had sent word that he wouldn't be able to join her for lunch, she'd been planning this meal, knowing that he would be returning after his first full shift. She'd meant to lay a beautiful table, have the house tidied just so and set hot food in front of him as soon as he walked through the door.

But from the beginning, events had conspired against her. The weather had closed in again, and what had begun as a simple snowfall soon became an all-out blizzard. Because of that, the other women had not been able to drop by for another visit before going to the cook shack. Willow had grown to rely on having them help with the children for a few minutes so that she could change her clothes and ready the table, so she'd immediately fallen behind in her preparations. Even Mr. Creakle and Mr. Smalls had been pulled away from their guard duties when they'd been summoned with many other off-duty miners to help clear the roof of the storehouse. Because of its large size, the structure had a flat top, and the accumulation of snow was threatening to bring it all down. Since the storehouse was vital to the camp's survival, anyone not assigned to mining work had been enlisted.

Already worried by the figure she'd seen watching the house that morning, Willow had tried to concentrate on her tasks. But the weather had made the children fractious. Their pitiful cries had eased only when Willow held them and walked around and around the keeping room. Because she could feed only one of them at a time, their schedules had become staggered, and it seemed she had no sooner fed and calmed one infant before the other would begin to cry.

Since she'd spent so much time with the babies, the laundry had begun to pile up. A stack of soiled diapers waited in a basket at the side door, a mortifying symbol for all the world to see that she was unable to cope. By mid-afternoon, Willow was exhausted and her plans for the perfect dinner gave way to something hot to eat. Dishes began to mount in the sink. She grew jumpy, listening for a creak on the stoop to signal that Creakle or Smalls had returned, or that Charles had come home early—anything that might mean she could catch just a few minutes sleep so that she could think coherently. But every time she was sure she heard a noise, she would step to the window to see…

Nothing. Nothing but wind-driven snow flinging itself at the glass.

Yet even in that nothingness…she felt as if she were being watched.

A sob rose in her throat, but she pushed it back. She wasn't some hysterical ninny. She had no reason to cry. She'd endured far worse than a few sleepless nights and some dirty dishes.

So why did she feel so…weepy?

A bang at the door caused her to start and she whirled to stare at the rough wooden planks. For a moment, she couldn't move, a sense of doom growing in her chest.

What if it was Jenny's killer?

What if—

"Willow? It's Charles."

She rushed toward the familiar deep voice as if it were a lifeline. Throwing the bolt, she whipped open the door. Then, before she could speak or even move to allow him room to come inside, she burst into tears.

Chapter Fourteen

To his credit, Charles didn't turn and run. Instead, he strode toward her, slamming the door shut behind him. Then, before she could even explain, he pulled her into his arms.

"What's wrong?"

Willow could hear the alarm in his voice, but she couldn't seem to form words, so she clung to him, her fingers digging into the muscles of his shoulders. All the frustrations of the day, her fear, her loneliness, her weariness, poured from her in a storm of emotion. Only after he held her for long, aching moments was she able to stammer, "B-babies crying…window…s-someone…"

Then the sobs made even those words incomprehensible.

To his credit, Charles seemed to know what to do. He enfolded her even more tightly in his arms, offering her his warmth and strength. He made soft shushing noises, much as he would when Eva cried as if her heart would break if her bottle was too long in coming.

Willow tried to calm herself, but his tenderness caused her to cry even harder.

Charles was such a good man—the kind of person any

woman would want to marry. But she knew that as soon as he saw the mess around him, he would throw her out into the snow. He'd always kept his house neat and orderly. He would have no use for a woman who couldn't do the same.

"Willow, Willow. Talk to me," he murmured next to her ear. "Please, talk to me. Has someone hurt you?"

She shook her head against his chest.

"Are you sick?"

"N-no."

"Then what? Tell me so I can help you."

She sobbed, then finally stammered, "I—I'm a h-h-horrible wife. A h-h-horrible mother."

"What? Why would you say such a thing?"

He drew back so that he could look at her. But Willow found it difficult to meet his gaze.

"I—I burned the d-d-dinner and the children were crying. There're diapers on the doorstep and dishes in the sink. And...and..."

"And you're wonderful," he whispered. "Wonderful."

She tried to shake her head, but he drew her close again, rocking her slightly.

"Maybe it was too soon for me to go back to the mine."

The statement was so shocking, so completely unexpected, it was her turn to draw back. "No! It's because of me that you lost your job in the first place! I should be able to cope with everything. I shouldn't be—"

"Stop it. You haven't done anything wrong, Willow."

"But..." Her eyes flooded with tears again. "The mess."

He smiled, his eyes crinkling at the corners. "I don't see a mess."

"But—"

"I see a *home*, Willow. This..." He gestured to the

room around them. "This is the first sign of life this house has ever had. Before you and the twins came, I had four walls and shelter from the cold. But now..." He shook his head with something akin to wonder. "Now, I see life and motion and purpose."

He cupped her face with his palms. Those broad, strong palms. And the tears nearly came again—not from distress this time, but from the way that he made her feel.

Loved.

Cherished.

"I should have told you how you amaze me," he continued. "You're kind and loving and honorable. Any man would be proud to have you as his helpmate. And the fact that you've managed to juggle as many of these new duties as you have amazes me. In the space of a few hours, you became a wife and the mother of twins." His voice rose in emphasis. "Any other woman would have had time to come to terms with those facts. Instead, you've married a stranger and adopted Adam and Eva into your heart as if they were your own. I think that's amazing."

She tried to shake her head again, but he held her fast.

"Amazing," he whispered again. "And I should have helped more."

"No, you've—"

Again he stopped her.

"Yes. I should have helped you with the midnight feedings last night. Instead, as a thoughtful wife, you let me sleep so that I could be well rested when I returned to work. I doubt you've had more than three hours sleep in the last twenty-four."

Again, the telling tears gathered.

"Any man would be lucky to have you as his wife, Willow."

She opened her mouth, knowing that he needed to

know the rest. But she hesitated, fearing that Charles wouldn't be so quick to praise her if he knew that she was the product of a less than sterling past. Her father had been imprisoned for debt. And a childhood spent at a charity school had left her barely able to read and write. She couldn't imagine how any man—especially one as honorable as Charles—could know such things and continue to regard her as his equal. As his partner.

Tears flooded her eyes again, plunging down her cheeks.

Charles frowned, wiping them away with his thumbs.

"Shh. Shh. You're worn-out, ye are." His brogue, which was usually no more than a soft lilt, became more pronounced. "Right now, me dearlin', ye need sleep. Get yourself up to bed and I'll bring ye a tray. Then, after you've eaten, I want ye to sleep."

"But—"

"Shh. I'll have no more arguments. Tonight, I'll take care of the wee bairns."

"But dinner—"

"I'll rescue what I can, and barring all else, I can manage an egg and some tea."

He placed a kiss on her forehead.

"Upstairs wi' ye."

Reluctantly, she broke away. But even as she regarded the messy keeping room, the dirty dishes, and heard the first faint baby grumbles coming from Adam—who would soon want to eat—she felt an inexplicable lightness settling around her heart.

"Maybe I should wait until—"

"Go."

She would have stood her ground and argued further, but the gentleness of Charles's expression was her undoing. Not wanting to fall to pieces in front of him again, she gathered her skirts and hurried upstairs.

"And how can such a wee laddie put away so much in that little tummy, eh?" Charles murmured.

He held Adam cradled in his palms, gently bouncing the baby, speaking nonsense to the bairn. The babe had finished his milk and issued a lusty belch, but he didn't seem inclined to fall back to sleep as his sister had done. Instead, he regarded Charles with wide blue eyes, appearing to hang on every word that Charles said.

The faint creak of a floorboard alerted Charles, and he looked up to find Willow peering at him from the top of the stairs. She wore that frilly wrapper that he had seen once before. The one with the pale little flowers and yards and yards of ruffles and lace.

"There's your mum. You'll have to tell her how we men held down the fort during the night. Nary a dish has been done, we're afraid to admit. Nor have we tackled the laundry. It seems we spent the night walking and rocking and talking, but that's a fine thing for a da and his bairns to be doing, isn't it?"

Adam's lips lifted in an expression that was half smile, half yawn, but Charles decided to interpret it as good humor.

"And how is Adam's mummy feeling this morning?"

Willow's smile was sheepish. "Much better, thank you."

"A night's rest is as good as a cure, isn't it, Master Adam."

The baby stretched contentedly.

"Aren't you supposed to be at work?"

Charles shook his head. "We're just about ready to blast the new tunnel. But with the funeral…"

He'd forgotten to tell her, but when she nodded, he realized that one of the other women must have relayed the information to her.

"What time will it be?" she asked.

"Eleven. I've arranged for Creakle and Smalls to come watch the children for us."

That caused a ghost of a smile. "I had planned to ask them as well, so I'm glad they already know." She shifted uncomfortably, her fingers pulling the neck of her wrapper tighter. Then she murmured, "I'll get break-fast started."

"No need. There's a plate waiting for you in the warm-ing oven. Nothing too fancy, I'm afraid. Just egg and toasted bread."

Willow padded barefoot toward the kitchen and Charles tried not to stare. She was a dainty lass, through and through.

She disappeared for a moment behind the partition, but he heard her soft exclamation. "You made toad-in-the-hole."

"Sorry. Told you my skills were a wee bit limited."

Willow appeared almost immediately, juggling her hot plate as she hurried to the table. "No, you don't un-derstand. At school, we were only allowed eggs on spe-cial occasions. And toad-in-the-hole? There was only one cook who would bother to take the time to make it."

"So you went to a boardin' school, then?"

She seemed to freeze at the question, then looked up at him with something close to guilt in her eyes. Charles watched as her skin paled, her freckles growing even more pronounced. She seemed to war with her own thoughts for a moment before saying, "I attended the Good Shepherd Charity School for Young Girls."

The pronouncement was made hesitantly, almost painfully. Then she looked up, clearly waiting for a response.

Not knowing what she meant for him to say, Charles offered, "Oh, aye? Did you like it there?"

"No!"

The word burst from her lips so forcefully that Adam started in Charles's hands, his little head turning toward the sound.

Charles had the feeling that he'd suddenly stumbled into a famed minefield.

"It must have been hard for you. Being away from your family."

"My mother had already passed away by that time. Da and I tried to keep up, working in the mills and all. But there was an accident. A boiler exploded and he was badly burned."

Too late, Charles realized he knew so little about Willow that he'd blundered into painful territory.

He knew enough about the culture of mining communities to anticipate what had happened next. A mill wasn't so different. Like Batchwell Bottoms, the factory had probably provided company housing, company meals, company stores. But if a man couldn't work, he'd be cut loose.

"So, even though the accident occurred through no fault of his own, he was...let go?"

Willow regarded him with surprise. "Yes," she whispered.

"How long was he out of work?"

"He never really recovered enough to...go back to work."

"Ach, lassie," Charles said, his heart aching for what must have occurred. With no job, Willow and her father would probably have been penniless and homeless.

"I tried to keep up with my own mill job at the time."

"How old were you?"

"Ten."

Charles regarded her in disbelief. Child labor was an all-too-real fact in England—in America, too. But in his opinion, it was a horrible practice. As much as he'd deplored his own existence in the foundling home, at least he'd been kept out of the workforce until he'd been old enough to ken the dangers.

Willow poked at the toasted bread on the plate, then at the egg that had been cooked into the hollowed-out spot in the center.

"We were able to get by for a time, but then the debt collectors began gathering." She met Charles's gaze again, her shoulders stiffening in a way that was at once defiant yet wary. It hurt his heart, the way she seemed to brace herself for criticism. "They sent my father to debtor's prison and me to Good Shepherd."

For a moment, she looked so young, so fragile, that Charles could imagine how she must have looked all those years ago. He could all but see her standing on the steps of the charity school, her hair a wild tangle of curls, her cornflower-blue eyes too large in her face, her freckles the only spots of color to her pale skin.

"Ach, lassie, you must have been so frightened."

Her brows creased in confusion. Somehow, she seemed puzzled by his response.

"You don't hate me?"

"Hate you?"

"I—I came into your house under false pretenses. My father was a debtor. He was sent to prison."

Charles lowered Adam into the basket, tucked the blanket around him, then turned back to Willow.

"And that has aught to do with you. By my account,

it was a string of unhappy accidents that led to such an unfortunate situation, not a lack of character. But then, the whole idea of debtor's prison has always left a bad taste in my mouth. In my opinion, men such as your father need a hand up, not incarceration."

He'd said the wrong thing again. Her eyes were filling with tears.

He hurried to kneel beside her.

"Please, don't cry. It rips me up inside when you're sad. There's nothing on earth that I want more than to make you happy."

She blinked quickly, wiping at the moisture beading on her lashes.

"You don't understand. I'm not like the other girls." She waved a hand in the vague direction of the Dovecote. "I'm not pretty or refined. I went to a *charity* school— and even the other students there looked down on me. They said the stain of my father's actions would be my burden to carry for the rest of my life. That I would have to live in penance—"

"Stop!" Charles stood, pulling her into his arms, his chest burning with a slow, simmering anger.

What kind of people would say such a thing? To a child who had already had her whole family torn away from her through no fault of her own?

"They were wrong, Willow. About you and your father. If anyone is to blame, it's whatever faulty equipment or negligence or…act of nature caused the mill's boiler to blow. It's untenable that anyone—let alone a teacher or a person who has control over a child—could ever say such a thing. And for it to be a charity school…" He drew back so she would see the fierceness of his expression. "The Bible defines charity as 'the pure love of Christ.' What you experienced wasn't love."

She looked up at him with such wide, disbelieving eyes that he couldn't prevent himself from saying, "They should have loved you, Willow."

Then he brushed his lips over hers, willing her to believe him, to know that she was loved.

Even if he couldn't bring himself to say the words aloud.

While Willow finished her breakfast, Charles went outside to clean the snow away from the stoop and make a path to the lean-to and the road, then milk the goat.

Unaccountably, she was grateful to have a few minutes alone to absorb everything that had happened.

He'd kissed her.

Not a peck on the cheek like they'd shared at their wedding. No, it had been filled with tenderness and devotion.

And that had been *after* she'd confessed the truth about her father and her upbringing.

She felt a prickle of tears, but forced them away. No more crying. No. More. If anything, she should be shouting from the rooftops.

Charles didn't look down upon her for being the daughter of a debtor, as so many men would have done. He didn't question her own morality or her reputation.

If anything, he understood.

The fact still shuddered through her in a wave of astonishment. The headmistress of Good Shepherd had never passed up an opportunity to warn Willow that her prospects for marriage were ruined and that her reputation as a woman of good character was already irreparably destroyed. Again and again, she'd informed Willow that there was no future for her other than a life of drudg-

ery. The best she could hope for would be a service position.

That was why Willow had been willing to agree to
a marriage of convenience. If she were meant for such
a life, she would rather choose it under her own terms
than Mistress Owl's.

But Charles hadn't seemed to see such limitations. In
fact, he seemed to think that she'd been wronged.

Taking her empty plate to the dry sink, she set a pot
of water on the stove to heat for washing, then hurried
upstairs to change her clothes.

Mindful of the fact that the funeral would be held later
that day, she briefly considered whether she should don
her old Sunday-best dress. It was the only thing she had
that was pure black. But even as she reached for it, she
hesitated. So much had changed for her—and in such a
short amount of time. She wasn't the same person who
had hidden behind the ill-fitting clothes from a charity
box. Now…

She was Charles's wife.

Even if it only lasted a little while.

In the end, she chose a black skirt and a black-and-
gray tweed jacket. She was pressing against the boundar-
ies of mourning, but since she'd have her cloak on most
of the time—and it was black as well—she didn't think
anyone would think ill of her choice.

As she rushed downstairs, she found Charles with his
hands braced on the table, leaning over to study the chart
that they'd made.

"Come look at this," he said, without turning around.

She moved beside him, and when he looked up, he
opened his mouth to say something, then seemed to lose
his train of thought.

"You look so bonny."

He spoke with a tone so full of wonder that she could scarcely credit the comment was meant for her.

Her hands smoothed down the ornate jet buttons of the jacket. "It's just something that Lydia gave me. I don't have any pretty things of my own."

Charles's lips twitched. "I know."

Her mouth dropped open, and he laughed.

"When are you going to burn those ugly black tents you wore those first few weeks you were here?"

"There's nothing wrong with them!"

"There's everything wrong with them," he said wryly, then straightened. He reached to caress her cheek with one knuckle. "I'm guessing they were more offerings of charity by your charity school?"

She nodded.

"Then you should burn them."

"You can't possibly mean that! They still have plenty of wear in them."

"And every time you wore them, you'd be reminded of the unkind people who forced you to accept them."

"I could cut them down and make something," she offered. But she was losing the power of her argument.

"I'd be happy to burn them for you."

"You will *not*!"

"Then I'll have Sumner or Lydia do it for me. I'm sure if I asked, they'd be willing to do it."

"You will do no such thing, Charles Wanlass!"

Her retort merely caused his smile to widen—and the effect was intoxicating. The hard angles of his face relaxed, became almost boyish.

"Only if you promise never to wear them again."

"I..." She wanted to tell him that he was ridiculous, but she couldn't say the words. Not when so much of what he'd said was true. He'd filled her life with so much joy that she couldn't bear the thought of wearing the dresses that had brought her so much humiliation. "I promise," she finally said.

His eyes crinkled at the corners as his smile became an all-out grin.

"Good. Now, come here."

Before she knew what he meant to do, he tucked her between his arms, then pointed to the chart with one hand.

"I've crossed out some names. I had a chance to go through the shift logs in the mine, and these men were on duty."

He pointed to a host of eliminated suspects.

"Which leaves only three names," Willow said breathlessly.

"Three *miners*. Theo Caruso, Francis Diggory and Orie Keefe." He pointed to a separate list that still contained Misters Hepplewhite and Wilmott, and the train employees.

"I don't think Mr. Hepplewhite or Mr. Wilmott should be part of our list. Jenny was joining her *husband*. They were already married."

"True." Charles picked up a pencil and drew a line through their names. "That means we've narrowed the list down to eight. That's considerably smaller than it was, *and* we've eliminated the two miners, Wilmott and Hepplewhite, who live in the block where Gideon traced the blood trail."

"Oh!"

Willow wriggled free from his loose embrace, hurrying to open the drawer where the linens were stored. Digging to the bottom, she withdrew Jenny's journal.

"I was able to retrieve this from the Dovecote. It's Jenny's."

He opened it, rifled through the pages for a moment, then met Willow's gaze.

"Did you read it? What did she write just before she died?"

Willow hesitated, then mentally kicked herself. Charles had been so accepting of everything else, why not confess her final secret?

"It's written in script. I never learned to read script. I barely learned to read or make my block print."

There was no shock, no dismay. If anything, his features became even kinder. Handing her the book, he said, "Then tuck it away again. We'll look at it together. Tonight. After the funeral."

He couldn't have known that with that simple response, he mended a hole in her heart that had been there since she'd been forced to leave her father. In that instant, he'd conveyed to Willow that it didn't matter where she came from or what circumstances had led her to his door.

He cared for her.

Just the way she was.

"Thank you, Charles," she whispered.

His brows rose.

"For what?"

She wasn't sure how to explain—not without encouraging the return of her tears. So she smiled and said, "For helping me. For helping the twins."

His eyes grew warm and gray, like a lake after a refreshing summer storm.

"There's nothing that I've ever wanted to do more."

Chapter Fifteen

Before dressing for the funeral, Charles went outside one last time, intent on gathering enough firewood for the rest of the evening and the following day. Even more importantly, he wanted enough dry firewood on hand for Willow to use while he was at the mine. He would have to leave long before dawn. He and his men would be blasting the tunnel in between the shift change, and it was Charles's custom to check the charges and the priming cord again and again to make sure that everything was properly set and every safety precaution had been taken. That meant that Willow would be on her own for a few hours, and he didn't want her going outside. He could milk the goat before he left, lay the fires, and then the house would be warm for his family when they awoke.

He was reaching for the ax that was kept on a hook in the lean-to when a deep voice said, "Let me do that. You're so absentminded lately, you'll probably lop off your own foot."

Charles glanced over his shoulder, but didn't rise to the bait. "Hello, Gideon. How are the Pinkertons?"

"Nervous. It seems that the brides are being more docile than usual. Except for the ladies who keep sneaking over here between mealtimes, there haven't been as many attempts by the girls to slip the coop, if you'll pardon the pun."

"Maybe they've finally resigned themselves to being under your men's guard."

Gideon made a noise that was half laugh, half groan. "I doubt that."

He grabbed a log from the pile, set it on the stump that Charles reserved for that purpose, then swung, slicing it neatly in half.

Normally, Charles would object to anyone taking over a chore that he regarded as his own. But Gideon seemed to need the exercise to take the edge off his mood, and Charles...

Well, he was feeling just fine.

He leaned a shoulder against the door frame and relaxed even more as Gideon sliced the halves into quarters, then tossed them into a pile.

"Then what do you think is going on?"

"They're either spooked by Jenny's murder..."

"Or?"

"Or they're planning a revolt."

Charles rolled his eyes—a reaction that seemed to upset Gideon even more.

He tossed the wood aside and grabbed another log, then shook his finger at Charles. "You mark my words. I wouldn't put it past them."

"And what are they going to revolt against? They've got the Dovecote to live in, access to the cook shack. They have their own doctor, their own medical facilities...what more could they want?"

Gideon shook his finger again, opened his mouth, shut it, then confessed, "I don't know. But if something happens, no doubt Lydia Tomlinson will be at the heart of it."

Charles couldn't help grinning. "Do you really think she'd be so...devious?"

"Yes."

"To what end?"

"I don't know!"

Gideon set another log on the stump.

He seemed to chew on his thoughts for a few minutes, all the while adding to the pile of firewood. At this rate, Charles wouldn't have to split logs for a week.

"I tell you, Charles, you've got to get back onto that pulpit."

Charles wasn't sure how the conversation had circled back to his former role as lay preacher.

"Why?"

"Because they can't seem to find anyone who will stick. Fredrickson was the first man they appointed. The poor fellow was so terrified, I thought he'd shake right out of his boots. Didn't come back again. Then it was Lester Dobbs. That man could talk the hind leg off a mule, but he spent the whole time reading so softly from the Bible that no one could hear him. I hear tell that Bottoms relieved him of his duties..." Gideon affected a quavering voice that sounded remarkably similar to Phineas Bottoms.

"Next, they asked Theo Caruso."

Charles straightened, recognizing one of the names left on the chart listing Willow and his suspects.

"Caruso? How'd that go?"

Gideon tipped his head back, resting the ax on the stump, his expression becoming pained.

"Honest to Pete, Charles. I've never heard anything quite like it. That man rails on and on about the wages of sin and where we'll all end up if we didn't repent. If

I'd had to listen to him much longer, I wouldn't have had the will to live."

Charles couldn't help laughing. "What do you know about the man himself?"

"He's new. He hasn't been here for more than…six months? He works with the mules, bringing the ore out of the tunnels, so you probably wouldn't have had much contact with him."

Gideon shot a meaningful look at Charles.

"I'm beginning to believe the man has a guilty conscience," Gault continued. "Maybe that's why he can't seem to get off the subject of death and sin and the punishments reserved for the wicked."

Charles wanted to pepper Gideon with questions. But he'd learned long ago that the man clammed up if he felt he was being interrogated—which was probably why he and Lydia didn't get along too well. She tended to needle the Pinkerton with questions.

Why do we have to go to the Dovecote now?

Why do we need so many guards?

Why? Why? Why?

Again, Gideon shot Charles a look. Then he said, "Jonah and I caught him with a bottle of whiskey about a month back."

Charles straightened. Here in Bachelor Bottoms, that was a serious offense. Even the most minor infraction could be grounds for dismissal. Bringing a bottle of alcohol into the valley would be enough for a man to be sacked.

"Do the owners know?"

"Bottoms knows. Jonah and I went to him first. You can bet that if Batchwell had found out, he would have been hollering so loud the mountains would come down. If the pass hadn't already been closed from the avalanche,

Caruso would have been out on his ear. But Bottoms hauled the man into his office and tore a strip out of his hide, I'd wager. Found out later that Theo's on probation. I was ordered to search his rooms and check on the man every now and again, make sure he was on the straight and narrow. If he can keep his nose clean until spring, he'll still have his job."

"So, that's the end of it then?"

Gideon paused again. He'd worked up a sweat and he ran the back of his arm over his forehead. "I don't know. I still feel like there's something...off about the man."

"In what way?"

He squinted against the weak sunshine trying to break through the trees. "I can't put my finger on it. He's a hard worker and clearly loves the Scriptures, but..."

"But what?"

"I don't know. He seems...troubled. No, he seems tormented. Especially the past few weeks. Even Sumner commented on it after one of his sermons."

Charles filed that information away. Maybe Willow could talk to Sumner and see if the good doctor had anything more to offer.

"Please, Charles," Gideon said, resting the ax on his shoulder. "I would take it as a personal kindness if you would get back to your preaching."

"Who's doing it now?"

Gideon closed his eyes and took a deep breath, as if gathering his strength. "Klute Ingraham."

At that, Charles laughed. Klute Ingraham was a portly miner with a shining bald pate, a rotund belly and a fondness for taxidermy. His donation to the creature comforts of the women in the Dovecote had been a trio of ferrets dressed like clowns.

"It's not funny," Gideon said, sounding like a disgruntled little boy. "You know how the man talks. He starts out reminiscing about the Garden of Eden, which reminds him of his grandmother who made wonderful bread, which he's never had as good as a day at the sea-shore in Maine, where they have marvelous clams that can bite you as easily as a fox, which, by the way, is the subject of his latest taxidermy opus."

"Opus?"

Gideon laid his hand on his chest as if taking a vow. "I am telling you the honest truth. That was the subject of yesterday's Devotional. He spent a solid hour detailing the methods employed to divest the poor little critter of its fur. I thought the women were going to be sick—and Miss Tomlinson turned around to glare at me! As if it were *my* fault the man was off his rocker."

"Did he ever get the sermon back on track?"

"Only after a great deal of noisy throat clearing by Batchwell. About the last five minutes, he finally man-aged to tie in a spiritual element by announcing that the unfortunate creature was destined to be part of a still life entitled *Wasatch Winter Wonderland,* in which Klute intends to pay homage to God's glorious creation of the Uinta Mountains."

"But the Wasatch Mountains are an entirely different range than the Uintas."

"You know that, and I know that. But Klute seems to think that a diorama involving a fox, a beaver and a duck are the perfect means to portray God's creative powers here in the Territories."

Charles chortled even harder at that.

Gideon pointed an accusing finger. "You're laugh-ing now, but wait until he comes to visit. He told me in passing that he was running out of ideas for subject mat-ter." Gideon's expression became positively beseeching.

"Please, for the sake of the community's spiritual welfare. Come back."

Charles opened his mouth to refuse. But then he said, "We'll see."

Bending, he scooped up an armful of wood. But he'd taken only a few steps toward the door when Gideon called after him, "I'm going to take that as an agreement!"

Willow was not a complete stranger to the mines. Her own father had briefly worked in a tin mine when she was small, before he'd taken a job at the woolen mills in Lancaster. But she'd never been inside one.

As she and Charles approached the yawning opening, her steps faltered. Charles had explained that, because of the weather and the deep layers of snow, it would be impossible to bury Jenny in the cemetery on the hill outside town. Short of dynamite, nothing would penetrate the frozen ground. Because of this, the miners had long ago dug a special tunnel that they used for interring their dead. A space would be excavated into the wall to hold the remains. Then the casket would be covered with earth, rocks and timbers, and the place would be marked with a plaque.

Charles bent to murmur, "Some people have an aversion to dark, close places. You don't have to go in if you don't want."

She shook her head. "No. I'll go."

He reached to lace their fingers together. "Hold on to me. If you find that you can't tolerate it anymore, you don't have to say anything. Tightly squeeze my hand and I'll take you back outside."

Willow nodded, even though she knew she wouldn't

accept the offer. She had to see this through to the end. She owed it to her friend.

They stepped inside, following the narrow rail lines that stretched into the distance. A few hundred feet into the tunnel, just as the shadows had begun to close around them, lanterns had been placed at intervals to drive away the darkness.

"These lanterns are made so they can't start a spark, and the rail lines are for the ore cars. See how they branch off from one another in the distance?"

She nodded, knowing that Charles was attempting to draw her mind away from the thought of stepping deep underneath the mountain.

"One of them heads north, the other south. Right now, we have mules who do most of the work of pulling the cars to the surface, but in time, we'll be converting to a steam locomotive system."

As they followed the tracks deeper into the mine, Willow was surprised to find that the tunnel wasn't at all what she'd expected. She'd heard her father complain about the damp, close confines of the tin mines, but here, the air was cool—not cold—and dry.

They approached the spot where the ore lines branched into opposite tunnels. Between them was a roughly constructed building with windows that looked out into the mine.

"This is where I spend part of my day when I'm working," Charles said, pointing to the door where someone had painted Office on a splintered board. "I meet here with Jonah and my crew before we head underground."

The darkness increased as they moved farther from the main entrance. Here, the miners had braced the walls and ceilings with timbers, and the openings gradually became narrower. The air grew heavy with the scent of earth and something that smelled like gunpowder. Occasionally, the rail lines would split into new tunnels that were identified with plaques painted with numbers.

"In this section, all the tunnels have been given odd numbers. The other side has all the evens. Can you feel the slight breeze?"

"Yes."

"The tunnels have to be kept well-ventilated to prevent the buildup of dangerous gasses and to provide fresh air for the miners. Because of that, you'll find offshoot shafts that lead up to the surface to help circulate the air."

"I thought the mine would be…damp."

Charles grimaced. "Some of the newer tunnels can be wet and muddy. Even the older ones get their share of water in the spring when the snow melts. But up here, we have drainage channels that help to keep the moisture at bay."

They moved several hundred yards down the line. Soon, the lanterns were spaced farther apart, so they moved from one puddle of light to another, until Charles drew her to a halt in front of a narrow opening.

"Still okay?" he murmured.

"Yes." The word was little more than a puff of sound.

"The walls will be closer here. But I'll stay by your side."

She nodded. Unlike the other openings they'd passed, this one hadn't been numbered. There were no rail lines leading inside.

Charles led her forward, through a narrow passage. No lanterns had been hung here, but she could see a golden glow at the end.

Her fingers tightened around Charles's and she tried not to think about the tons of mountain above her, kept at bay with little more than timbers. But soon, they stepped through a doorway and the space opened into a wide square chamber. In this spot, the walls had been lined floor to ceiling with rough-hewn timbers and she could see where brass plaques with names and dates identified the resting places of those who had been interred.

To her surprise, she found that she and Charles weren't alone. Many of the mail-order brides were present, as well as the Hepplewhite and Wilmott families, and a few employees from the ill-fated train. Several of them held bunches of holly or pine boughs in lieu of flowers. Toward the back of the group, at least two dozen miners ringed the room. They had removed their helmets, but held them under their arms so that the attached safety lanterns could provide them all with light.

"There would have been more people in attendance if Jonah had allowed it. The miners drew straws to decide who would come to pay their respects. The brides decided among themselves."

Willow's gaze swept the room, her throat growing tight with emotion. Jenny had associated very little with the miners. Willow was touched that so many had wanted to come to the funeral.

The ranks parted, allowing Willow and Charles to move closer to the far wall. There, Jenny's coffin rested on the ground. The planks had been removed from the wall, exposing a hole dug large enough to hold Jenny's remains.

Willow blinked away the tears that threatened to fall.

"Thank you all for coming." The murmured conversation ceased as Jonah Ramsey stepped in front of the coffin.

"It is a sad occasion any time this chamber is needed, and this event proves to be no exception. Indeed, this passing seems more tragic than most, since the life that was taken was that of a young mother and her unborn child."

Emotions rose in Willow's chest. She gripped Charles's hand, and he wrapped his arm around her shoulders, drawing her to his strength and warmth.

"As you know, there were many more who would have been in attendance had the space allowed," Jonah continued. "We are a small community here at the Batchwell Bottoms Mine. But we have been blessed these past few weeks by the presence of our unwitting guests. Jenny Reichmann was one of our stranded passengers. She was marooned here, against her will, through an act of nature. And because of that, she will never have the opportunity to reunite with the husband who, even now, waits for her arrival."

A sob pushed from Willow's throat as she remembered how Jenny had spoken of the man who'd stolen her heart. To hear her talk, her husband had been the stuff of dreams, a romantic hero who had swept Jenny off her feet and promised her the world.

"Any death diminishes us as a community. I know that the women of the Dovecote sorely miss their friend. The rest of us will mourn the fact that we never really had a chance to know her."

Willow didn't miss the fact that Jonah had been vague about the cause of Jenny's death. There was no mention of the fact that her life had been stolen through a supreme act of selfishness.

Murder.

Was the culprit here? Standing among them?

Willow's gaze slipped over the other women. Iona, who pressed a handkerchief to her mouth to stifle her sobs. Lydia, who allowed slow tears to fall unfettered.

Sumner, who stood tall and stiff, her lips pressed into a tight line.

Then Willow's eyes slid to the miners, who stood stoic and iron-jawed. And she wondered…

Could one of you be responsible?

She'd seen plays where the culprit of a dastardly deed returned to the scene of the crime—or attended the funeral of their victim. Would the murderer be so audacious? So…despicable?

She eyed each one of the miners in turn. For the most part, they stared solemnly at the ground, or stood steely-eyed, gazing at their superintendent. Only one of them locked gazes with her. A burly man with muttonchop whiskers and deep grooves around his mouth. He held her attention for several seconds, nodded ever so slightly, then looked away.

Willow studied the brides next, a part of her balking at the fact that she could even consider them to be suspects. But Marie and Millie, Emmarissa and Greta, Myra and Miriam all seemed genuinely devastated by the loss of their own.

Beyond them were the families, the Hepplewhites and the Wilmotts. Mr. Hepplewhite shifted uncomfortably from foot to foot. He kept tugging on his tie. Mr. Wilmott, on the other hand, stared blankly into space as if he were deep in thought and picturing another time and place.

Against the far wall, the railroad employees stood slightly apart from the other mourners, she noted. They wore their uniforms and stood at attention as if they were soldiers on review. There was Mr. Beamon, the porter who had accompanied them all the way from Independence, and another man Willow vaguely remembered helping her with her trunk as she and Jenny had hurried to make their train in time. The final man, one who stood tall and grim in workman's coveralls, must have been the engineer or a stoker for the doomed train.

Were any of them responsible?

If so, would they actually plot to end the lives of two newly born babes?

Her gaze became keener, slipping from face to face. She became almost frantic in her inspection, looking for the slightest sign of malice or guilt. As Jonah continued his eulogy, the words washed over her, becoming a distant hum as her panic rose.

She knew the twins were safe. Creakle and Mr. Smalls had been more than happy to watch over them so that Charles and Willow could attend the funeral. But even with the reassurance that her babies were being watched by two heavily armed men who doted on their every move…

Willow felt an overwhelming urge to return to her children.

Hers and Jenny's and Charles's.

"Charles, as our spiritual leader, I wondered if we could ask you to comfort us all with a word of Scripture, then a prayer to dedicate her grave."

Beside her, Charles stiffened.

Willow knew he warred with his emotions. Since he'd resigned, he didn't feel it was his place to offer any religious instruction, especially after he'd told so many untruths in his efforts to protect the twins.

But when attention swayed in his direction, there was no censure, no judgment. Merely an expectation that he would step into the role he had donned upon the resignation of their official pastor.

Reluctantly, he stepped forward and turned to face the assembled group.

Almost immediately, Willow found herself flanked

by Sumner and Lydia. They linked their arms through hers, shoring her up.

"On this sad occasion," Charles began, his voice low and deep and filled with the same thread of grief that Willow herself was feeling, "I would like to quote from the Bible, 1 Thessalonians 4:13-14." He took a deep breath, his eyes closing. "'Brothers and sisters, we do not want you to be uninformed about those who sleep in death, so that you do not grieve like the rest of mankind, who have no hope.'" Charles's voice gradually rose in volume and intensity. "'For we believe that Jesus died and rose again, and so we believe that God will bring with Jesus those who have fallen asleep in Him.'"

A chorus of "Amens" punctuated the recitation. Then Charles bowed his head to pray.

Willow could no longer contain her tears as Charles appealed to God to accept Jenny into his fold, to offer her peace and happiness in the eternities. He appealed to the Lord to bless those who had been left behind, to strengthen them and shore them up as they mourned.

Although Willow had heard Charles offer his sermons in the past, the richness of his sincerity and the strength of his conviction rang from his words, affecting her more powerfully than they ever had before. Charles was no longer a stranger among a sea of strangers. She had seen him through good times and bad. She'd felt his strength and his gentleness. She'd witnessed firsthand the depth of his character and his capacity for compassion.

And she'd nearly lost him to the same evil that had taken Jenny.

Squeezing her eyes as tight as she could, she offered her own fervent prayer.

Please, Lord, help us to find the source of all this wickedness. Help us to find the person responsible for

Jenny's death so that her children can be safe. And please, please...protect the man I...

Love.

The word sprang into her mind, and she found that she didn't have the strength to drive it away. She might have known Charles for only a short time, but she already knew him better than she'd ever known another living soul. It was as if a part of her recognized him from another time or place. From the moment she'd joined him to protect the twins, she had felt something within her bloom. He was more than a friend, more than a helpmate.

He was Charles.

Her Charles.

"Dear Lord, at this time, we ask that you dedicate this spot as the final resting place on earth for the corporal remains of Jenny Reichmann. And in doing so, we know that her soul is now in Thy keeping. Amen."

Willow lifted her head, heedless of the tears that spilled from her lashes and plunged down her cheeks. Instantly, her eyes locked with Charles's. And in their depths she saw the same fire of determination that burned in her own soul.

They would find Jenny's killer and bring that person to justice.

Chapter Sixteen

After the funeral, the mourners gathered in the cook shack. Women from the Dovecote had laid out platters of sliced cold meats and cheeses, pickles and relishes, cornbread and rolls. Pots of hot coffee and tea stood on the serving counter next to stacks of mugs and plates. At the far end were pans of cobblers made from dried apples, cherries and raisins, walnuts and pecans.

As the men filled their plates, their conversation remained low and somber. The women stood uncertainly for a moment. After they served the meals each day, it had become customary for them to eat at the farm table in the preparation area. But today, the...*separateness* between the brides and the miners seemed wrong somehow. One by one, the women joined the men at the tables.

Willow and Charles found places at the end of a trestle table near the door. As they ate, the other occupants seemed to regard them as the closest thing to Jenny's next of kin. One by one, they filed by to offer a few words of comfort.

"My deepest sympathies, Mrs. Wanlass. Mr. Wanlass."

"It's a shame to lose anyone so young."

The men seemed genuinely mournful about Jenny's

passing. Inexplicably, their kind words helped Willow to cope with the situation. She'd been too young when her mam had passed to comprehend what had really happened, and her father...

He'd been buried in a pauper's grave before she even knew that he'd died.

"This must be very difficult for you, Mrs. Wanlass."

Willow looked up to find that the crew from the train stood at their table.

"Yes, thank you, Mr...."

"Niederhauser. I was the engineer on the train." He waited a beat before adding, "I take it that you and Miss Reichmann were friends."

"Yes, we met in Liverpool when we both began our journey."

"Then you must have grown very close."

"Mmm."

He opened his mouth, clearly intending to say more, but a glance in Charles's direction seemed to stop him.

"My condolences, ma'am."

Finally, all the attendees seemed to have said their piece, because Willow and Charles were left alone.

Willow stared down at her plate. She knew she should taste something. The brides had gone to so much effort— and once she returned home, she had so many things to do.

No.

Once she returned home, she would hold little Eva and Adam until she couldn't hold them any longer.

Charles took her hand and squeezed it.

"Eat," he said gently. "You need your strength."

She poked at her food. She couldn't ever remember being so exhausted.

No. Not exhausted.

Hollow.

Longing for a friend she would never talk to again.

Charles seemed to understand, because he didn't rush her. He allowed her to sift through her thoughts and catalog her memories, until finally, she cut off a small piece of ham.

The crowd thinned, and she could hear the women talking in low murmurs in the kitchen. After having volunteered at the cook shack herself, she found the familiar noises comforting.

And yet...

Her nape seemed to prickle, and she looked behind her, noting that the gentleman with the muttonchop whiskers was staring at her again.

"Charles?"

"Hmm?"

"Who's the man behind us?"

Charles glanced over his shoulder, then back again.

"Theo Caruso."

"Do you know him?"

"Not really, no. I've never worked with him on a shift. Why?"

"He keeps staring our way. He was watching us during the funeral, too."

Charles took her hand. "Stay away from him if you can."

"Why?"

His thumb rubbed over her knuckles. "I hate to say anything against a man without talking to him myself. But Gideon seems to think he's...troubled."

"Troubled?"

Charles shrugged. "I don't know much more than that. According to Gideon, he's broken one of the camp rules. Until we cross him off our list of suspects, I'd like you

to be careful. If he knocks on our door, don't open it unless I'm there."

"I won't."

But as she bent back to her food, the little hairs at her
nape still prickled uneasily.

When they returned home, Charles felt as if he'd been
toiling away at the mines with a pickax. His body was
exhausted, his mind numb. And all he craved was the
quiet peace of an evening with his wife and children.

Willow seemed to be of the same mind, because as
soon as Creakle and Smalls had said their goodbyes,
she'd shrugged out of her cape and jacket, and hurried
to where the babies lay sleeping on a quilt on the floor.
They would be needing cradles soon, something that
Jonah Ramsey had hinted was already being arranged.

Charles bolted the doors, lit the lamps and coaxed the
fire into rollicking flames. Then he shrugged out of his
own jacket. Before joining Willow, he removed the diary
from its hiding place and carried it with him as he joined
his wife in the wooden chair that had somehow become
his, while the tufted seat was now hers.

He didn't immediately open the book. Instead, he set
it on the floor.

While his back was turned, Willow had scooped
Adam into her arms. The wee lad remained asleep, but
Charles knew that didn't matter. He suspected that Wil-
low drew comfort from his tiny warm body.

Charles lifted Eva against him and was rewarded with
the barest slit of her eyes. For a moment, she seemed
ready to fall back asleep. But then her Cupid's bow mouth
opened and her tongue appeared. Slowly, sleepily, she
arched her back, blinked up at Charles, then smiled.

"She's smiling at me." He couldn't prevent the words that burst from his lips. Nor could he disguise his wonder.

"Sumner says babies can't smile this early. She says that the baby probably has a bubble in her stomach."

No. She'd smiled.

Charles rested his pinkie against the wee bairn's fist, and she reached out to grasp it, trying to carry it to her mouth.

"She's going to be a strong lassie."

Willow offered a wry grimace. "She'll have to be to keep up with Adam. He already has a stubborn streak."

Charles caught her gaze, and once again, his heart seemed to speak before his brain could think of the consequences. "We make quite a little family, don't we?"

Willow could have made light of his comment—and he almost wished she would. But her tone was soft and sweet as she offered, "Yes. We do."

The admission brought such a note of longing to the night that Charles found it almost painful to bear. There were still so many unanswered questions. Who had killed Jenny? Why were the children in danger? And what would become of their little family once the riddle had been solved?

Knowing that there would be no real answers that night, Charles shifted Eva to one arm, then bent to pick up the journal. "How far back should I go?"

Willow's brow creased. Then she ran a finger over Adam's brow, and darned if the little boy's lips didn't twitch at the corners.

"Last February? April? If the twins were born in January…"

Charles rested the book on his knee and rifled through the pages.

"February it is."

Then he began to read.

* * *

It was as if she was being offered a bedtime story, Willow decided. Charles's voice was deep and resonant, full of inflection and emotion. The entries read like a novel—a tempestuous romance, a declaration of undying love, a bittersweet parting. Willow had to keep reminding herself that the words had been written by a real person and not one of the Brontës.

For hours, they pored over every page, while outside the wind began to blow, rattling the windows and causing the lantern flames to dance from a stray draft. In all that time, Jenny never mentioned the name of the man who had courted her. She merely referred to him as "Beloved."

Through it all, the babies woke and were fed, played, fussed, then fell asleep again. Yet Willow noticed that Charles seemed as reluctant as she was to place them back in their basket.

The last few entries were the hardest. Jenny spoke of her excitement at traveling west to meet up with her Beloved. How she counted the days, the hours. She spoke of the devastating power of the avalanche that had swept their train from its tracks, then awakening to the fear that her baby had been harmed, her joy when she felt it move inside her. Then suddenly, she wrote: *I've seen my Beloved! And even though I've confronted him, here in a place where I've been forbidden to be, I can't regret following him.*

Charles glanced up. "She saw him? In Bachelor Bottoms? So, was this where she'd secretly planned to come all along?"

Willow opened her mouth to agree, but something was needling her, flirting at the edge of her consciousness. Something important that she needed to grasp before it flitted away.

Oblivious to her unease, Charles continued to think aloud. "Then the person responsible has to be a miner. We've got three company men on our suspect list. Theo Caruso, Orie Keefe and Francis Diggory. I know for a fact that Theo joined us less than six months ago. Orie in the summer. Either one of them could have been the man who jilted Jenny. That ring they found clutched in her hand could have come from any of them."

Yes, yes, it all made sense.

Except...

And then it hit her, the fact that had slipped through her fingers.

"Charles," Willow said slowly. "Charles, I think we've overlooked something. An important clue."

He met her gaze, his excitement dimming.

"Charles, in the diary, she never mentioned *marrying* her Beloved."

Charles's eyes widened, and he leaned back in his chair. "Which means we've increased our suspect list again."

"Yes. But we've found a stronger motive, as well."

Willow shivered, dragging the quilt tighter around her neck. A peek beneath her lashes assured her that it was still early. Dawn hadn't yet begun to rim the mountains. Peering over the side of the cot, she saw that the children slept soundly. It wouldn't be long before they would awaken for their meal, but for now...

She would settle back beneath the covers and enjoy the last few minutes of sleep.

But even as she wriggled deeper into the puddle of warmth she'd created, she became more conscious of the cold. Her feet were chilled, her fingers stiff. Her nose felt pinched and icy.

Blinking, she cast a glance toward the window, wondering if it had somehow come open during the night. But the curtains were still.

She shivered and threw back the quilts. Blindly, she felt around for her slippers, but her toes seemed to have turned into blocks of ice.

Charles had told Willow that he would set the fires before he left. He and the rest of his crew had finished laying the charges for the new tunnel, then had kept a crew of Pinkertons guarding them overnight. They'd all met early this morning to detonate the explosives before the early bird shift came to work.

Fearing the children had grown cold, as well, she threw an extra blanket over their basket and quickly dressed in her warmest day gown. Then she grasped the basket and hurried downstairs.

Just as she'd feared, it was obvious that Charles had laid and lit the fire, but somehow, it had gone out. She rearranged the logs and began again. The fire that finally caught seemed smoky, making her wonder if snow had been blown down the chimney.

While the flames struggled to light the larger logs, she moved into the kitchen to poke up the coals on the stove. Again, she could see evidence that Charles had started the process. A teakettle had been set on one of the burners and a pail of snow waited to be melted. But when she touched the surface, the metal was stone cold.

She bent to peer into the grate, only to discover nothing but black ashes.

She quickly set a new fire, then hurried back to the fireplace.

"What on earth?"

The flames had finally begun to grow, but instead

of the smoke rising upward, a black cloud billowed into the room.

Too late, she realized that the chimney wasn't drawing properly. But by now, the logs had caught fire and the blaze grew stronger with each passing moment.

"No, no, no, no, no!"

She whirled toward the kitchen for the pail of snow, only to discover that smoke poured from the range, as well.

A glance toward the children revealed that she didn't have much time to act. Grabbing a carpetbag, she hurriedly gathered a few of their things together—diapers, bottles, a change of clothing from the drying cord, extra blankets. Then she looped her arm through the handle and reached for the twins.

Not taking time to put on her coat, she rushed outside. She wasn't sure what had happened to keep the chimney and the stovepipe from drawing, but she couldn't afford to stay indoors any longer to investigate. Nor would she leave the children alone out of doors. She would hurry down to the livery. If Mr. Smalls was there, she could ask for his help.

She dodged toward the lean-to, where the children's sledge had been stored, and stowed the twins in the box, the carpetbag on the bench. Then she pulled the children into town. But when she reached the livery, she discovered that the doors were locked. Too late, she realized that Creakle and Smalls had probably been summoned to the mine with the rest of Charles's crew.

Anxious, she gazed around her. But the street was curiously empty.

The Dovecote.

There would be Pinkertons outside the women's dormitory. She could ask them for help, then take shelter with the other women until someone could check on the chimneys.

Grasping the handle of the sledge, she ran toward the far end of town, then turned down the lane. Her boots slipped and skidded in the snow, and her breath came in deep, shuddering breaths that seemed to burn in her lungs before escaping again in a puff of white.

She was nearly there when she saw a movement at one of the windows. Seconds later, the door whipped open and Lydia ran to meet her.

"Willow, what's wrong?"

Willow nearly collapsed in her arms. "The house. There's smoke building up and I had to get the children out. I didn't have a chance to put out the fire in the hearth or…"

By this time, some of the other women had begun to hurry outside.

Lydia directed them with one hand, the other still supporting Willow's quivering frame. "Marie, Greta! Take the babies and their things inside. Myra and Miriam, go round up our guards—especially Mr. Gault, if you can find him. Tell them to double-time it to the Wanlass house before the whole thing burns down."

A raw sound of distress burst from Willow's throat. "I've got to go back! I can't let anything happen to Charles's home!"

"Nonsense. This is a job for the men. It's about time they did more than lollygag around here watching a bunch of women who can take care of themselves."

In the distance, Willow saw a pair of men easing out of the pine trees just as Myra and Miriam approached. Within seconds, they were running toward town.

"See?" Lydia said. "It's all settled. Now, let's get you warmed up inside. You're going to catch your death out here."

* * *

Charles whistled under his breath as he approached the row house. Nothing on earth could compare to a job well done. This morning, they'd managed to lay the rest of the charges that he'd planned, and then complete a controlled blast. The rock face had come down, just as he'd hoped it would, revealing a thick seam of silver. He'd wager that the seam would continue on another hundred or so feet beneath the mountain, maybe more. Even now, crews of miners were clearing up the debris, sorting the ore from worthless rock. As they worked, another team erected support beams and braces to ensure the safety of the corridor.

Normally, Charles would remain in the thick of it. There wasn't a job in the mine that he hadn't done before—nor did he feel that any job was beneath him. But this afternoon, he wanted to eat his midday meal at home.

Home.

The word had the power to sizzle in his chest like primer cord. For the first time in his life, he actually knew what it meant. Home wasn't a place or a structure. It was a *feeling.* A sense of *belonging.*

And that, more than anything else, drew him away from the mine, away from the secret seams of ore the blasting had revealed, away from friends and coworkers.

So that he could go home.

Shoving his hands into his pockets, he hunched into the collar of his coat. He suspected a storm was brewing, even though he could see patches of blue showing through the clouds. True to form, January in the Uintas alternated between frigid temperatures and blizzards, and cold, clear days that tempted a person to think about spring, even though the warmer weather was months away.

At least Charles hoped that a real spring was months away. He wasn't sure what he would do once the pass cleared. It wasn't a decision he could make on his own anymore. He and Willow needed to talk. More than anything, he was hoping to convince her to abandon her earlier plans and remain with him.

But not today.

He glanced up, wondering if he could catch a peek of Willow's shadow behind the curtains, then stumbled to a stop.

The door hung open on its hinges.

The chill that raced through his body had nothing to do with the cold. He burst into a run, taking the steps two at a time.

"Willow!"

The cry bounced hollowly off the walls, but there was no answer.

"Willow!"

He pounded upstairs, slammed open the door to her room, then searched in his own.

Nothing.

His heart began pounding in his throat and he checked the rooms again, not knowing why he did so. There was no place to hide in the row house. Not for a grown woman and...

The twins.

"Sweet Heavenly Father," he whispered under his breath. "Please, please let them be safe. Let them all be safe."

He rushed downstairs again, growing conscious of the cold. How long had the door been open?

At the same moment, he noted the sharp scent of smoke, and his gut tightened.

No, no, no! He should have arranged for Creakle and Smalls to stay with her.

But he'd needed all his men with him.

And he'd known that Lydia and Iona would be dropping by after breakfast, as well as several other women. He'd thought that Willow would be safe enough until afternoon.

He heard a thump on the stoop and rushed to the door. When he discovered Willow pulling the sledge, and the babies nestled safe in the box, he couldn't control the words that burst free.

"What on earth have you been doing? You need to stay home, in the house, like you've been told to do. Don't you ever do that again!"

The moment the words crossed his tongue, he knew they were a mistake. They'd been uttered harshly, accusingly, laden with the temper that he'd fought for years to contain. In a flash, he'd become the bully that he'd fought to leave behind him since he'd been an adolescent in Aberdeen.

He saw the effect of his harshness in the shattered expression that crossed Willow's features. In an instant, her confidence fled and she became the shy, fearful woman that she'd been when she'd first entered Bachelor Bottoms.

Willow didn't know where she was going. She merely turned and ran.

Despite the cold, her cheeks burned with heat. She'd been a fool. After playing the part of Charles's wife, she'd begun to believe that it could be real. She'd forgotten that he had other goals, other priorities. He'd been allowed to return to work, and in doing so, his world had opened up for him again.

But hers was oh, so small. It had always been small.

The mill.

The charity school.

And now…

Charles's house.

His children.

Him.

How had she allowed this to happen? How had she allowed him to become the center of her small universe? How had she let herself think, even for a moment, that someone like Charles—a man who was strong and handsome and smart—would ever consider someone like *her* a suitable companion? A woman who hadn't learned to read until she was nearly thirteen, who still struggled to form her letters in a legible manner. If she hadn't forced herself into his home, he could have found someone else to help him. Someone clever, like Lydia or Marie.

The street ahead of her shifted and seemed to slip sideways. Too late, she realized that she was weeping openly, her sobs punctuating the air she gulped into her lungs. She blindly sought somewhere—*anywhere*—she could go to lick her wounds. A place she could be alone, so that she could draw the tattered remains of her selfworth together, enough to at least pretend that she was like the other girls.

She wasn't sure how she found her way, but suddenly looked up to see the back of the Meeting House before her. Tucking the sledge against the wall, she scooped up the twins and prayed that the doors weren't locked during the day.

Her chin trembled when the knob of the rear door turned easily in her hand. Slipping inside, she tiptoed through the private office to the large meeting area beyond.

She'd never come into the building from this direction. It seemed odd and slightly sacrilegious to use the same entry as the pastor. She crept past the raised dais and the tufted chairs reserved for Batchwell and Bottoms, then past the lectern to the center aisle. Automatically, she sank onto one of the benches where the women sat during Devotional. To her relief, there was a lingering warmth to the building, especially here, near one of the many pot-bellied stoves that were used to warm the chapel.

Hugging the children to her chest, she tried to remind herself what was really important. Her feelings didn't matter a hill of beans next to keeping the twins safe. And she'd done that. Despite what Charles had said, they couldn't have stayed in the house. Not with all that smoke. Things could have been different if she'd been able to find help faster but...

No.

She'd done her best.

A scraping sound caused her to pivot on her seat, to find a huge figure silhouetted in the doorway. Too late, she realized that she and the children were alone, unarmed and completely unprotected, when the man stepped inside and the door snapped shut behind him.

Instantly, she recognized one of the miners who'd been at the funeral. The tall, imposing fellow with the mutton-chop whiskers who had stared at her so intently.

Theo Caruso.

One of the men on their suspect list.

She vainly tried to think.

Was this the person she'd seen watching the house? She'd caught only a glimpse of him from behind. But it had to be the same man.

Didn't it?

She saw his hands ball into fists and.release, ball into fists and release.

"I've been tryin' t' get you alone."

His voice was deep, raspy, more growl than spoken words.

"I'd like t' see the children."

Willow's arms tightened around the twins. Her heart was beating so fast that she could hear the blood roaring in her ears.

"Stay where you are!"

She jumped to her feet, but the heel of her boot tangled in the hem of her skirts. For a moment, she swayed, fought for balance.

The man lunged toward her just as the outer door opened.

Once again, she saw little more than a silhouette in the doorway. But she knew each plane and angle of that figure as intimately as she knew her own reflection in a mirror.

Charles.

She instinctively ran toward him, rushing past the miner so quickly that he didn't have time to react.

"Take me home!" she said frantically. "Now!"

Chapter Seventeen

With every step they took back to the row house, Charles prayed that he could find the words to make up for the way he'd treated her so harshly. How could he reassure Willow that he would never want to offend her, that it was his cursed temper that had landed him in trouble again?

But then, he'd never been honest enough with Willow to confess his troubles from the past. He'd had the perfect opportunity when she'd told him of her own upbringing—and he knew, deep in his soul, that she would never fault him for his uncertain parentage or his years in a foundling home. Even so, he'd balked at that final piece to his nature, the temper that had caused him to pummel a boy for calling him names.

He'd hesitated in telling her everything, because he hadn't wanted her to become afraid of him.

But she was afraid of him now.

Since he'd taken the job of pulling the sleigh with the twins, she purposely stood apart from him, walking with her head down, her eyes on the road—and that fact crushed his heart even more. Over the past few days, he'd seen her blossom from a shy little rabbit to a warrior.

Then he'd crushed her spirit with a few careless words.

He'd thought it would be best to wait until they were safely home before he spoke to her, but he couldn't bear her silence anymore.

"I'm so sorry, Willow."

She didn't respond. The only sound was the crunch of their footsteps in the snow.

"When I returned home to find the door open, the twins gone... I can't explain the fear I felt."

"In the future, I'll be sure to leave a note so you know where to find Adam and Eva."

Her voice was flat and his heart twisted even more.

"And *you*, Willow. I was so worried about *you*."

When she looked at him, her eyes were filled with shadows. "But I'll only be here until the pass melts."

The words struck him to the core. From the beginning, he'd tried to remind himself that the time would come when Willow would want to continue on her journey. She'd had plans for her future before meeting him. But with each day that passed, he'd begun to believe that their arrangement could become permanent. That somehow they could be a real family.

A real couple.

Charles knew that he could do no better than having Willow Granger as a wife. She was generous and loyal and fiercely protective. She would be a wonderful helpmate to any man.

If only she weren't committed to another.

"Is that what you want?"

The words escaped from his mouth before he could stop them. But even though he regretted his awful timing, he had no desire to recall them.

Willow grew still, her breath hanging in front of her like a gossamer cloud as she peered at him. She seemed to be warring with her thoughts, and Charles prayed that she would remember the good times and not his anger.

If she would only give him a chance.

"Charles! Willow!"

The mood shattered as Gideon Gault loped toward them. For the first time that Charles could remember, he wished his friend would go away, if only for a few minutes.

"I'm glad I caught you." Gideon lifted his hat in Willow's direction. "Ma'am."

"Mr. Gault."

"That was pretty smart thinking on your part, Willow, getting out of the house as quickly as you could."

Charles didn't miss the pointed look that Willow shot in his direction.

"And I'm glad you came to my men for help rather than anyone else."

If Gideon didn't stop talking, Charles was afraid he'd never have a chance to make things right with Willow.

Gideon shifted even closer, his voice dropping. "Did you have any problems with your fireplace last night?"

Charles thought of the huge blaze he'd fed as he and Willow had read Jenny's diary. "No, why?"

Rather than answering, Gideon asked another question. "What time did you leave for the mine?"

"About four."

"Did you set a fire?"

"Of course. The house had grown cold through the night and I wanted to warm things up for Willow and the twins."

"When I woke, the fires he laid hadn't started," Willow interjected.

"It's a good thing they didn't."

Gideon swept his hat from his head and plunged his

fingers through his hair. "After my men arrived and put out the fires, we had a look around the place. We found some tracks in the snow round the back of your house, as well as an old ladder from the livery. Someone climbed onto your roof and shoved blankets down your chimney and stovepipe. If those fires you laid had kept burning… Willow and the children could have smothered from the smoke before they ever woke up."

A giant fist seemed to close around Charles's chest. He watched as the color drained out of Willow's face.

The burst of anger that he'd felt merely an hour ago was nothing more than a spark compared to the rush of fury that stormed through his body—a good portion of it directed at himself.

Someone had tried to kill his family. Had very nearly succeeded. If it hadn't been for the hand of Providence extinguishing the early fires and Willow's quick thinking, he would have returned home to something far worse than an empty house.

"Gideon, can you accompany Willow and the twins home and stay with them until I get back?"

His friend nodded, settling his hat back on his head. "Sure. What is it you need to do?"

"I'm going to speak to Smalls and borrow a sleigh from the livery." Charles turned to Willow. "I want you to empty out the trunk at the bottom of my bed. Fill it with a few changes of clothing for both of us and whatever the babies will need. Gather up the chart and the journal—"

"Journal?" Gideon asked.

"We'll explain later." He returned his attention to Willow. "I'll be back as soon as I hitch up the sleigh. I'm moving you and the twins to the Dovecote. It'll be safer there. You'll have the women to help you and the Pinkerton guards to make sure that no one gets in or out of the dormitory without going through them first."

He looked toward Gideon for confirmation and his friend nodded.

"I think that's a good idea. What with blasting the new tunnel and guarding the ore coming out of the mine, my men are spread pretty thin. I've tried to have someone keep an eye on your place, but the help has been spotty at best. This way, you'll have round-the-clock protection—and after what's occurred, I don't think any of the brides will squawk about the added protection around the Dovecote."

With each word, Willow's eyes had grown wider, and she'd unconsciously moved closer to the twins.

"Whoever is doing this seems to be growing more desperate," Charles said. "Maybe it's time we flushed him out."

"But how?" she whispered.

"You said Jenny's things were searched."

"Y-yes. Things on her dresser were merely rearranged, but her trunk was a shambles."

"Did the culprit take anything?"

"Only the rattle."

"So they weren't just looking for valuables?"

"I don't think so. If that were the case, they would have taken the silver comb and mirror on her dresser, or the gold carbobs and coins she'd hidden in her trunk."

"Do you think they were looking for the diary?"

Willow nodded. "They would have found the rattle quite easily, but the condition of the belongings in her trunk seemed to indicate they'd kept looking."

"What diary?" Gideon asked again.

Charles held up a hand. A part of his brain worked to figure things out as he spoke.

"I think we can assume that whoever is responsible for Jenny's murder would have known quite a lot about her movements. They would have known what room she had at the Dovecote and that Willow shared the space with her."

"So when they couldn't find the diary..." Willow whispered.

"They assumed you had it." Charles grimaced. "It might explain why someone was watching the house. Maybe they hoped you'd leave it empty at some point."

"But I did leave. The day the girls brought the sledge, I went to the Dovecote."

"And who's to say our own things weren't searched as well, while you were gone?"

Willow's eyes widened. "I—I did feel like something was...out of sorts when I came back, but I couldn't put my finger on it. Even so, they wouldn't have found anything. I didn't bring the journal back until that afternoon."

"So maybe the blocked chimneys were a second attempt to flush you out of the house."

Gideon shook his head. "When she came tearing out of there, he'd know that she would run for help. There wouldn't be time for another search." His hand gravitated toward the butt of the revolver holstered at his hip, and his voice grew steely. "More than likely he was making an attempt to corner the one person who could still uncover his secrets."

Charles felt a cold finger trace down his spine.

"Willow."

When they arrived at the Dovecote, Charles was relieved that Gideon Gault took the lead with the other women. In a tone as smooth as silk, the Pinkerton informed them all that, due to the lingering smoke, it wasn't healthy for Willow and the babies to remain at home for the time being, so would the women mind if the Wanlass family stayed in the dormitory?

The women had immediately bundled Willow and the children inside.

Leaving Charles standing outside in the cold.

As the door shut behind them, Charles sighed. Was this a sign of the future? Would he soon have to watch Willow and the twins move away from him?

"Don't take it personally."

He looked up to see Dr. Sumner Ramsey walking toward him. She was without a coat, so her arms were folded around her for warmth, but her expression was welcoming.

"It's the baby effect," she murmured.

"The baby effect?"

"As soon as a baby enters a room, it doesn't matter what other diversions are present, the baby will get all the attention. The women would leave Willow out here in the snow, too, as long as the babies came inside. Eventually, they would realize they'd forgotten her and come looking."

For a moment, Charles was horrified at the callous description. Then he realized Sumner was teasing.

"Don't worry about it. They'll be plying you with more cookies and cocoa than you can tolerate, soon enough. Bring the sleigh around the back. I think the best thing for your little family is for you to take over the dormitory infirmary for the time being. The bed and dresser I used before I married are still there, and we can shift the medical furniture to bring in some more comfortable seating. It will be your own little home away from home until things can be sorted out." She shot him a warning glance. "Just make sure you do your sleeping in the barn. If you and Willow plan on an annulment, I won't have any rumors circulating about her after the fact. And there's nowhere in the Dovecote for you to sleep on your own."

"Yes, ma'am."

Charles grasped the horse's bridle, leading him around the large building that had housed the brides for nearly a month.

"I assume that all this talk about smoke is only part of the truth."

Charles nodded.

"We're afraid it might have been another murder attempt."

Sumner regarded him with open horror. "Against Willow? And the children?"

"Yes. At the very least, our suspect did his best to get her alone and unprotected. If she hadn't run toward the Dovecote and the Pinkertons…"

"This has got to stop."

"I couldn't agree with you more." Charles thought things over carefully before asking, "Could you and Jonah linger in town tonight? At least until the other women have gone to bed?"

"Sure. Why?"

"I think it's time to lay a trap for Jenny's killer. And I think it's going to take a joint effort. If you could bring Jonah to meet with us, I'll let Gideon know. Willow and I will fill you in on what we've pieced together and then we can all come up with a plan."

Sumner's brown eyes glinted with determination and her chin tilted to an angle that Charles remembered from those early days in the valley when she'd been wrangling with Jonah over the treatment of the stranded passengers.

"How about eleven o'clock?"

* * *

After the bustle of the day and the way the ladies had spoiled the children, Charles and herself, Willow had thought the women would never go to bed. But by eleven o'clock, an eerie silence hung over the Dovecote.

Sumner's office had undergone a transformation. Jonah had taken his wife's supplies to the infirmary in town, proclaiming that anyone needing care could go there, whether or not Batchwell complained.

Willow's brows had risen at that remark. In the past, Jonah had been a company man through and through. But since marrying Sumner, he'd softened toward the other women and their plight.

Once the examining table and patient cots were removed, the women had brought a settee, a rocker and a pair of chairs into the room. In anticipation of their guests, Charles and Willow had arranged the trunk in the middle, then spread out the chart and placed the journal on top. Now the two of them sat in silence, the ticking of the clock in the main room marking the minutes.

"How much longer?" Willow whispered.

Charles took out a pocket watch and glanced at the face. "It's eleven. But I'm sure they'll wait until there aren't any lights in the windows upstairs."

He rested his elbows on his knees and laced his hands together. "I was wrong to speak to you so abruptly, Willow."

She shook her head, continuing to pat Adam softly on the back. The baby had fallen asleep some time ago, but his weight against her chest and the sweet scent of his skin grounded her. Since Eva would rouse soon for her feeding, Willow planned to hold him as long as he'd allow it. Then she would take Eva into her arms. "It doesn't matter, Charles."

He looked up then, his expression pained. "Yes. It does. When I walked into that house and found it empty, I was so scared. I thought that someone had broken in and taken—" he swallowed "—had taken my little family. And I couldn't bear it. When you showed up I didn't think." He shook his head. "I lashed out."

"I should have left a note. I should have—"

"No!" His gaze became fierce. "You did the right thing. You packed up everything that was important and you went for help. That's exactly what you should have done." He gripped his hands together, loosened them, gripped them. "You've been very honest with me. You've told me all about your upbringing—and it doesn't matter to me. It really doesn't. But you should know at least as much about me."

Willow couldn't account for the expressions that flashed across his face—resignation, sadness, defiance.

"I'm from Scotland, originally."

Willow's lips twitched. "I think everyone is aware of that."

"Do you know what a wanlass is in Scotland?"

"No."

"A wanlass or windlass is a winch for moving heavy objects. I was given that surname because I was found in a basket on the doorstep of the Grottlemeyer Foundling Home. The home is well-known in the area for the wanlass that brings water up from the well."

"Oh."

"Ironic, isn't it? That a pair of twins would be left on my own doorstep."

Willow's hand spread wide over Adam's back as she tried to imagine what Charles must have looked like all those years ago. Chubby cheeks? Blond curls or a shiny pate?

"I have no idea when I was born or where. Much like the twins, my only belongings were a few changes of clothing—fine clothing made of silk and linen. The blanket was also of good quality, edged in very expensive lace. Then, at the bottom of the basket, was a silver box. It looked like something a woman might have on her dressing table."

He stood and paced to the fireplace. "It would have been better for me if I'd arrived in rags. The rumors started before I could even understand the maliciousness behind them. Somehow, the other children decided that I was the unwanted offspring of a titled family, or the unfortunate result of an affair."

Again, the similarities to the children were remarkable.

"In any event, I became a target for teasing and pranks. I think that, underneath it all, the other children feared that someone important would come to claim me—a foreign prince or a titled nobleman—while they would be left behind." He sighed. "In any event, I was ostracized. I became impatient. Angry. If someone so much as looked at me wrong, I lashed out. I lived with one goal—get them before they could get me." He stared into the flames, seeming to see into the past. "I developed a temper. A fierce temper." He met her gaze and said softly. "I hurt someone, Willow. Another boy called me a vulgar name and stole the silver box. Then he threw it into the sea."

Charles's fingers curled into fists, but he consciously relaxed them. "My temper exploded. I'd always thought that the box might allow me to track down my kin one day. Then, in an instant, it was gone forever." His eyes grew dark and stormy. "I hit him, Willow. Then I hit him again. And again. And again. If Phineas Bottoms hadn't been walking down the street that day…"

His expression filled with regret and remorse—something Willow would never have thought possible. In her eyes, Charles could do no wrong. She never would have supposed that he had his own demons plaguing him.

When he spoke again, his voice was rough with emotion. "I have fought so hard to put that boy behind me, to tamp down my temper, to be the man that I should be." She saw a sheen of tears in his eyes. "Then when I couldn't find you…that temper came raging back and I hurt the one person that I should have been protecting."

Before Willow could respond, they were interrupted by a knock at the door. Gideon poked his head inside.

"Is it safe to come in?" he murmured.

Charles bent to fuss with the fire, and realizing that he needed a moment to compose himself, Willow said, "Yes, do, Gideon."

She lay Adam in a wooden crate that the women had lined with blankets. Jonah had attached a pair of rockers to the bottom to fashion a makeshift cradle. Eva lay in an identical contraption. Jonah had then confessed that—since the twins were growing so quickly—he'd already begun to make the babies proper cradles which would be his and Sumner's combined wedding and christening gifts to the Wanlass family.

"Jonah and Sumner are right behind me." He scraped his feet against the step to remove the snow from his boots, then entered. "We'll have another blizzard tonight, I wager. I'll be glad when January is over."

Willow automatically looked toward Charles, only to discover that he was watching her.

Please don't let winter end too quickly.

As soon as the pass melted, the two of them would need to decide, once and for all, how to proceed with their lives.

Gideon's prediction held true. Before the man could cross to the fireplace and hold his hands out to the flames, there was another knock on the door.

This time, Charles let Jonah and Sumner inside.

"Hello, everyone." Sumner began tugging off her gloves. "And how are the twins?"

She hurried over to peer into the cradles, then shot a look at Charles and said, "See? Even I'm not immune."

Willow gazed questioningly at her friend, and Sumner grinned. "I'll fill you in later."

After reaching to tuck the blankets around Eva, she sat beside Willow on the settee. Her eyes immediately fell on the chart.

"Jonah, come look at this. They've really narrowed things down."

Gideon took the rocker and Jonah the chair opposite his wife. But just when they'd all focused on the chart, the door to the main room swung open.

"Would anyone like coffee?" Lydia whispered.

Immediately behind her was Iona, who added, "We made a fresh pot. And there's leftover plum buckle from dinner."

Charles shot a narrowed glance at Gideon.

"Don't look at me," his friend grumbled, jumping to his feet and reaching for the tray filled with mugs and saucers.

"Oh, please," Lydia said dismissively, going around the room with the coffeepot. "We knew something was up between Charles and Willow the minute she claimed to have given birth to twins."

"What?" Willow gasped.

Iona settled into the seat that Gideon had abandoned and reached out to pat her hand. "Sweetie, you were a little shy in the beginning, but you weren't pregnant. Especially not with twins."

"But...you didn't say anything when Charles and I... when we..."

Lydia touched her shoulder as she crossed behind the settee. "Because we'd already heard about Jenny's murder. It didn't take too long for Iona and me to surmise the twins belonged to Jenny." As she filled Willow's cup, she met her gaze with kind eyes. "Any of us would have done what you did to protect those babes. And since Charles had stepped up to help you—" Lydia winked in his direction "—we knew you'd be in good hands. Our only concern was whether you were willing to take such a drastic step."

As the conversation rose and fell around her, Willow found herself watching Charles.

He seemed just as distracted. Their gazes connected for long moments, and in the depths of those quiet, gray eyes, she saw the man she'd always seen. A good man. An honorable man. A man who'd been willing to throw away his job to take care of the twins.

And her.

So much had changed between them—within them—that the word *drastic* didn't apply anymore. Their marriage had never been a hardship. If anything, it had become an unwitting blessing.

She couldn't help shooting him a soft smile—and she watched as he seemed to sag in relief. He rubbed his eyes as if they were tired.

But had she seen a glint of moisture there?

He'd asked for her forgiveness, and she would give it to him—how could she not? He'd made a mistake, spoken hastily. If anything, that burst of temper had made her feel more like his equal. For so long, she'd heard the

praises of Charles Wanlass, the man that the other miners called The Bishop. The lay pastor. And she'd feared,
deep down, that he was too perfect for the likes of her, a
poorly educated girl from humble beginnings.

But he wasn't the saint she'd supposed him to be.

He was a man.

He was her husband.

In that instant, she knew that whatever the spring
thaws might bring, she would not be joining Mr. Ferron
in California. She would write him a letter of apology,
explain that she had changed her mind and that she would
find a way to repay him for the passage he'd sent to her.

But she wouldn't marry him.

She'd already married the man she loved—although
she'd done things out of order. And if winter could hold
on just a little longer...

She'd find a way to convince him that their borrowed
family should remain together.

Chapter Eighteen

Willow linked her arm through Sumner's and tried to alter her gait to her friend's longer strides.

"Are you sure that we won't get in trouble for this?" she murmured under her breath.

Sumner shrugged. "We have our guards and we have a legitimate reason for being in town."

Willow had grave doubts about the latter part of that statement. Sumner, as a physician and Jonah's wife, might have been given more liberties in moving around Bachelor Bottoms, but Willow was sure that such allowances did not extend to her.

Sumner squeezed her hand reassuringly. "Just follow my lead. I may have to adjust my remarks extemporaneously."

In an effort to flush out the culprit who had killed Jenny, Willow and Sumner had been enlisted to set the first phase of their plan in motion. As subtly as possible, they would cast hints that Jenny's diary had been found.

"What if the men don't spread the word?"

"Don't worry about that. If you get more than one miner together, they'll gossip like a pair of fishwives. I've seen it happen often enough."

They waited for a sledge to pass, then crossed the road.

But rather than going to the cook shack, they moved one door down, to the company store.

A bell jingled overhead as they stepped inside.

Willow's eyes grew wide as she absorbed the wonders of the establishment. The walls were lined from ceiling to floor with shelves, and those shelves held every possible commodity that could be imagined—shirts, pants, suspenders, socks, shoes, food stuffs, tools, bridles and tack, books, sweets, brooms, dustpans, hip baths and horse troughs. A rolling ladder—the kind that Willow had seen only once, in a public library in Liverpool—maneuvered around the room on a brass track. Glass-fronted counters flanked the space in a U, holding even more treasures: musical instruments, toiletries, pen sets, ties, pocket watches, chains and fobs.

In the center was a potbellied stove surrounded by chairs and small tables. Several miners hunched over checkerboards. At the sound of the bell, they'd grown still, as if participating in a bizarre form of freeze tag.

"Good day, gentlemen!" Sumner called out blithely, either unaware or refusing to acknowledge the effect she and Willow were having on the all-male establishment. "Mr. Grooper."

Mr. Grooper hung halfway up the ladder, one foot on an upper rung, one hand reaching toward a box of soap powder. He remained there for a good minute, blinking furiously, as if he were in the grips of a mirage. Then his Adam's apple shifted as he swallowed.

"Miss… Miss… Miss… *Mrs.* Ramsey. Miss… Miss… Miss… *Mrs.* Wanlass."

The weight of so many stares was enough to root Willow to the floor, but Sumner held her arm and pulled her resolutely in her wake.

"Mr. Grooper, we wondered if we could confer with you on a somewhat...*personal* matter."

Although none of the other men moved, Willow could feel their attention shift to the shopkeeper. Just as Sumner had predicted, the store became so quiet that the pop of a log in the stove caused the wizened man to start, then cling to the ladder when he nearly lost his balance.

"Of—of course, ladies."

He abandoned the soap powder altogether and scrambled down the ladder. Then he leaned across the counter. His eyes, magnified by his spectacles to twice their size, pinned them with an inquisitive stare.

"How may I help you?"

Sumner also leaned close, dropping the pitch of her voice to a conspiratorial level, despite the fact that she could still be heard by every man in attendance. Willow smothered a smile when she heard the chairs creak, as if the miners were leaning toward them as much as they dared.

"We realize that we are making our plans...prematurely. It will be a month—perhaps two or three—before the pass opens. But we have been gathering up Jenny's belongings."

Grooper shook his head. "Poor, poor girl," he murmured.

"Yes, indeed. It's a horrible business, her death." Sumner sighed. "Mr. Grooper, we're aware that, at the time being, any mail or shipments to and from the mine are...well, impossible."

He nodded.

"But we wondered if you could clarify a few things for us."

"I will certainly try."

"Could you tell us how soon we might be able to mail something to the outside world? Will we be able to get something through once the snow in the pass begins to melt? Or will we have to wait until *all* of it is gone?"

Behind his spectacles, Mr. Grooper blinked, then

cleared his throat importantly. "No, ma'am…ma'ams. Although you—the women, the mail-order brides—will probably be stranded here until the snow is completely gone…" he shifted a receipt pad, a string holder, his pen and inkwell, until they lined up on the blotter like soldiers on a field of green "…certain pieces of correspondence are of a more…important nature. We have sorted the mail thus far as to priority. As soon as a man can get through with a horse, he will begin taking weekly trips to the nearest railway station, where they will be forwarded to Ogden."

Mr. Grooper paused and stared at them, then continued "Did you have something you wanted to mail?"

"Yes, we do." Sumner leaned closer. "I hope I can rely on your discretion."

"Of course, Dr. Ramsey." He leaned forward in turn. "I take it that this correspondence is of a…*personal* nature?"

"Indeed. As you know, Jenny Reichmann's passing has been a tragedy to our community."

"Mmm." He nodded gravely.

"But what makes it even more tragic is the fact that none of her family has been notified yet. Although we will eventually arrange for a trunk with her personal belongings to be sent back to England, we thought that we could…soften the blow, so to speak, by mailing a letter of explanation, along with Jenny's journal."

"Oh!" His brows creased for a moment before he offered, "But wouldn't it be faster—and much cheaper—to forward it to the husband she was supposed to meet in California?"

Sumner glanced over her shoulder, as if to ensure that no one was eavesdropping—even though there wasn't an ear in the room that wasn't turned toward them.

"You see, we happened to glance through Jenny's entries—just to see if there were any clues as to what might have happened to bring her to such an untimely end."

The man made an indistinct rumbling noise before offering, "Of course, of course. A totally reasonable action."

"In doing so, we discovered that Jenny wasn't married at all."

Mr. Grooper's mouth formed a wide O and the tips of his ears flushed pink.

"She was seduced, Mr. Grooper. Seduced in the most despicable manner. Then her seducer abandoned her."

The shopkeeper seemed to be at a loss for words on how to respond.

"It is possible that her entries may have given clues to the identity of her attacker. After the shift changes tonight, Jonah, Gideon and Charles will be meeting at the mine offices to reread the last few pages to gather evidence." Sumner's voice dropped to a stage whisper. "I do believe that they are very close to making an arrest."

Gooper grumbled and burbled unintelligibly in a way that was part alarm, part excitement.

"In any event," Sumner continued, "we came to the conclusion that, as soon as an arrest was made, the diary should be returned to her loved ones. For safekeeping."

"Ye-e-es. Yes, I can see why."

"So, if we were to make arrangements for its being mailed, we would want to ensure that it would be kept… secure."

"I could lock it in the safe, then send it with the first man to head out of the valley."

"Brilliant!" Sumner slapped the counter with a glove-covered hand. "You are a wonderful, wonderful man to do this for us, Mr. Grooper."

"Ooh, well, I…"

"We will come back to the store as soon as Gideon

Gault has apprehended the man," Sumner said with a beaming smile. "In the meantime, could I possibly purchase two of your finest peppermint sticks?"

The shopkeeper hurriedly reached for the candy, nearly knocking over the jar in the process. As he slipped the sweets into a small paper bag, it didn't seem to occur to him that the women had been forbidden to enter the store, let alone buy anything.

Sumner reached into her reticule and removed a penny, which she placed on the blotter. "Thank you kindly."

Then she and Willow turned to make their way toward the door.

Willow had to admire the way Sumner exited the establishment, like royalty bidding farewell to an audience. She nodded, waved, called out the names of several miners for a more personal touch. But finally, just when Willow feared that she might burst out laughing, they stepped into the cool, crisp January air.

"You are shameless!" Willow said under her breath when they'd crossed the street again. "I don't think I've ever heard anyone offer so many tall tales with such a straight face."

Sumner grinned. "That's why you brought me along. We both know that you wouldn't have been able to say any of it without giving yourself away. You're a horrible liar." She dug into the sack and removed one of the peppermint sticks, then handed the sack to Willow.

They were walking slowly now, enjoying the brief hint of freedom and the warmth of the sun on their faces. It didn't really matter that a pair of Pinkertons followed in their wake.

Willow lifted the sack to her nose and inhaled. Her eyes briefly closed as she absorbed the heady scent. Memories washed over her and she was thrust back in time to her childhood, when both her parents had still been employed at the mill and Christmas brought a sack of nuts, peppermints and an orange as a gift from the owner. Her father had taken as much enjoyment as Father Christmas himself to award Willow with the treats.

"Do you think they took the bait?" Willow wondered.

Sumner stopped in front of the infirmary and gestured to the windows. In the bright sunshine, they reflected Bachelor Bottoms like a mirror.

"See for yourself."

Willow broke off a piece of the peppermint stick and placed it on her tongue. Then she watched in amusement as many of the men who'd been in the company store came bursting outside. They moved in all directions— some stopping other miners on the streets, others dodging into the barbershop or the cook shack.

With luck, the word would spread like wildfire and entice the killer to come out of hiding.

"Do you think this will work?" Willow asked, as her humor seeped away beneath a deep-seated fear. Not so much for her, but for the twins, who were so small, so helpless, and the men who would lie in wait at the mining offices later that night.

"It has to work," Sumner answered with equal gravity. "It's time all this violence comes to an end."

"I don't understand why we have to leave the Dovecote," Willow said—and not for the first time. Shadows were beginning to fall outside. It would soon be time for Devotional, then dinner.

"Jonah and Gideon and I agree that it will be easier to protect you and the children if you're away from the other women. At the Ramsey house, you'll only need a few guards. No one can enter that valley without being seen for miles."

"But at the Dovecote—"

Charles took her arms, rubbing his palms up and down their length in reassurance.

"If you stayed here, there are too many ways someone could involve the other women in an effort to force our hand. Even with guards, the women are coming and going all night. They'll be attending the Devotional, then many of them will stay to help in the cook shack. Gideon already has every man on his crew spread as thin as they can go. If you're off company property in a secure location, he has more Pinkertons who can help us."

The arrangements had already been explained to Willow once before. But when the time had come to put their precautions in place, she'd balked. She couldn't bring herself to leave Charles. Not like this. Not with so many things unsettled between them. She had to tell him that she'd forgiven him for his rash remarks, that she understood him much better now. He needed to know that she'd decided that she would not be continuing on to California. Heaven help her, if she could drum up the courage, she would tell him that, if he'd have her, she would remain his wife. And if he wouldn't...

She couldn't bring herself to think of that event. She knew that if spring arrived and they decided to remain a family, sacrifices would have to be made.

But right now...

"Charles, I... I don't want to go."

"I know, Willow. But it will only be a few hours. Overnight at best. Once you're at Sumner's house, you'll have time with your friend and you'll forget about everything we're trying to do here in Bachelor Bottoms."

She opened her mouth to correct him, to tell him that she'd been trying to say that she didn't want to leave him. Ever.

But his eyes were so shadowed and worried, she realized that this was the worst possible moment to unburden herself. Once Jenny's murderer had been caught, there would be plenty of time for all that.

She nodded, allowing Charles to help her fasten her cloak and lift the hood over her hair.

"I've got the babies' things in the box of one of the company's sledges. Is there anything else you need?"

You. Just you.

But since she couldn't say the words aloud, she shook her head.

"Go on, now. Head outside and I'll carry the twins."

She stepped into the cold, her gaze automatically heading toward the mountaintops. Gray clouds were piling up, warning of a change in the weather. But they should have time to ride to the Ramsey homestead three miles away.

She hurried to the sledge, waiting patiently as Charles maneuvered the basket into the space under the bench. Adam seemed to sense that an adventure was underway because he flailed his arms, dislodging the quilt. When the cold air hit his face, he squinched his eyes shut, a furrow of dislike appearing between his brows.

"Serves you right, laddie. It's too cold out here for wee adventures. You'll have to wait a month or two."

Charles tenderly covered the baby with the quilt again, tucking the corners more securely around the edges. Adam squirmed in protest, but thankfully, he didn't cry or wake his sister.

"You next."

When Willow gathered her skirts and tried to find the iron rung with her toe, Charles stopped her.

"Let me."

Before she knew what he meant to do, he grasped her

around the waist and lifted her onto the sledge. Then he continued to hold her for long, aching moments.

"You know that I wouldn't have aught happen to you or the babies, don't you?"

She nodded.

"This will all be over tonight. It has to be. One of those three men will flinch and try to get the diary. Then life can return to normal."

Except that Willow didn't know what "normal" meant anymore. So she clung to the rest of his statement.

They had winnowed the list of suspects down to three men.

Theo Caruso, the miner who had tried to take the babies in the Meeting House. Francis Diggory and Orie Keefe.

One of them was a killer.

"Be careful. Promise me you'll be careful."

Charles offered her a half-cocked smile that wasn't entirely convincing. "I promise. Don't forget, Ramsey and Gideon will be there with me."

He held her hand until she'd taken her place on the bench. Then he draped a woolly bearskin over her lap and tented it over the basket.

The snow squeaked as he crossed in front of the team, double-checking the traces as he went. Finally, he climbed up and sat beside her. "You're sure we have everything we need?"

She glanced behind them, taking in the small trunk that held a change of clothes for her and the babies, as well as spare blankets and diapers. Next to that was her carpetbag, which was filled with the feeding bottles and two crockery jugs filled with goat's milk. Then in the corner between the bench and the box, more ominous than the rest, leaned Charles's rifle.

"Everything's here."

"Good." He slapped the reins and offered a soft, "Hiyah!"

The sledge skidded slightly to the side, then righted itself behind the team as they began to pick up speed. For long minutes, they traveled with only the rush of the sleigh runners and Adam's soft baby grunts and coos to accompany them.

"I think Adam likes the ride," Willow said with a smile.

"Aye. He'll be like his da, loving the outdoors. No one will fence him in."

"Is that why you're a miner? To avoid the fences?"

He nodded. "In part, although some might argue that the tunnels are more confining than any office could ever be. But it's more than that. The mines saved me. The moment Phineas Bottoms put a helmet on my head and a pick in my hand, I had a way to earn my worth. I was useful. Needed. In control of my own choices."

Willow knew exactly how Charles felt. In her time with him, she'd grown more confident than she would have ever thought possible. She'd found her own purpose with the children.

And her husband.

Please, please, Father in Heaven, let it be the start of many more such days.

Willow opened her mouth, needing to tell Charles how he had changed her life. But a sudden sharp *crack* split the silence of the night. Just as quickly, the horses bolted. Willow bent to steady the basket, then cried out when she felt a blow to the head.

Without warning, the night sky seemed to fill with sparks of light.

Then everything went black.

Chapter Nineteen

Charles grappled to make sense of his world as everything seemed to happen at once. The horses leaped into a gallop, Willow gasped and wilted beside him, and a squall of protest signaled that Adam had decided he'd had enough of his new adventure and he wanted to be held.

Crack.

Instinctively, Charles bent low as he recognized yet another rifle shot. Grappling with the reins, he glanced over his shoulder. A horse and rider were galloping hard toward them.

He glanced at Willow's limp form and a panic unlike anything he'd ever experienced gripped his throat.

Dear Lord above, please let her be safe. Let my whole family be safe.

Crack.

The wooden box of the sledge splintered behind him.

The familiar anger rose within him. But there was a difference this time. He wasn't the inexperienced youth who raged out of control—or even the man who'd let his frustration control his tongue.

No. This time, he was a husband and a father, and he

would protect his family at all costs. But he would do it with a clear head.

Without thinking, Charles transferred the reins to one hand, laid the other around Willow to steady her on the seat, then pulled hard to the left. The horses tossed their heads in confusion, but followed his lead, angling sideways before he brought them to a sudden stop. As he did so, the sledge skidded sideways, sliding, sliding.

Knowing that the rider wouldn't have time to react, he didn't reach for the rifle. Instead, as soon as the sledge was steady, Charles whipped open his coat and reached for his revolver. Jumping to the ground, he planted his feet firmly and aimed. But not for the heart. He wouldn't have another near death on his conscience. Not when he had so much to live for. Nothing would prevent him from giving every ounce of his affection and dedication to his loved ones.

He shot high and wide, startling the horse and making it rear. The rider, who'd been sighting down his rifle, was caught unprepared. His arms flew wide as he hung in midair. Then he was tumbling backward into the snow.

Charles ran toward him, noting that the rifle was a good yard away from their assailant—but not out of reach if the man lunged.

When the culprit scrambled to his knees, Charles shot to the right, mere inches from his fingers.

"Don't move!"

The man didn't listen. Instead, he flung himself forward.

Charles aimed carefully and pulled the trigger. A blossom of blood appeared at the side of the man's hand and he yowled, rearing back, cradling his wrist.

Charles slipped and slid through the snow, managing to snatch the man's rifle from the drifts and fling it well

Instead, things had gone horribly wrong, and she'd summoned the last of her strength to take her children to safety, to yank away Niederhauser's wedding ring, to provide them all with the clues to her attacker.

A thundering filled Charles ears and it took him a few moments to realize that it wasn't his blood pounding in his ears. Looking up, he saw two riders galloping toward him. He lifted his revolver, prepared to defend his family yet again. But then he recognized Gideon's familiar blue uniform and Jonah's fierce expression.

He waited until the men skidded to a halt and dismounted.

"We heard the shots," Gideon said, unholstering his sidearm.

"This the guy?" Jonah asked, his brows furrowed over his dark eyes.

"Yeah. Edgar Niederhauser."

"You're kidding." Gideon squinted at the man in the shadows.

"He's got a rifle over there." Charles gestured to the spot with one hand. "Get him back to the camp before he can hurt anyone else." He suddenly became aware of the high-pitched wailing of the twins. "I've got to see to my wife and children." Charles was already walking backward toward the sound.

"Do you need help?" Gideon asked.

"I don't think so. I'd rather have this fellow as far away from them as possible."

"Are you going to head to the homestead?" Ramsey shot him a concerned gaze.

"I don't know yet." He scrambled to think. Willow might need medical attention. But Charles couldn't ignore the powerful—almost *primal*—need to see them all safely home.

Seeing that the men had things in hand, he ran as fast as he could to the sledge, skidding around the back so that he could approach the bench from Willow's side. To his infinite relief, he saw her reach out and brace a hand against the rail. Then she straightened, bringing a hand to her head.

"Willow!"

She looked at him, blinking, then offered him a woozy smile. Her eyes grew clouded in concern. Her fingers tenderly probed a goose egg that was swelling on her forehead. "The babies…"

"They're unhurt. I think they're scared from the horses bolting."

Willow frowned, as if suddenly remembering. "There was a noise. Then Adam cried out. I reached to steady the basket, but I must have hit my head on the arm of the bench."

Charles lifted questing fingers. "Are you sure you're all right? I can take you to Sumner. She can examine you to make sure."

She shook her head, then winced. "No. I'm fine. Really."

Willow bent to pull the quilt aside. As soon as the twins saw her, their cries eased and they looked up at her with brimming eyes and trembling chins.

Despite the cold, she scooped Adam up, handing him to Charles, then reached for Eva. Within minutes, the twins' frightened sobs disappeared beneath weary hiccuping sighs.

"There, there, little love," Willow whispered to Eva.

"And look here at our brave laddie." Charles found himself drinking up the sight before him. Two contented children.

And a wife.

In that instant, she met his gaze and blurted, "I love you, Charles Wanlass. I don't want to ever leave you."

She loved him.

He wanted to shout the words from the mountaintops, then offer his own words of adoration. But first, he needed to be honest. Completely honest. If this whole affair had taught him nothing else, it was that secrets could have unintended consequences.

When she would have spoken again, he said, "Wait, Willow, wait. Before you say anything more, there's one last thing about me that you need to know. When I told you of my past, I wasn't completely honest. I was up front about the teasing and the boy that I pummeled. But I didn't tell you everything. I…" He took a deep breath, surprised at how so many years of silence had made his confession all the more difficult. "The fact of the matter is… I hit that boy. Again and again and again. His words—the name he'd called me—filled me with a rage like I've never experienced before or since. I watched through a red haze as my fists struck him over and over."

Her eyes grew dark. Troubled. And he rued the fact that he'd been the one to dim their light.

"If Phineas Bottoms hadn't been walking down the street that day. If he hadn't decided to intervene, to pull me off… I would have killed that boy."

Charles waited for her to say something. *Anything.* But rather than speaking right away, she bent to place Eva in the basket. Then took Adam from his arms. When the two were safely tucked inside and covered by the blanket again, she climbed down from the sledge.

Charles braced himself. Since she'd taken such pains to speak to him, face-to-face, he knew that she would reject him. In the past few days, he'd shown her that he could have a formidable temper.

But to his surprise, she cupped his face in her hands. "But you *didn't* kill him, Charles."

"Willow, I'm no better than Edgar Niederhauser. I could have beat that boy to death."

"But you *didn't*. And you're nothing like Edgar Niederhauser. You learned from your mistakes and vowed to do better. *Be* better. How could you compare yourself to that man? You *care*, Charles. You care for these miners. You minister to their spiritual needs and provide them with friendship and support. You dote on these twins. You've offered them a home and safety and love." Her voice dropped to a whisper. "And you care for *me*, Charles."

"I love you, Willow. I *love* you."

In a moment, the shadows in her eyes disappeared. Joy filled her features, enveloping her much like the ethereal glow he remembered from the painting of the ghostly protector that had fascinated him so much as a child.

She was so beautiful.

"Will you marry me, Willow?"

She grinned.

"We're already married."

"Then will you *stay* married to me? Forever and ever?"

"Yes, Charles, yes."

He pulled her into his arms, absorbing her happiness, her warmth, her *love*.

"Are you sure?" he murmured against her ear.

She drew back, her arms still looped around his neck. "Yes. I love you, Charles Wanlass. *You.* Just as I know you love the real *me* with all my faults and foibles. The journey we've taken before meeting one another doesn't matter. What matters is how we continue from now on. Together."

They embraced again. Soon, they were interrupted

by the sound of someone clearing his throat. Looking up, they found Gideon and Jonah grinning at them. Between them, Edgar Niederhauser stood, handcuffed, his head hung low in defeat.

"Have you made up your mind about whether or not you'll be going on to the homestead?"

When Willow would have stepped away, Charles kept an arm looped around her waist. "If it's all the same, I think we'll be going home."

He glanced down at Willow and she offered him a quick nod of agreement.

"Then would you mind giving Niederhauser a ride as far as the jail?" Gideon asked.

Within minutes, Edgar Niederhauser was trussed unceremoniously in the back of the sledge with a length of rough rope they'd found in the box. Gideon tied his horse to the side rail, then climbed in, taking up the spot opposite the man, his revolver held loosely in his lap.

"Don't you move, you hear?" He nodded in Charles's direction. "That one might think twice about shooting you, but me? I wouldn't bat an eye."

Gideon looked up at Willow and offered her a faint wink, then said, "Whenever you're ready, Charles."

"If you two don't need me tonight, I'll head home to Sumner and tell her what's happened," Jonah said. "We can sort out everything else in the morning. Batchwell and Bottoms will want to be briefed, so we may as well meet together. Say, the private dining room at the cook shack? Nine o'clock?"

Gideon looked hopefully in Charles's direction. Charles knew that he and his men had been watching the women's comings and goings round the clock for the better part of a week. He doubted that any of the Pinkertons had enjoyed more than a few hours of sleep a night,

and he was sure that Gideon, as their leader, had amassed
even less. Clearly, he was hoping to lock Niederhauser up,
post a guard, then give his men permission to stand down.

"Nine o'clock will work fine for me—as long as Willow won't need me to help with the bairns."

She smiled, her mitten-covered hand stealing into his.

"I'm sure that I'll have a houseful of brides, by that
time. You won't be the only ones needing to give a briefing. The women will want answers, as well." Her eyes
twinkled. "And they'll probably have a lighter guard than
usual."

Gideon's laugh bounced off the hills and mountains.

"Aptly put, Mrs. Wanlass. Aptly put."

Long before they entered town, they heard the sound
of the alarm bell in the distance.

Willow gripped Charles's arm.

"What else could have happened?"

He grinned, his teeth flashing in the gathering darkness.

"I think that bell is letting everybody know that Jonah
and Gideon might need help apprehending Jenny's murderer. The whole town probably heard the gunshots."

Just as he had supposed, as they entered the main road
that led to the mining offices and then to the mine, men
began gathering on the boardwalks, the alleyways and
the street. As the sledge neared the livery, Smalls burst
out, jogging alongside the conveyance. Women rushed
from the cook shack and more came running from the
direction of the Dovecote.

As Charles pulled to a stop in front of the offices and
Gideon ushered Niederhauser into one of the jail cells in
the stone basement, the crowd pushed closer, clamoring
for an explanation.

Finally, when it became apparent that no one intended to leave, Gideon held up his hands to silence them.

"Settle down, settle down! We've got a pair of sleeping babes nearby, and we wouldn't want to wake them."

The noise instantly decreased, becoming a soft murmur instead.

Gideon sighed and stared at the tips of his boots. When he looked at the crowd again, he said, "I'll give you ten minutes in the cook shack to explain everything. Then each of you will return to your own homes. We've had enough excitement here at Bachelor Bottoms to last a lifetime. Tomorrow, you can gab, gossip and discuss all of the events to your hearts' content. But *this evening*, unless you're doing a shift in the mine, you're all going to get a good night's sleep."

He led the way toward the cook shack, and the group followed as if he were Moses leading the Israelites out of Egypt.

Willow fought the urge to giggle. Poor Gideon. He looked grumpy and grumbly and ready to turn in—just as he'd urged everyone else to do. But she also knew that his efforts would provide the distraction for Charles and her to slip away unnoticed.

As if to validate her suspicion, the Pinkerton briefly glanced over his shoulder and touched a finger to the brim of his hat. Then he reached to pull open the cook shack door.

"Ladies," he murmured, as the miners allowed the women to precede them. "Please tell me you have cookies left from dinner."

"We have pie, Mr. Gault," Iona replied, reaching up to pat him on the cheek like a doting aunt. "Cherry or apple."

He slapped a hand over his heart in a showman's display of delight. "You are an answer to prayer, Mrs. Skye."

As the last of the women stepped inside and the miners pressed in behind them, Creakle toddled toward Charles and Willow.

"How 'bout if Smalls and me put the team away fer you, Mr. Wanlass."

"That would be a monumental favor, Creakle. Smalls."

Smalls gripped one of the horses by the bridle.

"We'd be glad t' be of service, Charles," Creakle said with a doting smile. "The two of you are prob'ly plumb tuckered out."

Smalls nodded, waiting patiently as Charles jumped from the bench, then circled the sledge to lift Willow down. As soon as her feet had touched ground, he reached for the basket.

For a moment, he nudged the blanket down, just to check. Willow felt a surge of joy when the two babies blinked up at him, then grinned.

It didn't matter to Willow—nor, she suspected to Charles—that Sumner had said the babies couldn't smile yet. Willow chose to believe that they somehow knew that they were safe. They were loved.

"Only a few minutes more," Charles murmured, touching Eva's nose so that she blinked, then Adam's chin.

The baby made a noise that could have been a coo of contentment.

He tucked the blanket around them again, then hefted the basket against his chest. "They're growing fast. Jonah said he's just about finished making them proper cradles. Now that the blasting has been a success, maybe I'll linger around the house for a day or two while the ore crew catches up. Besides a place to sleep, the babes will require somewhere to store their clothes—and I'm thinking you'll want a wardrobe for all your dresses. I'm not the craftsman that Jonah might be, but I can still get the job done."

"I'd like that."

When Charles would have handed the basket to Willow, Creakle quickly offered, "Don't worry 'bout yer trunk none. Smalls an' me will bring everything by as soon as we've seen t' the team."

"Thank you, Mr. Creakle. Mr. Smalls." Willow shot each of the men a grateful look. "I am so indebted to you both. I don't know what I would have done without all your help these past few days."

The men nearly glowed from pride, their chests puffing out in importance.

Willow linked her hand through Charles's arm and they pointed themselves toward home. But they'd gone only a few yards when a shape stepped out of the shadows.

For a moment, Willow started as she recognized Theo Caruso. But the man's expression was so miserable that she forced herself to relax.

They had Jenny's murderer. If Theo Caruso had been connected to the events, somehow, Niederhauser would have said something.

Wouldn't he?

Theo had his hat in his fists, and his broad fingers mauled the brim. "I wanted to apologize, ma'am. I realize now that I must have scared you. In the Meeting House. That wasn't my intention, honest it wasn't. And if I unsettled you… I am so, so sorry. You see, the last correspondence I received before the pass closed up was a letter from my mother. Gladys, my sweet dear wife, had just given birth to twins—two boys!" He beamed with pride, but then the joy dimmed ever so slightly. "My mother said that Gladys was poorly after the births and the children were small. Then… I didn't hear anything more. I thought… I *hoped*…that if you wouldn't mind, I could hold your babies. Just to…be close to my own babes, even if it was only for pretend."

Willow felt her eyes prick with tears. Sumner had often lamented over the sacrifices that the miners endured, living away from their wives and sweethearts, fathers, mothers and children. It was a lesson that the good doctor had learned the hard way, while she had balked against the rules of Bachelor Bottoms. This poor man represented all that these men endured in order to provide a better life for their loved ones.

She released Charles, crossing to stand near the large miner and put her hand on the man's arm. "Mr. Caruso. Would you like to join us for dinner tomorrow?"

He opened his mouth, but struggled to make any sound come out. Finally, he nodded.

"I take it that you work the day shift?"

Again, he bobbed his head.

"Charles and I will be attending the evening Devotional." She glanced over her shoulder. "I think it's time we both drew solace and strength from the services. But if you're agreeable, we'll have dinner soon afterward."

The huge man seemed to melt in relief. "I would be honored, Mrs. Wanlass." He glanced beyond her to add, "Pastor."

"Good. We'll see you then."

Theo nodded, obviously embarrassed by the moisture that gathered in his eyes. Then he hurried to the cook shack.

Charles caught up to where Willow stood.

"You're a good woman," he said, his voice ringing with pride.

And love.

She linked her hand through his arm again.

"And you're a good man, Charles." She looked up at him, and even in the early twilight of a Uinta evening, she could see the happiness in his expression.

"I think we'll have a beautiful life together."

He nodded. "I do believe your words will prove prophetic."

Then they settled into an easy walk, moving toward home.

* * * * *

If you loved this sweet historical romance,
pick up the first book
from author Lisa Bingham's miniseries
THE BACHELORS OF ASPEN VALLEY

ACCIDENTAL COURTSHIP

Available now from Love Inspired Historical!

Find more great reads at www.LoveInspired.com

Dear Reader,

I hope that you enjoyed *Accidental Family*, Willow and Charles's story. The book is a special one to me since I am the mother of three adopted children. Those of us who have found our families through this route have a deep love and gratitude for the birth mothers who have entrusted us with their children. I am so indebted to Melanie, Joy, and LaToya. As an adoptive mother, I know that our Heavenly Father takes great care in guiding all those involved in arranging these special families. I know that my own three babies were all miracles on Earth.

As a little side note, Charles's character was loosely based on one of my own ancestors, my great-great-grandfather, James Wanlass. Much like Charles, my great-great-grandfather was an infant when he was left at the door of a foundling home wearing clothes too fine for his station. He was then given the name Wanlass because of a nearby windlass. Much like Charles, rumors surrounded his arrival—that his parents died in a carriage accident or that his mother died in childbirth and his father, a ship's captain, left James at the orphanage, then was lost at sea. James left the orphanage as a teenager to work in the coal mines and then as an iron worker. He became a lay minister soon before emigrating from Scotland to Utah Territory where he became a farmer. It must have been thrilling for a poor orphan from Scotland to claim his own piece of land in the American West.

I love to hear from my readers. If you'd like to get in touch with me, you can reach me at my website, www.lisabingham

author.com, or through my social media sites on Facebook, www.Facebook.com/lisabinghamauthor, or on Twitter, @lbinghamauthor.

All my best to you,

Lisa

We hope you enjoyed this story from
Love Inspired® Historical.

Love Inspired® Historical is coming to
an end but be sure to discover more
inspirational stories to warm your heart
from **Love Inspired®** and
Love Inspired® Suspense!

Love Inspired stories show that
faith, forgiveness and hope have the power
to lift spirits and change lives—always.

Look for six new romances every month
from **Love Inspired®** and
Love Inspired® Suspense!

Get 2 Free Books,
Plus 2 Free Gifts—
just for trying the Reader Service!

"Mr. Halloway." The soft voice near his side added to his
disorientation. "Are you in pain?"

Ivory-skinned and hazel-eyed, with a halo of red-gold
hair, the woman from the train came into view. She had
only a scrape on her chin as a result of the ordeal. "You
fared well," he managed.

"I'm perfectly fine, thank you."

"And the children?"

"They have a few bumps and bruises from the crash,
but they're safe."

He closed his eyes with grim satisfaction.

"I'm Marigold Brewster. Thank you for rescuing me."

"I'm glad you and your boys are all right."

"Well, that's the thing..."

His head throbbed and the light hurt. "What's the
thing?"

"They're not my boys."

"They're not?"

"I never saw them before I boarded the train headed for Kansas."

"Well, then—"

"They're yours."

With his uninjured hand, he touched his forehead gingerly. Had that blow to his head rattled his senses? No, he hadn't lost his memory. He remembered what he'd been doing before heading off to the wreckage. "I assure you I'd know if I had children."

"Well, as soon as you read this letter, along with a copy of a will, you'll know. It seems a friend of yours by the name of Tessa Radner wanted you to take her children upon her death."

Tessa Radner? "She's dead?"

"This letter says she is. I'm sorry. Did you know her?"

Remembering her well, he nodded. They'd been neighbors and classmates in Big Bend, Missouri. He'd joined the infantry alongside her husband, Jessie, who had been killed in Northern Virginia's final battle. Seth winced at the magnitude of senseless loss.

Seth's chest ached with sorrow and sympathy for his childhood friend. But sending her beloved babies to *him*? She must have been desperate to believe he was her best choice. What was he going to do with them?

Don't miss
THE RANCHER INHERITS A FAMILY
by Cheryl St.John, available April 2018 wherever
Love Inspired® Historical books and ebooks are sold.

www.LoveInspired.com

LIHEXP0318